KT-501-650

PRAISE FOR *BEING BILLY*:

'*BEING BILLY* WAS A TOTAL **PAGE-TURNER** – AUTHENTIC AND GRITTY. BILLY'S VOICE DOESN'T FALTER ... SPIKY, BRAVE AND **COMPASSIONATE**' – JENNY DOWNHAM

'**A WONDERFUL BOOK**' – MORRIS GLEITZMAN

'A FREQUENTLY HEART-BREAKING ACCOUNT OF ONE BOY'S ROUTE – **KICKING AND SPITTING** – THROUGH THE CARE SYSTEM' – *BIG ISSUE*

'**MOVING AND POWERFUL, I LOVED IT**' – SOPHIE MCKENZIE

'**LIKE KEN LOACH FOR FOURTEEN-YEAR-OLDS,** WITH ALL THE HEART AND HUMOUR AND COMPASSION THAT THAT IMPLIES' – *TRANSMITTER*

'POWERFUL, HEART-BREAKING, HONEST AND HOPEFUL – A STRONG, THOUGHT-PROVOKING DEBUT' – CATHY CASSIDY

'**COMPELLING** EMPATHETIC AND HOPEFUL' – *SUNDAY TIMES*

'REMAINED WITH ME LONG AFTER FINISHING THE FINAL PAGE; **THE TRUE MARK OF A GOOD READ**' – PHILIP ARDAGH

'LIFE-AFFIRMING, REDEMPTIVE AND REALLY JUST **RATHER GOOD**' – *GUARDIAN*

'IT'S FRIGHTENING WHEN A DEBUT NOVEL IS AS GOOD AS *BEING BILLY*' – MARCUS SEDGWICK

'EARLE HAS CREATED A COMPLEX AND MEMORABLE CHARACTER IT SOON BECOMES IMPOSSIBLE NOT TO ROOT FOR' – KEITH GRAY, *SCOTSMAN*

'**PHIL EARLE WRITES STARKLY BUT SENSITIVELY** ABOUT DAMAGED CHILDREN IN THIS BRILLIANT PAGE-TURNING NOVEL. **IT MOVED ME TO TEARS**' – JACQUELINE WILSON

Phil Earle was born, raised and schooled in Hull. His first job was as a care worker in a children's home, an experience that influenced the ideas behind *Being Billy* and *Saving Daisy*. He then trained as a drama therapist and worked in a therapeutic community in south London, caring for traumatized and abused adolescents.

After a couple of years in the care sector, Phil chose the more sedate lifestyle of a bookseller, and now works in children's publishing. He lives in south-east London with his wife and children, but Hull will always be home.

www.philearle.com

Books by Phil Earle

BEING BILLY
SAVING DAISY

spinebreakers.co.uk

SAVING DAISY

phil earle

PENGUIN BOOKS

PENGUIN BOOKS

Published by the Penguin Group
Penguin Books Ltd, 80 Strand, London WC2R ORL, England
Penguin Group (USA) Inc., 375 Hudson Street, New York, New York 10014, USA
Penguin Group (Canada), 90 Eglinton Avenue East, Suite 700, Toronto, Ontario, Canada M4P 2Y3
(a division of Pearson Penguin Canada Inc.)
Penguin Ireland, 25 St Stephen's Green, Dublin 2, Ireland
(a division of Penguin Books Ltd)
Penguin Group (Australia), 250 Camberwell Road, Camberwell, Victoria 3124, Australia
(a division of Pearson Australia Group Pty Ltd)
Penguin Books India Pvt Ltd, 11 Community Centre, Panchsheel Park,
New Delhi – 110 017, India
Penguin Group (NZ), 67 Apollo Drive, Rosedale, Auckland 0632, New Zealand
(a division of Pearson New Zealand Ltd)
Penguin Books (South Africa) (Pty) Ltd, 24 Sturdee Avenue, Rosebank,
Johannesburg 2196, South Africa

Penguin Books Ltd, Registered Offices: 80 Strand, London WC2R ORL, England

penguin.com

First published 2012
001 – 10 9 8 7 6 5 4 3 2 1

Text copyright © Phil Earle, 2012
The lyric 'All the other girls here are stars, you are the northern lights' taken from the song 'Kathleen'
written by Josh Ritter 2004. Published by Touch Tones Music Ltd
All rights reserved

The moral right of the author has been asserted

Set in 10.5/15.5pt Sabon
Typeset by Palimpsest Book Production Limited, Falkirk, Stirlingshire
Printed in Great Britain by Clays Ltd, St Ives plc

Except in the United States of America, this book is sold subject to the condition that it shall not, by
way of trade or otherwise, be lent, re-sold, hired out, or otherwise circulated without the publisher's
prior consent in any form of binding or cover other than that in which it is published and without a
similar condition including this condition being imposed on the subsequent purchaser

British Library Cataloguing in Publication Data
A CIP catalogue record for this book is available from the British Library

ISBN: 978-0-141-33136-2

www.greenpenguin.co.uk

MIX
Paper from
responsible sources
FSC
www.fsc.org FSC™ C018179

Penguin Books is committed to a sustainable
future for our business, our readers and our
planet. This book is made from paper certified
by the Forest Stewardship Council.

*This book is dedicated to my friend, Jonny John-Kamen,
who closed all the boxes . . .*

*and to my incredible parents, Neet and Ray, who sealed
them shut.*

All the other girls here are stars, you are the northern lights
Josh Ritter, 'Kathleen'

My name is Daisy Houghton.

I'm fourteen years old.

Six months ago I killed my dad.

It wasn't premeditated or bloody. I didn't even have to lay a hand on him.

Speaking to him was enough.

He didn't know what was coming. How could he? All he was doing was protecting me. Doing what any parent would do.

I should have realized, though. Seen the danger in what I was doing. That what I had to tell him was too great for anyone to carry.

If only I'd kept my mouth shut. If I had done, he'd still be around, and I'd be at home.

Instead I'm here.

In a room with plastic windows and a bed that's bolted to the floor.

It's not prison, but that's where I deserve to be.

I know what you're thinking by the way.

Where's your mum? Why aren't you home with her?

That's the problem.

I killed her too.

CHAPTER 1

You can tell how good a party is by the time that the walls start sweating. I'm not an expert or anything, far from it. It's just something I've noticed. Probably because this is the eighth Friday in a row that someone from our school has opened their house to everyone on Facebook. You'd think after seeing the results once *they'd* think twice, but nope. Here we were again.

From the moisture sliding down the walls, this party was a ten. In fact it was turned up to eleven. The bass was bouncing off the walls, the floorboards squeaking and swaying, threatening to give in well before eleven o'clock approached. As I watched the sea of bodies bounce in front of me, beer spraying everywhere in celebration, I had to rein myself in. Remind myself what I was doing here.

I took a sip of beer. Well, it had been beer to start with, but as I'd slowly siphoned it down my throat I'd popped back to the kitchen a few times and topped the bottle up from the tap. It didn't taste great, but it kept up the illusion.

That's the secret, you see. That's why I'm here at all. It's all about showing your face. Do that and you're fine. Ironically, it's when you're almost invisible that the trouble starts, because that's when you become a target. From there they start digging around for stuff that they can throw back at you, personal stuff, the stuff you try to bury, out of reach of anyone, yourself included.

I think I've got it mastered now, the balance. I don't miss a party, even if I have to blag my way in, and while I'm there I get around, speak to as many people as I can. I'm not averse to dancing or anything either, but not if the lads involved are anything like fit. I don't need that kind of complication. Neither do they.

I just work the room, building on the conversation from last time, giving them a bit more info without ever throwing them anything too juicy, nothing they can latch on to.

God, it sounds terrible, doesn't it? Makes me sound so cynical. Like the kind of people I hate. But it has to be done.

I've chatted to half a dozen people tonight, or tried to. It's almost impossible to make yourself heard over the music rattling your senses, but I enjoyed what I heard. In fact, maybe a bit too much. I think I drank the first third of my beer too quickly and gave more away than I should've. Still, a trip to the tap soon rectified that problem and since then it's been fine. All in hand.

People kind of know what I am.

The kooky one. The one who loves the cinema, never shy of an opinion on what they should and shouldn't be watching. And I'm comfortable with that. There's a cool, a kudos to it that buys me immunity from the harsher kids homing in on this month's victim.

Looking around the place, I made a call. The house was

bulging and I knew it would be forty-five minutes tops before a neighbour called the police in. So I decided to give it another five before sloping off home.

After a quick dance with a couple of girls in my year, I motioned to my empty bottle and walked in the direction of the fridge. They'd never know I was heading for the door instead.

I was only three paces from it when someone got in the way, derailing my best intentions.

Rob Stearn. The best and worst person possible. If there was anyone I could lose control in front of, it was always going to be him. I pulled my shirt sleeve down, keeping everything in place and hidden, before sliding a lick of hair behind my ear. A single movement that made me look both stupid and up for it at the same time.

'All right, Daisy. You off?'

I heard him, but because of the music made out that I hadn't, buying some time as he repeated himself.

'Yeah,' I yelled in his ear, leaving him to recoil slightly. 'Got to meet someone.'

'What, your dad picking you up?'

It was a loaded gun of a question. Answer wrongly and I'd be labelled as a kid on a curfew, enough of a reason for people to start zeroing in. So I pulled on my slyest grin and fired back at him.

'Not my dad, no. Right gender, but definitely not related.'

The lie stuck to my teeth, but he seemed to buy it, a flash of disappointment in his eyes. He recovered quickly, shoulder-bumping me gently before telling me to have a good night. 'I'll see you Monday,' he added, before disappearing back into the crowd.

Watching him go, I felt a stabbing regret that I'd said what I had, knowing he'd find someone else in there happy to entertain him for an hour or two.

I pulled my coat on, feeling like it weighed fifty kilos, and squeezed through the front door, head down. Nobody seemed to see me go.

The wind slapped my cheeks as I turned the first corner towards home, but I barely felt it. I'd done it again, ghosted through the night exactly as I'd wanted to. A small prickle of pleasure passed through me, but I didn't listen to it, I just let it pass. There'd be plenty more nights like that to come.

CHAPTER 2

The classroom was buzzing with stories of Friday's party when Mr Hobson made his first entrance.

In fact he could've been stood there for five minutes, soaking up what was being said before any of us noticed he was there.

'OK, everyone. Throw your attention this way, will you?'

Excited chatter gave way to surprised whispers, all of them asking who this was at the front of the class. Whoever it was, it certainly wasn't Miss Addison. There was no smell of cats or questionable blouses in sight, and the other girls in particular looked delighted.

'Thank you very much. As you can tell, I'm not who you were expecting. Miss Addison has unfortunately been taken ill. It's unlikely she'll be back this term, or even before the summer break, so in the meantime you'll be having me instead.'

'I wish,' whispered a voice beside me, loud enough to start a ripple of giggles. That was the thing about Donna Riley. She had a line for every occasion. Funny or cutting, it didn't matter. She'd provide it, and as a result she was every teacher's worst nightmare.

I looked up at the new guy and tried to work out if he could withstand a broadside from her. There weren't many who could.

Leaning back in my chair, I swivelled towards her, waiting for the attack, but it didn't come. This wasn't her normal strategy. Usually she was the first one to get stuck into the new blood. I've heard her bombard teachers with question after question, usually before they've had time to write their names on the whiteboard.

But with this one?

Nothing.

At first I wondered if she had a different game plan. Maybe she was bored of the obvious approach, but as the minutes went on, and the introductions were finished, there wasn't a peep out of her.

But she was definitely checking him out.

In fact, she couldn't take her eyes off him. She even laughed at some lame gag he cracked, which drew confused looks from the rest of the class, who were also waiting for her to pounce.

'How old do you think he is?' she whispered to me.

I didn't have a clue, but begged my mouth not to say something daft. She wasn't the sort to make a prat of yourself in front of, unless you wanted to be humiliated as well.

I checked him out properly. He was at least ten years younger than any of the other teachers we had. He had short, scruffy hair and looked reasonably smart without trying too hard. One of those guys who could get away with a jacket and jeans without looking like an embarrassing relative.

'Don't know – early thirties or something?' I whispered, hoping it was the right answer.

'Nah, he's younger than that. He can't be more than twenty-five.'

With that, she lifted herself off her chair, craning for a better view as he wrote on the board.

'What are you doing now?' I laughed.

'Keep it down, will you? I'm checking out his hand.'

'What for?'

'To see if he's wearing a ring.'

The snort was out of my mouth before I could stop it, prompting Mr Hobson to turn on his heel and leaving Donna to look like a complete goon.

'Sorry, Miss . . . er?'

All eyes fell on her, and for the first time she didn't have an answer. Not one that was funny anyway.

'Er . . . It's Donna, sir. Donna Riley.'

'And did you want something, Donna? I'm all for respecting teachers, but you really don't need to stand in my presence, you know.'

Poor Donna. She looked gutted. Especially at the sneers and giggles from the others. I cringed at what would come next. With her back to the wall, she could be pretty damned venomous, and I hoped none of it was coming towards me.

'Was just checking out your . . .'

She wasn't going to come clean, was she?

For the first time, he looked mildly impatient.

'My what, Donna?'

'Your . . . handwriting, sir. Miss Addison's was a mess.'

Mr Hobson glanced over his shoulder, as if only half-believing what he was hearing.

'And is it legible?' He sighed.

'Looks tidy to me, sir.' Donna grinned, a semblance of confidence returning to her face. 'Very tidy indeed. Keep up the good work now, won't you?'

She sat back down with a smile, happy she'd not made a *complete* prat of herself.

'Oh, he's a feisty one, isn't he?' she whispered, before leaning even closer. 'And no ring either. So do us a favour, will you, Daisy? Keep an eye on him for me.'

'Eh?' I mouthed. 'Why?'

'I want to know if he's checking me out, that's why!'

She was insatiable, but I knew I had to do as she said. I'd be stupid not to.

So for the rest of the lesson, I forced myself to check him out. Or rather, check out where his gaze was aimed.

And do you know what? Donna was right. Well, partially.

Because every time I raised my eyes, he was checking someone out. Or at least I think he was.

But it wasn't Donna he was looking at.

It was me.

CHAPTER 3

My heart always quickens when I come home from school.

Silly really, that I still feel like this at the age of fourteen, but every time our front door comes into view, for a split second, I think that she's going to be inside. Waiting for me.

For as long as I can remember, it was always about the three of us.

Me.

Dad.

And Mum's shadow.

When I was younger, I used to get really carried away making up rules, stuff that if I kept to, then she'd be there when I closed the door.

If I can get home without standing on a pavement crack, she'll be there.

If I reach the gate before that bus passes, she'll be waiting for me, arms open.

But no matter how carefully I stepped, or how quickly I ran, she never was.

And I was always disappointed.

I can't help myself even now. My mind still wanders

occasionally into stupid games, no matter what I tell it. It's just the games that have changed.

If I can open the gate as the song on my iPod finishes, then maybe . . .

I think it's the window above the front door that gives me hope.

Don't laugh. I'm not going mental. It's true.

Because it's Mum's window. The one she made herself.

She was a real 'doer' apparently, my mum.

So when she and Dad moved into the house, she set about putting her stamp on the place.

Starting with the front door. Or rather, a piece of glass that sat above it.

'It was the first project she took on when we moved in,' Dad had told me. 'It didn't matter that the wallpaper was peeling off the walls, or that the hot water didn't work. She just got fixated on that bloody piece of glass.'

'I don't get it,' I'd replied.

'That was just the way her mind worked. She reckoned that we'd decorate the walls a hundred times while we lived here. But that piece of glass? Well, once it was done, it would be there forever. It was like she wanted to leave her legacy as soon as she arrived. Like she knew she wouldn't be here for long.'

I loved that window more than anything else about our house. The time she must have spent putting every shard of multicoloured glass in place. I had images of her in my head, sat up until dawn, fingers cut to ribbons, until the sun was complete.

And now, when light shone through it, her multicoloured, fractured rising sun, it made perfect sense.

Even on the drabbest days, when the hall light forced its way through the glass, well, it lit up the whole street. It was impossible to look at it and not have hope. Not believe that the person responsible for it would live forever.

Walking up the path, I lift my chin and close my eyes to its glare, breathing in its warmth.

I push through the front door, my pulse quickening slightly.

'Hello?' I yell, my voice questioning just who might shout back.

There's a clatter of a bottle, then the door to the kitchen slides open and, for the millionth time, my crazy dreams die.

'Hi, Dad,' I whisper, as he smiles, pulling me into his arms, like we haven't met in years.

'Cup of tea?' he asks.

'As long as there's biscuits,' I reply.

His laugh is long and smoky. 'Naturally. You can't have one without the other. You do the boiling. I'll get the dunking material.' And with a peck to the top of my head, he turns and heads for the cupboard, leaving me to smile guiltily and wonder how I lucked out so much.

Me and Dad are all about routine. Like the home-time tea and dunking sessions. It's a ritual that only lasts fifteen minutes, or three Rich Teas each (chocolate-covered if we're feeling decadent), but it happens Monday to Friday without fail, as soon as we're both home.

It's not as if the tea prompts any deep conversation or anything either. Just the bog standard 'How was your day?'

routine. I suppose it eases us into the evening gently, reminds us both that we're not on our own.

I often wonder if Dad feels the same as me when he walks down the path at night. Does he dare to dream as well when he sees her window?

There have been occasions when I've seen disappointment on his face as I come through the door, because no matter how much I might look like her, it'll never be enough.

'Right, then,' he yawns, pushing his glasses on to the top of his head. 'On to the big decision. Whose turn is it tonight?'

'Mine,' I say without hesitating. 'You chose *The Shining* last Friday. I've barely slept since.'

'You big wuss!' He grins. 'We watched it at your request I seem to remember, and we watched it early on. So don't blame me.' He reaches into his cardigan pocket and pulls out his tobacco, tossing it on to the table. 'So what's it going to be, then?'

I say nothing and smile. Dad groans theatrically.

'Again? How many times is that this year?'

'Not enough.' I smile, before adding, 'Six.'

'Well, let's get tea out of the way, then, shall we? We can't keep *Shawshank* waiting, can we?'

Tea can't pass quickly enough, but to be honest, with our cooking skills, it never takes long to make. Fridays are all about stealth, though, about getting to the main event with the minimum fuss and maximum speed.

I love films.

No, let me rephrase that.

I LOVE films.

Love them at the cinema. Love them at home. On a

laptop. An iPod. Whatever. I don't care where or how I watch them, as long as I get my fix.

TV's fine, but there's something different, something purer about a film. About condensing a whole story inside a couple of hours.

My earliest memory (at least I think it is, though I may have blocked every other early thought out on purpose) is of sitting in this huge room, surrounded by other kids all as wide-eyed as me.

And then the lights went out.

And I was scared.

But only for a second, because then there was colour, and noise, this overwhelming, ear-filling noise, followed by laughter, and chases, and tension and happiness. And then it was over, and I cried all the way home because I wasn't allowed to stay and watch *The Jungle Book* again.

To be honest, Dad probably felt like crying too, because I've inherited my love of film from him.

He's a real fidgeter, though. When you talk to him, he's forever nibbling at his nails or jiggling his legs. But when he's watching a film, he's motionless. Well, almost. His eyes never shift from the screen. The only thing that moves is his hand to his mouth as he draws on his cigarette or swigs from his wine glass. Sometimes even that's too much of a distraction for him and he leaves the fag dangling from his mouth, inhaling intermittently as ash falls unnoticed on to his jeans.

I suppose I should mind about the smoking, but I can't really. I know it's killing him, burning his lungs and rotting his throat, but it's part of him. I can't imagine him not sat in the open bay window, blowing smoke into the night as he polishes his lighter over and over again on his jumper. The Zippo lighter Mum gave him on their wedding day. His initials scratched into its surface.

I don't smoke.

I've tried it.

Obviously.

It felt like hot gravel being tipped down my throat. Where's the attraction in that? But rolling them? Now, that is addictive. Dad only smokes rollies, so when he's sat by the window, eyes fixed on the screen, I sit and occupy my hands, making his cigs for the next day.

I love the way tobacco smells. I can never believe that something so sweet-smelling can taste so foul, but I love rolling it in the papers, and the feeling of satisfaction as the pile grows on the coffee table.

Even Dad's impressed when he collects them at the end of the night.

'You're going to want paying for these works of art soon,' he says, though the smile on his face disappears as he adds, 'You'd better not be rolling anything else but tobacco, you know.'

'What do you mean?'

'When you're with your mates. Weed or anything.'

I shove him playfully, although it's not as if I've never been offered it.

'You're joking, aren't you? How would I afford it on the pittance you give me?'

He leans down and plants a kiss on my forehead, an ashy, sour-wine kiss. 'I'm off to bed. Make sure you don't leave the TV on standby.'

'Yeah, yeah,' I sigh, 'I know. Save the planet, blah, blah, blah.'

He offers me one last smile before backing out of the room, his eyes not leaving mine, like he fears it could be the last time he sees me.

I hear him shuffle up the stairs, his bedroom door closing, so I reach for the remote and flick *The Shawshank Redemption* back to the opening credits.

My eyes retreat to the screen, pushing away the thought of Dad hiding his loneliness from me. I mean, we all have our secrets.

Me more than most.

CHAPTER 4

The central heating had clicked off by the time I woke, the cold air nipping at my exposed skin.

The clock told me it was half past three and I groaned in protest before stretching for the corner of my duvet.

A slicing sensation in my arm stopped me before I could reach it and suddenly the truth of what I'd done slapped me across the face.

It'd happened again. I'd given into it, hadn't I?

My left hand moved hesitantly down to my right arm, tackling the job that my eyes were too ashamed to. The pain on contact shocked me upright, forcing me to look at what I'd done.

Initially there was nothing to see but a bulky wad of gauze, but as I teased it away from my skin I was left in no doubt. Around the cut was a drying patch of blood that had been staunched by the padding, but the wound itself was still angry, bleeding in protest as I pulled gently. Reaching to the floor with my good arm, I grabbed a fresh piece of gauze, plus the Savlon. Taking the cap off with my teeth, I smeared it on to the gauze and pressed gently, wincing as the cream fought with the cut.

The nail scissors were sat on another piece of gauze, at the end of the bed where I'd left them, the bloodstains wiped off, alcohol applied. I'd clean them again once my arm was sorted.

Being methodical about it all helped somehow. God knows there was no method to the rest of it. The rest of it was anarchy, this sudden wall of panic that I couldn't fight off.

When the fear first came six months ago, I could beat it with deep breathing and pacing around. It scared me, but not enough to bother Dad with. I just put it down to hormones, and there was no way Dad was going to talk to me about that.

It's about more than that, though. I've known that ever since the pacing stopped working. At first I upped the ante a bit, splashing my face with cold water, pressing my forehead against the condensation on the bedroom window. But that didn't cut it either, not once I'd found Mum's report and seen for definite what I'd done to her.

From that point on, a couple of months back, the fear had come thick and fast. Not every night at first, it picked its moments, overpowering me when I was at my most tired, most stressed. Teased me it did, working me up into such a sweat that I started to pinch at the skin on my arms, doing whatever I could to jolt myself to my senses.

That worked too for a while, until the fear got wise to it, pressing the accelerator so hard that a pinch didn't touch the sides. Until there was nothing left to do but turn to the nail scissors in my bedside drawer.

I winced at the shame of it, casting my eye at the skin

above my right elbow, the series of nicks and lines that sat in various states of repair. Some of them were long shallow scratches; others were short sharp nicks, clustered together like an *equals* sign. Not that any of them gave me the answer.

The only thing I knew was that the scissors worked. Why or how I had no idea, but to be honest that didn't matter. For now it was enough – it had to be, until I worked out what to do to make the fear go away for good.

What I couldn't afford to do was let it get in the way of school, of fitting in. If I started to show weakness now it would only make things worse, give them an opportunity to see what I was really about, and I couldn't let that happen.

Gingerly I stood, wrapping the duvet around me without reducing pressure on the gauze.

Stop the bleeding. Check it's clean. Bin all the evidence. Get some sleep. Follow those steps and I'd be OK. It was simple if I just followed the instructions.

When my eyes managed to open, they were greeted by a sight I hadn't expected.

Dad was perched on the edge of the bed, cup of tea in hand, cigarette tucked behind his ear.

'You look like I feel,' he said softly. 'There's a cup of tea there for you. Couple of dunkers too if you want them.'

'You been up long?'

'Few hours,' he lied, the wet hair slicked back on his head giving the game away. I watched him closely enough to know that the first thing he did every morning was have a shower.

I rolled towards my tea, the first real movement I'd dared since coming round, aside from blinking. But as I pushed my arm beneath me to sit up, I felt a white-hot pain shoot up it and I fell on to my back, swearing madly.

Dad was up in a flash, his arms on my shoulders, 'Daisy? What's the matter?'

'Nothing.'

I glimpsed under the duvet as discreetly as I could, and saw that my arm was covered in a crusted brown mess, the material sticking to it in places. It looked like a toddler had been finger-painting with it.

'Didn't sound like nothing. What's hurting? Let me look.'

I recoiled, tucking my arm beneath me, trying to ignore the second wave of pain, which made me want to be sick.

'I SAID IT'S NOTHING! Listen to me, will you?'

Dad was practically blasted off the bed with the force of my words. I'd never spoken to him like that. Never had reason to. And he didn't know what to do as a result, except back away slowly towards the door.

'OK. Sorry. I'll . . . er . . . I'll wait downstairs for you. Make you another tea.'

I could see his hand shaking as he reached for the handle, the colour in his face draining away.

I cringed as the door closed softly, knowing I'd hurt him as much as I'd hurt myself.

With the balled-up bedding under my arm, I plodded down the stairs towards the kitchen.

Dad was lost in his mug, a coffee as black as his mood steaming in front of him.

I scooted behind him, hoping to get to the washer without him noticing my bundle, but as I tried to ram it through the door, it unravelled just as Dad turned towards me. He clocked the large patch of blood on the corner.

'You all right?' he asked, his eyebrows turning up. 'You have a nosebleed or something?'

My mind froze as my hands went into overdrive, shoving the load into the drum as quickly as I could, hoping the exertion would mean the blood rushed to my hands instead of my cheeks.

'Daisy?' Dad repeated. 'I said, is everything all right?'

'Yeah,' I said, wobbling as I pulled myself to my feet. 'Yeah, fine.'

'Was it a nosebleed?'

I fixed him with a look, a desperate lie flitting into my mind just in time.

'No, Dad,' I mouthed slowly, 'not a nosebleed, no. Believe me –' and at this point I put a full stop between each word – 'I. Don't. Think. You. Want. To. Know. Know what I mean?'

Dad stared at me for a second longer than I thought he would, until the world's biggest penny dropped and the prospect of talking about periods scared him half to death.

'I'll just finish your tea,' he blushed, jumping to his feet and hiding behind the kettle.

I exhaled deeply, hoping I could breathe out the shame of the lie before Dad got back to the table.

Sliding a mug towards me, he stroked my head softly with his other hand, an action that made me want to confess everything.

Unfortunately he didn't give me a chance.

'You got plans for today?'

I shrugged. 'Nothing exciting.'

'Well, I reckon we can remedy that. There's a double bill on at the Ritzy. Couple of spaghetti westerns that I haven't seen in years. I reckon you'd love them. Do you fancy it?'

It wasn't the kind of thing I ever said no to. Not out of duty, although I knew it made him happy. I gave him the biggest smile I had, nodding so hard I must have looked weird.

'Are you sure you're OK?' he asked. 'You know, if something's bothering you, you can tell me. You know that, don't you?'

I couldn't look him in the eye and diverted my gaze to my cup instead.

'I'm fine,' I gulped. 'Just tired. But thanks. And the same applies to you.'

He looked confused.

'You know, if anything's bothering you. I'm here for you too.'

It was an invite to talk about her, to tell me how much he missed her. But he didn't, he just mirrored my reaction and studied his drink.

That was all I needed to know. He wasn't all right, and neither was I, but at least we had Clint Eastwood to take our minds off it, for a few hours at least.

CHAPTER 5

English lessons had taken on a new dimension since Mr Hobson's arrival, to the female half of the class at least.

Suddenly, chairs were occupied as soon as the bell went and the classroom shimmered with the amount of lip gloss being applied. It was funny to watch, there was no denying it.

Donna Riley stood at the front of the admirers' queue, her skirt getting shorter by the lesson. What I didn't expect, though, was to be enrolled in her plan to impress him.

'I need you to help me,' she beamed, no trace of embarrassment on her face as she sat beside me.

I was tempted to look around, to make sure she wasn't speaking to someone else.

'Do you reckon you can get him over here more often? To our desk?'

'Who?'

'Hobson, you fool. You're good at this English stuff, know what buttons to push. So I need you to ask the right questions. Ones that'll get him over to us.'

I was stumped. She wasn't someone you said no to, not unless you had a death wish, so I grinned knowingly, nodding along.

Somehow I got my expression wrong, as she fixed me icily.

'I don't want you trying too hard to impress him or nothing. You just need to get him over here at least once a lesson. That way he'll keep noticing me.'

'What's the best thing to ask him?'

'I don't know. You're the brain. Just ask him about apostrophes or something. Nothing impressive, mind. I need him to see *me*, don't forget.'

I tried the expression again, more successfully this time, which was a huge relief.

And so, for the next couple of lessons, I played my bit part in Donna's plan, waiting for her to nudge me under the table, egging me into some crappy question that I already knew the answer to. It usually got Mr Hobson over to us, and as expected Donna did her best to flutter her eyelashes or giggle at what he said, whether it was funny or not.

To be honest, I don't think he had a clue what was going on, but he was a lot more patient with me than he was with her, humouring me despite my ridiculous questions. I thought I still caught him looking my way, fixing me with this hesitant smile for a second too long, but I pushed it to the back of my mind, thinking he was probably just waiting for my next inane question.

I was doing my job, pleasing Donna as much as I could, but eventually, about three weeks in, the wheels fell off.

'From reading your creative work,' he crowed, 'it's become clear that a number of you don't understand the importance of dialogue. How it can sometimes tell you more about a character's state of mind than even the finest piece of prose.'

He was met by a sea of blank faces. But I knew where he was going.

'So,' he continued, 'I'm going to show you a scene from a film. But my question to you is "Why?"'

Shoulders shrugged. Heads dropped to avoid making eye contact and I felt a dig in my ribs from Donna.

'Do you know?' she whispered, but as I leaned over to fill her in, we were interrupted.

'Miss Riley!' came his voice, a hint of irritation in it. 'Do you already know the answer?'

Donna stared at me pleadingly, but what was I going to do? Send her a text? I just shrugged and mouthed 'Sorry'.

'What about you, Daisy?' I thought I heard his voice soften, but could've been wrong. 'Come on. Share it, will you?'

I felt my cheeks burn as eyes spun towards me, waiting for me to make Donna look stupid. I was ready to shake my head and blend in, when he interrupted again.

'I think you know the answer to this, Daisy, don't you? Even if you don't, give it a go.'

And before I could stop myself, I spoke up.

'Because in cinema dialogue is all you have? You haven't got prose, so you have to let the characters fill in the gaps with what they say.'

'Hallelujah,' he shouted. 'Spot on. Take a bow. Now, all of you, I need you to watch this scene. It's only three minutes long, but it tells you more than ten pages of description could.'

And as he dropped the blinds and hit play, I felt a buzz of appreciation ripple through me. As well as a fierce glare from Donna.

She found me during the lunch hour. She didn't take me aside to a quiet place and give me a slap. That wasn't the way she rolled. She was into ritual humiliation, the thing I feared most.

'Everything OK?' I asked, already knowing the answer, feeling eyes falling upon me, sensing a battle.

'OK?' she barked, with an expression usually reserved for the kids she despised. 'What do you think? I looked like a complete twat in there. How do you think I feel?'

'I'm sorry,' I offered, feeling my guilt levels rise. 'I tried to give you a heads up, didn't I?'

'Not very hard, though, eh?'

'What do you mean? He was looking right at us. I could hardly write it down for you, could I?'

'Obviously!' she huffed. 'But there is such a thing as saying nothing at all, you know.'

'What?'

'You could've done what I did. Said nothing and looked stupid.'

I couldn't help but laugh. 'But that's crazy.'

Before I knew it, the gap between us shrunk to nothing.

'No, I'll tell you what's crazy. It's crazy that I asked for your help and that you chose to throw it back in my face. Doesn't that seem like an odd choice to you?'

It did. I knew it did, as I'd seen what she'd done to other kids who'd done the same. I couldn't let that happen to me, not if I wanted to hold everything together and keep everyone at a safe distance.

'I'll sort it out,' I gabbled, wiping a mixture of my sweat and her spit from my face. 'He'll have forgotten all about it by the next lesson and I can throw you some good examples of dialogue working. He'll love that.'

She looked at me like I was talking Japanese.

'Too late for that now,' she sneered. 'They mark your card soon as they meet you, this lot. Best thing you can do now is keep a low profile. Stay out of my eyeline and out of his good books. I'll be watching you. You hear?'

I didn't have a chance to nod before the bell rang and the corridor swelled with other kids, leaving me to fight my way against the tide, towards the exit. I knew where I had to go to sort out my head and it wasn't here.

CHAPTER 6

Taking refuge in a cinema wasn't a new experience. Dad and me had been hiding in them for as long as I could remember, but doing it during school time? It was risky, but it had to be done.

I shaded my eyes as I approached the exit doors, preparing for a rare blast of sun on the other side. There was nothing worse after a film than a bad case of sun blindness.

Although the screening finished twenty minutes after school did, I still had to be careful as I left. Didn't want anyone clocking me, wondering how I'd got into town so quickly. This was the fifth time I'd risked bunking off and so far everything had worked out tidily. No one, it seemed, suspected a thing.

I wasn't daft about it. I registered in the afternoon before ducking out, had even forged a letter from Dad once about a hospital appointment. Didn't want anyone getting suspicious or anything. Plus I was canny about what I was wearing when I arrived at the Ritzy. One sniff of a school uniform and I'd be shown the door, so I always switched my jumper and school shoes as I left, adding this flowy scarf I had, plus a shed-load of lip gloss. The hope was that I passed for a sixth-former on a free period, and despite sweaty palms each time I bought my ticket, no one seemed to look twice.

By the time I hit fresh air, I'd forgotten all about the film I'd seen. For the first painful time in my life, it was unimportant. What mattered was that I was out of the glare at school, my absence limiting the damage I could do by simply being there, especially in Hobson's lessons.

The run-in with Donna had scared me, made a nonsense of the balancing act that I thought I'd perfected. I couldn't risk another cock-up in front of Hobson: Donna never gave second warnings. I'd been lucky to get a first.

Hobson didn't help things either. He'd continued using films in a number of his lessons, and when no one came up with the answers quickly enough, I was his default setting. Not that I gave him anything. Not a single answer. It wasn't worth the risk, regardless of how easy the questions were.

He was bemused by my sudden lobotomy. He looked at me in such confusion, like he knew that I was doing it on purpose. After a couple of lessons where I refused to answer, he kept me back on my own, earning me a glare from Donna for my trouble. I couldn't win.

'Is everything OK, Daisy?' he asked.

'Sir?'

'I'm slightly worried about you, how you've been these last couple of weeks. You've seemed a bit, pensive. Not the same person you were when I arrived.'

'Don't know what you mean, sir. Everything's fine.'

Donna's head appeared in the window of the door, irritation plain to see.

'I got the feeling that film was your thing,' he added, looking for a way in. 'I was surprised, given what you'd said before, that you didn't know the answers this time.'

'Must've got lucky, I suppose.' My feet were shuffling towards the door.

'I'm right, though, aren't I? Films are something you love, aren't they?'

It seemed an odd question, but I shrugged it off, not wanting to give him anything to lengthen the conversation.

'They're all right,' I mumbled. 'Can I go, sir? I've got to get home quick. I've something on.'

Still frowning, he nodded, and after checking the coast was clear I made a swift exit towards the river path and home.

That's when I'd decided on doing the occasional bunk. It seemed the safest option, away from either Donna or Mr Hobson. And the cinema was the perfect place to disappear.

Or at least it had been, but as I walked down the cinema steps I crashed headlong into someone, bumping them off balance, jarring my scarred arm in the process. They seemed to bounce back in slow motion as I recognized them.

It was Mr Hobson.

I'd have bolted if I thought it would do me any good. And if he hadn't launched into a conversation.

'Daisy? What are you doing here?'

There seemed no option but to tell him the truth.

'I presumed when I didn't see you in class this afternoon that you were ill. I certainly didn't expect this.'

I braced myself for a lecture, or for him to drag me back to the head's office, but that wasn't what I got.

'Is the lesson so bad that you felt you had to do this?' he asked, almost hurt.

'It's not about the lesson, sir. There's nothing wrong with the lesson.'

'So why bunk off? It's hardly what I expected of you. You always seemed so . . . keen?'

It wasn't a question I could answer. Not without unpicking all my hard work and leaving me with a slap from Donna. Strangely, neither option appealed, so I came up with a complete lie.

'Just couldn't face it today, sir. It's the first time I've done it. Really.'

'And was it worth it?'

'Sir?'

'The film. Was it any good?'

There was a smile on his face. It didn't belong there, not in these circumstances, but he genuinely looked amused and interested.

'It was . . . pretty, well, average really. Just some rubbish rom-com.'

'Nothing worse than a disappointing film. It always seems like such a waste. And there are so many brilliant romantic comedies as well. Have you ever seen *When Harry Met Sally*?'

I shook my head.

'And you call yourself a film fan? That's more disappointing than finding you bunking off! You should do something about it.'

The whole conversation was baffling. I didn't know if that was my cue to smile and walk off or what, but he had one more thing he wanted to say, the smile disappearing as he started.

'Daisy, all jokes aside, you've put me in a difficult position. You know I have to think of your welfare and let the school know what's gone on. What would we have done if something had happened while you were meant to be in our care? I know you're nearly fifteen, but you're still vulnerable. There are people about who would still look to take advantage of you.'

Shit. Dad was going to be asking a lot of questions now, ones I didn't want to answer.

'But I see your potential as well, Daisy. And I don't want you getting a reputation in school for a one-off mistake. And this is a one-off, isn't it?'

'It is, definitely.'

'OK. So let's chalk this one up to experience, shall we? I can keep a secret if you can.'

The relief was so great I wanted to kiss him. Naturally I stifled that feeling.

'That would be magic, sir. I won't do it again.'

His grin was back. 'Make sure you don't. We have to trust each other, you hear? Otherwise I'll be in as much trouble as you. There's one thing you need to do, though, Daisy. And that's really think about why you've done this. And if you need help in doing that, then ask. There's something special about you and no one wants to see you struggle when there's no need.'

His words punctured me slightly, because he'd been honest when all I'd done was lie. They made me realize what I'd been storing up and how heavy it suddenly all felt. In an instant tears came to my eyes and I lifted up a hand to shade them.

'Are you sure you're OK?' he asked.

'Sure, thank you,' I gabbled, before walking slowly away.

'You know where I am,' he yelled as a parting shot.

I did know, because each time I glanced back he was still there, smiling kindly.

CHAPTER 7

Dad realized there was something wrong when I didn't wolf my tea down. We both knew there was a DVD to follow, which was usually enough to get me past a plate of beans on toast in minutes. Spearing them individually must have said a lot.

'You all right?' Dad asked.

'Yeah, course.'

'I put chilli powder on them, the way you like it.'

'Cheers.' I skewered another one.

'And Marmite on your toast too.'

'I know. It's perfect, ta.'

He studied me and I could feel his concern, but didn't know what to do about it. Not without making him uncomfortable.

That's how it worked every time I brought Mum up: he'd sweat, mumble and eventually get so fidgety that I'd let the subject drop. Usually, I couldn't put him through it, as much as I needed to hear about her.

It was his reluctance that had forced me behind his back and into the loft. I'd been desperate to find something that pulled me a bit closer to her – photos, letters, anything. But

I hadn't expected to find the report from the hospital, a single piece of paper that turned everything on its head and pointed the finger directly at me.

The thought of it now made my arms prickle and pulse race, but as much as I wanted to burn the report or bin it, anything to deny its existence, I couldn't. Instead it sat in my drawer, ready for the next time I needed to punish myself.

'Daisy, are you listening to me?' His hand on my scabbed arm pulled me back into the room and out of my chair. My sudden movement was enough to get him on his feet too. 'What is *wrong* with you tonight?'

'Nothing's wrong. I'm just tired, that's all.'

'Has something happened at school?'

'No, of course not. School's fine.'

'Is it something I've done, then?'

He looked so wounded before even hearing an answer that I shook my head.

'Is it the film I chose? You know we don't have to watch it tonight.' His eyes sparked up. 'We could go out. There's a new comedy on at the Ritzy, the one you wanted to catch. Why don't we go see that instead? A midweek treat.'

I couldn't do the Ritzy, not after being there a couple of hours ago. What if someone recognized me, commented on me being back so soon?

Anyway, that wasn't the point. I couldn't do any film tonight. I didn't want to escape. I wanted to talk about Mum for once, instead of pretending she'd never lived.

'Do we have to?'

He clutched at his chest, feigning a heart attack, a desperate bid at humour. 'What. Did. You. Say?' he gasped, which made me testier than I should've been.

'Jesus, Dad,' I snapped. 'Don't make me out to be some kind of freak. I just don't fancy it for once, that's all. We could do something else, you know. Other people do.'

He tried to look confused, but I reckon he knew what I wanted to talk about. Walking to the kettle with his back to me confirmed it. He'd do anything he could to not chat about Mum, and for once I wasn't prepared to let him.

'You know what we could do?' I said, too much steel in my voice to sound anything but antagonistic. 'We could go up into the loft and dig out some photos of Mum. Find pictures we could put around the house.'

He didn't turn as he stirred his tea mechanically. 'We already have photos of her out.'

'We have two, Dad,' I yelled, 'and one is by your bed! She's hardly everywhere we look. Why can't we spend an hour, thirty minutes even, choosing some pictures I could put in my room or in the lounge.'

I realized what my brain was doing. It was trying to force him up there, not to find photos, but for him to notice that the hospital report had gone and that I'd found it, to back him into a corner so he had to acknowledge what I'd done to her. I wanted him to get angry with me and shout at me, because then it would be out there and maybe in time he might forgive me. Perhaps then I could fight the fear away, maybe then I could stop hurting myself.

But he wasn't going to give. I saw his shoulders slump as he turned to me, his brow creased deeper than ever before.

'I can't, Daisy. Not tonight.'

'Then tomorrow maybe. Or the weekend. I don't mind when it is.'

'Stop HASSLING me!'

The volume blew a gust past my ears.

He never shouted. At anyone, never mind me. Part of me wanted to turn and throw a strop out of the room, to show him how upset I was, how much this meant. But I never got the chance, because he was through the door before me, each footstep on the stairs an avalanche.

CHAPTER 8

The landslide didn't stop at home. It became more and more difficult to keep my feet at school too, especially now my cinema trips had been rumbled.

I tried hard to keep a lower profile than ever, but seemed only to find ways of drawing attention to myself.

In a single day I managed to walk into an open locker door (almost decapitating myself) and embarrassed myself hideously in a PE lesson (me and hockey sticks never did go together) before dropping my lunch tray in front of the whole school. It was like someone had a humiliation magnet trained on me, and to cap it off we had English last period, another pitfall that I doubted I could avoid.

To help me further Donna cranked up the pressure as we marched in.

'I'm expecting great things from you today, hear me?'

After ten minutes I could feel the sweat pooling on my back. I had to feed her some info that would help, because the alternative didn't bear thinking about.

Salvation eventually came about half an hour in when Hobson asked a question about a prologue. I scribbled the answer furiously in my exercise book, almost breaking the page with my nib, before thrusting it under Donna's nose. Her hand shot up instantly, blurting the answer out proudly despite not having the foggiest what it meant.

Mr Hobson stood in shock for a second before beaming widely.

'Excellent answer, Donna. Spot on.'

Modest as always, she stood and curtsied to the class, quickly unpicking the work she, or rather I, had done. She didn't stop beaming for the rest of the lesson, except to grill me for more answers.

'Good to see you pulled yourself together,' she said as we stood to leave.

'I'm doing my best,' I answered, trying to act casual, though I must have sounded desperate.

'Well, you've a long way to go yet. Don't forget that.' And with a final snarl she upended my bag on to the floor, its contents skimming over the tiles, including the case that held my scissors and lint.

Fortunately she didn't look back, soaking up giggles from the others as she paraded out. I was on my knees in a flash, scuttling around until I spotted my tin.

I was unravelling quickly. I needed to get everything in the bag and home before anything else went wrong.

'You've missed some stuff over here,' sighed Hobson, bending to retrieve my gym kit. I took it meekly, not daring to look at him. 'Oh, and there's this too.'

He had my tin. I could hear the scissors rattling inside and prayed he couldn't work out what it was for.

I snatched this time, eager to have it in my hands.

'Steady on, Daisy. I'm trying to help.'

'Sorry, sir.' I blushed. 'Just in a rush to get home.'

'Well, let me help you, then.' He turned to pick up my bag, delaying a second with it before coming back to me.

'It's like the Tardis, this thing. I can't believe how much stuff you fit in it. So, how are you? How's . . . things?'

'Fine,' I mumbled. 'Great.'

'Really? It's good to see you back in class, but it's only really in body, isn't it? I didn't hear from you again today.'

I bit my lip at what I'd gifted Donna.

'What can I say?' I offered. 'I never was the sharpest tool.'

He sat on the desk in front of me with a sigh.

'What a load of bollocks.'

The sharpness of his words made me look at him.

'We both know that's not true. I look around the room and I see more potential in you than in any of the others.'

'Course you do,' I scoffed.

'It's true. You have something very special, Daisy. You're intuitive, instinctive, and it kills me to see you not fulfilling your potential.'

'I'm getting by.'

'But that shouldn't be enough for you. I've read your file in the office, spoken to the other teachers, and they'd like more from you too. I know there's something holding you back. I realize we've had this conversation before, but you need to know that whatever is on your mind, we can sort it out.'

'Honestly, sir, there's nothing going on.'

'Daisy, we both know that's bull.'

'How do YOU know?'

'Because I've been there, and I acted just like you,' he added quietly, before pulling himself to his feet. 'There were things I bottled up for a long time. Stuff that ate away at me, and until I got brave and told someone, someone I trusted, it messed me up badly. I don't want the same to happen to you. You're worth more than that, do you understand?' He laid his hand on my arm, my bad arm, but I didn't pull away in pain. Instead I felt a buzz ripple up it, all the way to my shoulder.

'Think about what I've said, won't you?' he said as he gathered his stuff and headed to the door.

'I will, sir. Thanks,' I answered, instinctively feeling for my scars, still sensing the rare good feeling that he'd left there.

I thought about little else all the way home. In a way he was right, I needed to unload, but I daren't. What I'd caused was so unforgivable, how would anybody understand or want to help? It wasn't as if I could talk to Dad either. It was hardly a roaring success last time I tried, and we'd barely spoken since.

I kept going back to something Hobson had said, that he'd been there, done the same as me, and I wondered, hoped even, that maybe he might be the one person who'd get it, who wouldn't laugh or run off in disgust. The thought of sharing started a new wave of fear circling me, forcing both my step and my heartbeat up from an amble to a jog. I needed to be home, in my room, where I could fend it off safely, where no one could see me or my scissors.

I managed it as well, or did for a while. Dad wasn't home, which calmed me a bit, and for once I kept the panic at bay with a shed-load of pacing about. I tried to force my head into other things too, thinking that unpacking my bag would divert my thoughts elsewhere, and it did until I found a parcel in the bottom of it, wrapped clumsily in brown paper. Frowning, I turned it over, fearful of it being a gag from Donna, another way of humiliating me. Binning it went through my head, but I couldn't shelve the curiosity and found myself peeling back the wrapping at the top right-hand corner.

Instantly I recognized the packaging. DVDs. Two of them, *When Harry Met Sally* (the film he'd banged on about at the cinema) and one called *Frankie and Johnny*. Both looked old, like they'd been on someone's shelf for years, and I frowned because I hadn't seen either of them. Both were rom-coms, identical-looking to the film I'd seen when he caught me leaving the Ritzy. There was a note tucked into one of the sleeves, a scrawl I could just about make out:

> *If it's comfort viewing you're after, try these two. I love*
> *'em! Don't worry about giving them back . . . I have*
> *spares . . . enjoy!*
> *TH*

He must have slid them in there when he was helping me with my stuff. But why hide it? In a way it didn't matter, it was the size of the gesture that counted. I couldn't remember the last time someone did anything like that, or knew me well enough to get it right. I was stoked and terrified in equal measure, but chose to push *When Harry Met Sally* quickly into the DVD player. Watching it would give us something to talk about, things that might allow me to get on to the stuff that really mattered.

CHAPTER 9

He was right about the films, both of them. All right, they were rom-coms like he said, a bit cheesy and soppy with inevitable happy endings, but that was what made them so great. They were like comfort food, perfect to escape into, away from all the other nonsense cluttering up my head.

When Harry Met Sally was so great I watched it every night for the next three days. I didn't share it with Dad either. I wanted it for myself for a change, plus it gave me an excuse to steer clear of him. From the maudlin look on his face he didn't look ready to talk about our argument either.

The most pressing thing was finding a way of thanking Mr Hobson without embarrassing myself in front of everyone else.

I couldn't march up to him at the end of the class without drawing unwanted attention, but also because his gift had kind of changed things in my head.

I started feeling nervy every time he walked in, and instead of not answering his questions for fear of Donna, I was silent for fear of him changing his mind about me, about me being special. I mean, he'd said that, hadn't he?

It was stupid, I know, but no one had shown interest in

me before, and it felt like he understood me, like he could see the thought processes behind my eyes. And if that was the case I didn't want to stuff it up, even if it meant I told him nothing else.

It took me about a week to find the opportunity to speak to him properly, and in that time Dad and me had spent zero time together. I couldn't remember when we'd last gone two nights without flopping down in front of a film, and it was eating at me, taking the shine off the positives I was feeling.

It had been a difficult day. I'd felt on edge, like the next humiliation was just ahead of me, and as a result I'd hung around in the toilets until most of the kids had gone – it seemed easier to do this than face the chance of one last run-in – and was just passing through the gates when Mr Hobson strode up next to me, looking like he could do the whole day over again.

I admired his energy, wanted to be able to suck a bit of it up and let it whiz round my body too.

His grin was infectious, and, it seemed, he knew it.

'Now that's what I like to see. A smile on your face.'

'Bit of a rarity, is it, sir?'

'Not just with you. With exams going on, I've never seen so many arsey people in one place.'

I'd had no idea that the other kids had stuff going on for them. Stuff that made them unhappy. I'd been so wrapped up in myself, going round in endless circles trying to work out how to deal with Dad, the fear and the fallout, that I didn't have space for anything else. And I couldn't see how that was going to change unless I unloaded it all somewhere.

'So what's news with you, then?' He'd obviously got bored of waiting for me to respond.

'Oh, you know, not much.'

'Seen anything good lately?'

'I have as a matter of fact.'

He knew which films I meant, he must have done.

'And what were they, then?'

'I think you know the answer already.'

'Well, I'm glad you liked them. They're definitely favourites of mine.'

My cheeks flushed as I tried to work out how to say thank you in a way that told him what it really meant. But typically I failed. Instead I went for the dumb option.

'Why did you hide them in my bag? Why didn't you just give me them?'

'Seemed like the right thing to do. You were so flustered with your stuff going everywhere, I thought you might explode if I sprung them on you. Anyway, everyone needs a surprise every now and then.'

'Well, it was definitely that.' I smiled from behind my fringe. 'Cheered me up it did. Big time.'

'So it should too. Modern classics. Both of them.'

I nodded before realizing I didn't know what to say next. He didn't either, and there was a moment that felt awkward. I wanted to fill it with something that would keep him talking to me. Beyond our conversation stretched another frosty night with Dad and I wasn't ready for that yet.

'You taking the path home tonight?' he asked.

I gazed across the road to 'the path', a concrete walkway that led down the river towards home.

How he knew it was always my route I didn't know, or choose to worry about. I nodded.

'Mind if I walk with you?'

'Er . . . no. I mean fine.'

We crossed the road and down the path in silence, my heart thumping, until we hit the river.

'I like this bit of town,' he said, as if almost to himself. 'Reminds me that we're not far from the sea.'

'Yeah.' I looked at the water, at the scum and rubbish that collected at its edges. 'Hardly attractive, though, is it?'

'Venice of the North!' He grinned. 'I like it. I've never lived on the coast before, so it's a bit of a novelty.'

I nodded, trying to look interested without being dorky.

'What about you, Daisy? You always lived here?'

'Yeah. Can't really imagine living anywhere else. Dad was born here too. Reckons there's no escape, says the road that comes in is strictly one-way.'

'And what about your mum? She local too?'

It felt like an innocent question, so I allowed myself to answer.

'Nah, she moved around loads when she was young. Her dad had some big job that took him all over the place.'

'Mine too,' he said with a sigh. 'Makes you want to find somewhere good and stay put. Is that what happened with your mum?'

I chewed the inside of my lip, wondering how to respond to that one. How much I could say without opening the box too wide.

'Yeah, probably.'

I waited for his response, my breath holding, hoping he'd move the conversation along.

'What does your dad do, then?'

'He's a sales rep for a publisher.' It felt good, safe, and I let the sentence out quickly in relief. 'Has been ever since I was born.'

'So he's a big reader?'

'Kind of. He does read and that. But he's more of a film man really.'

'Of course. That's where you get it from, eh?'

'Right.' It felt good to have had thirty seconds of comfortable conversation. Shame, then, that it came crashing down with the next question.

'And what about your mum? Does she work as well?'

I couldn't remember the last time someone asked me a question about Mum. Everyone knew she was dead, and that conversations about her were too. Everyone except Mr Hobson, who didn't know any better.

I'm not sure what my face was saying to him, but it must have been something grim, because it stopped him in his tracks.

'Daisy? Are you all right?'

I pushed some hair behind my ears and breathed in deeply, steeling myself.

'No, I'm fine. It's just . . . well, we . . . Mum's dead, you see.'

The words didn't feel any better out in the open. They never did. It felt like they paved the way to people seeing what I'd done to her. That it was only a few more questions until they worked out that it was all my fault.

'Oh, that's awful. And crappy of me to bring it up like that. Sorry, I didn't think.'

I tried to pull myself upright, pass it off as no big deal.

'Don't worry about it. How could you know? Anyway, it was a long time ago.'

We plodded on in silence. Minutes passed as we walked beneath the bridges that ran over the river. In that time I searched for a new line of conversation in my head. For anything that would take us away from dead mothers.

But typically, nothing popped up. Not even a fail-safe favourite film or actor to take us off on a tangent.

So much time had passed and I was so deep in thought that when his next words came, I had no idea what he was talking about.

'I've always hated that assumption about time.'

'Sorry?'

'That time makes it easier when it comes to death. It's never worked like that for me anyway. Not with my mum.'

I looked at him, trying to work out if I'd heard him right.

I threw his words up in the air to see if they landed in the same order.

Did he just say that he'd lost his mum too? And if it was true, then why wait those minutes before coming out with it? Why let the silence and awkwardness of what I'd said hang there?

I sneaked a look at him, to try and work out if this was just some weird wind-up, or whether he was spinning me a line to make me feel better.

But his face matched mine. He wasn't close to tears, or milking it like some crap soap actor. There was something

49

there. Something around his eyes that told me it was true, and it was a realization that bumped the fear closer to the surface, forcing me to breathe deeply and keep it in check.

Silence again, except for the gravel crunching underfoot and the hopes whirring round my head.

Hopes that finally, finally, I might have found someone who understood.

CHAPTER 10

I'd never really thought about walking home from school alone before. It had always been about getting from A to B, half an hour where I thought about what I might watch that night, that or beat myself up about something or other.

I saw the other kids trooping out in groups, bursting to share their news from the day, but I didn't envy them or wish it for myself. Or I hadn't until that first walk with Mr Hobson. After that night I wanted it all the time, the company, the banter, the smiles it brought to my face. And it had to be from him.

He didn't appear every day as school ended, and on those nights I'd meander down the path alone, turning every minute, desperately needing to see him trotting along to catch up. Sometimes he did, sometimes not. I even found myself slowing down as I left for the day, giving him time to gather up his stuff, increasing the chances of running into him 'accidentally'. It mattered that much, made the hugest difference to my mood for the rest of the day.

We didn't always talk about much. Well, apart from the obvious. He had weird taste in films, was always banging on about art-house things from directors I'd never heard of. I'd wind him up, telling him he couldn't possibly like them if he was into rom-coms, that he was a film snob. He always took the wind-up with a smile before dishing the abuse straight back at me.

We'd walk for a bit, and chat for a bit, and sometimes sit on this bench by a particularly ugly bit of the river, all silt and marooned shopping trolleys. Not that it mattered. I'd forget about everything apart from how I was feeling. How he was making me feel.

And how was that?

Well, it was just different.

Nothing corny or dramatic.

Half an hour in his presence stopped me drowning for the rest of the day, stopped me fretting about what might or might not get said to Dad when I pushed through the front door. He made me feel like I was worth something, like what I said counted. And it felt good.

'I worked out last night that this is the eleventh school I've taught in.' He sighed and sat down.

'And how long have you been doing it?'

'Couple of years.'

'Why move about like that? Wouldn't you rather stick around and get to know places better?'

'It hasn't appealed,' he sighed. 'Not since my mum died really. It's easier to keep moving around. New places mean new challenges. It stops me thinking about her and getting maudlin.'

His words hit me hard. At least he knew what it was he was trying to replace. I'd never had that luxury. I would have killed to have known Mum for even a year or two. The thought alone started the fear circling.

'This place feels different, though. Better.'

'Why's that, then?'

'Not really sure. I've taught in places with better resources and brighter kids, but your school has got under my skin, you know?'

He fixed me with a stare that made me nod automatically, although I didn't relate to what he was saying. I had no idea why this place would appeal to anyone. But I couldn't help hoping that I might have something to do with it. The fear laughed at the thought, causing my skin to prickle in embarrassment.

'So you think you'll stick around for a while, then?'

I cringed after saying it.

'Yeah, I reckon so. Miss Addison's no closer to coming back, so you're stuck with me for a while yet.'

'Donna will be pleased.'

'What is it with you and her?' he asked. 'Have you had a falling-out or something?'

'We were never friends to start with.'

'But I've seen the way she relies on you in class. She obviously looks up to you.'

'You're kidding me?'

'Well, she obviously sees that you know the answers.' He paused for a second, noticing the tension in me at the mention of her.

'Is she the reason you've been ducking out of class, Daisy?'

'No,' I lied, clenching and unclenching my fists to stop them fizzing.

'Because if she is, you need to do something about it. Or we do. You can't let one person get in the way of you progressing. Not when they have no interest in learning themselves.'

'It doesn't matter.'

I could feel my voice getting quieter, the bumping of my heart against my ribcage. I didn't like the digging, wasn't in control any more of where it was going. The fear loved it, started hanging on to me as my thoughts unravelled.

'Of course it matters. You need to do something about it. Talk to her. Sort it out. Or let us do it for you.'

'You have *met* Donna, haven't you?'

'I've seen her in every school I've been at, or variations of her. And you can't allow yourself to be scared of her, you really can't. It's not worth it. You're not scared of her, are you, Daisy?'

It wasn't a difficult question, or even a profound one. But for some reason it was all he needed to ask. Because it was true, I wasn't scared of her. I was scared of *everything*. And I was suddenly so overwhelmingly tired of feeling like it.

A gasp of sadness burst into my throat, taking me by surprise, pushing its way past my lips as a tear escaped from my eye.

Stupid. How could I be so weak?

He was on to it in a flash. Hardly surprising, as it was a pitiful sight, full of weakness.

He turned towards me, tucking his left leg underneath the other on the bench.

'Hey now, what's all this about?'

'It's nothing. I'm just tired, that's all. It's been a bit full on, what with everything.'

'And what *is* everything, Daisy? What is it that's getting to you?'

I shook my head, blowing deeply to calm myself down, aware of my heart speeding up.

'It's fine. You can tell me. Really you can. Whatever it is, I can guarantee you it's not as bad as you think. It never is.'

'I can't tell you.'

'Then you have to speak to someone else. You can't hold these things on your own. It's not fair to expect that of yourself. If you can't tell me, then tell your dad. Let him help you. Maybe he could come into school to see Donna's folks, set them straight on whatever's going on. I could even talk to him if you want.'

'I appreciate it, but there's no point. Dad's not . . . comfortable with stuff like that. He's not the talking type.'

'But he's your dad.' There was surprise in his voice that told me he didn't like the sound of this. 'If something is bothering you, he'd want to know, wouldn't he?'

'He's got his own stuff going on. Anyway, there's some things he just can't deal with. It's not the way he's made, you know?'

'Can you talk to him about your mum?'

All the tension in me leaked out at her name, at how simple the problem was to him. All I had to do was talk to Dad. It really was that simple, but it was also the one thing I couldn't do.

'Not about that, sir, no. I want to, and I've tried, but I can't. It's too difficult.'

'Why is it difficult? He's your dad. He must miss her too.'

'That's just it,' I moaned. 'I don't know how he feels. She's

55

this unspoken thing in our house. What I *do* know I've had to drag out of him and it kills him to talk, I can see it does. Anything else I found out, well –' I thought about the report and what it told me – 'I had to go searching for.'

He smiled at me sadly, his hands reaching gently for my shoulders, the same electric current rippling down them as when he touched me before.

'God, that must be so difficult. Believe me, I know.'

'You haven't seen how he looks at me sometimes. It's as if every time he lays his eyes on me, all he can really see is her, my mum. And all that does is break his heart all over again, that and make him hate me.'

I felt a whoosh of air escape from me as that final sentence left my mouth, a sentence that left me off balance and giddy, teetering into him, my forehead resting on his chest and my ridiculous tears soaking his shirt.

His arms snaked round my back and pulled me gently into him, his words in my ears.

'That's crazy. Why on earth would he hate you? You're his daughter. You're all he's got. Why on earth would he possibly hate you?'

I pushed my head further into his chest, so far that I feared I might knock him over. This was it. The last moment I could turn back. But I had to do it, even if it meant muffling the words so that if he did hear them, he wouldn't be able to push me away immediately.

'Because I took her away from him. I killed her. It's all my fault.'

My words bounced around the tiny gap between us.

I'd done it, spoken the words out loud that I feared the

most, the words that had been stuck in my brain for what felt like forever. I couldn't control it any more, it was out there, and I had to accept the consequences.

I felt my shoulders jerk as the tears struggled out of me and I braced myself, ready for him to push me away in disgust.

But he didn't. In fact he didn't move away at all. At first he whispered softly in my ear, telling me that everything was OK, that he understood. And as he told me, his upper body swayed slightly, taking me with him, rocking me like I was a baby.

I felt confused, convinced that he hadn't heard me, or understood what I'd said. I'd just told him that I'd killed my own mother and all he could do was coo in my ear. I had to put him straight before it made me any angrier.

I pushed my head back, trying to break his grip around me, forcing him to look at me.

'Did you not hear me?' I yelled in his face. 'I just told you I killed her.'

'And I heard you,' he said, his eyes not leaving mine as his left hand stroked my hair. 'But I don't believe you.'

'But you have to,' I spat. 'I've been trying to find a way of telling someone for months. I've read the report. It told me what I did. I can show you. You'll have to believe me!'

'It's OK, Daisy. I hear what you're saying. But I don't have to read anything to know what's true. And I know you don't have it in you. That's not you.'

I felt my body tense, the anger surge in me, and instantly I wanted to hit him, to hit him like I wanted to hit Donna. But he wouldn't let me. He just held on and told me again and again, 'That's not you.'

I don't know how many times he told me. It could have been five, it could've been fifty, but at some point something snapped and I couldn't listen to him any more.

'How is it that you think you know me, eh? How is it that you can sit there and tell me that I didn't do what I said I did? You don't know anything about me. You don't know how old I was when I did it, or how I did it. You don't know anything!'

But no matter what I threw at him, he didn't lose his temper or his grip. It was just the same expression locked on me, the same calming arm around my back, the same hand smoothing my hair.

I had only one thing left. Just one bullet that I could fire at him to prove he knew nothing, and without thinking I pulled myself out of his grip and ripped the sleeve of my right arm up past my elbow.

'Do you see this?' The anger in me was so loud that I looked at my scarred, scabbed arm for the first time with no feelings of repulsion. 'This is what I'm capable of. Can you see it? Well, can you?'

He nodded, his expression not changing for a second.

'Yes, I can see it.'

'Good. So don't tell me I'm not capable of hurting someone. If I'm capable of doing this to myself, how do YOU know what I could do to anyone else?'

'It's all right,' he said, and gently pulled my sleeve down. I tried to draw away, but somehow, with no force on his part, he wouldn't let me. He just buttoned my cuff and held on to me.

I struggled at first, but with little effect, and instead of the anger tears returned instead. Huge raking sobs that came up from my boots.

His quietening noises returned, soothing enough to fall into a rhythm with my crying, which slowly, slowly eased.

My head ached. Ached with the crying, with the size of the confession and the confusion of his acceptance.

But it was nothing compared to the confusion that followed as he pulled away from me and wiped away the tears before, slowly and deliberately, closing in to kiss me.

CHAPTER 11

Some of the best kisses in films are unexpected. Believe me, I've watched enough of them to know. I've seen kisses that caused fireworks to go off, the heavens to open or flowers to bloom as lips met.

But there was no romantic moment when Mr Hobson decided to kiss me, even though I'd daydreamed for weeks about how it might feel. After all, he was the person who finally understood me, the one I could trust to lay it on the line to.

For a split second I felt warmth, a relief that maybe I was worthy of someone's affections, but that was quickly replaced by the bizarrest of thoughts.

His name.

I had no idea what it was. Only that it started with T.

So he was Mr Hobson. Or sir.

And this realization shocked me back to reality.

All the other lads that I'd kissed, I didn't just know their names, but who they'd got off with before me. I knew their sisters or brothers. Some of them I'd known since I was five, had got changed in front of them before PE classes at primary school.

But with him? All I knew was that he was my teacher, that he was at least ten years older than me, that he liked films and that his mum was dead.

Other than that, nothing.

It wasn't bothering him, though. His hands were wrapped around my back and neck, pulling me even closer into him.

He felt too close.

Which was ridiculous, as that's generally the idea when you're kissing someone.

But his lips weren't soft any more and his hands weren't gentle.

I could feel the stubble around his mouth rubbing on my chin, a million miles away from the bum-fluff lads my age sported, and it felt alien, uncomfortable, wrong.

I tried to ease my mouth away from his, to force a word out, although what that word was going to be, I had no idea, but his grasp remained strong, his right hand sliding underneath my hair to the nape of my neck.

Squeezing my hands against his chest, I levered the tiniest of spaces between us, pulling my head back until I could smell his breath, growing staler by the second.

He opened his eyes as my lips left his.

'What's the matter?' he whispered, a look of bemusement on his face, which confused me right back, making me wonder for a second whether anything was wrong after all. But as soon as his lips forced themselves back on to mine, it was wrong all over again.

'Don't, sir.' The words escaped to the side of his lips, and he gulped, trying to swallow them before he had to listen to what they said.

I prised my head away still further as he advanced, offering him my cheek, my neck, anything but my lips.

'Please, don't.'

'What's the matter?' he mouthed, a trace of irritation in my ear.

'I don't know. Nothing, maybe.' Why I said that I had no idea, as there was plenty wrong, but all I could think of was his first name.

'Then it's OK. There's no one about. Let me look after you. That's what you want, isn't it? That's why we're here.'

He was right. That was exactly what I wanted.

But not like this, or here, or from him.

The only arms I wanted round me were Dad's, and I'd pushed them so far away lately that he was nowhere in sight.

I felt my weight falling backwards as he guided me towards the bench and started to panic as the force of his grip strengthened.

His calmness seemed to have been replaced by a frantic look as his eyes danced up and down the river, assessing who might be watching.

His right hand traced its way from my shoulder and down my arm as he tried to steer me around, but as it made contact with my cuts, I felt a strange sensation.

Instead of recoiling in pain it seemed to galvanize me, shock me into seeing that I had to get him off me, and quick. Again, I squeezed my arms between our bodies, but his will was stronger than mine, his breathing too.

I started to panic as I realized what I had got myself into, and my initial reaction was to shout at myself, to ask how I could have found myself here, with him.

But all my mind did was shout right back –

This is what you wanted, isn't it? It's no good wishing for something then complaining when it happens! Suck it up. You're the one to blame.

It was right, this was happening because I'd allowed it to.

I could've not waited outside school, or told him I wanted to be on my own when I walked down the path that first time. He was here because I asked him to be. It was no one's fault but mine.

But all the laying of blame didn't get me away from him or home safely. And if I was to manage that I had to get myself straight.

I bent my head to the left, craning to see down the path, desperate for a dog-walker, jogger, anyone to come into view, but there was nothing, no one.

I wanted to scream in frustration, but then I realized that *he* didn't know we were on our own still. He was so intent on devouring my neck that he couldn't possibly have been keeping watch as well.

It was all the encouragement I needed and I took a gulping lungful of air before bellowing straight into his ear, 'There's someone watching us, over there on a bike!'

Mr Hobson jumped back, his body spinning as he searched for who I'd seen.

In the time it took him to establish there was no one there and to shake the ringing from his ears, I stumbled away from him in the direction of home.

At first, for a glorious moment, I thought that was it: that I'd scared him enough to turn and sprint in the opposite direction. But the slapping of my footsteps were soon matched by his as he bounded up beside me.

'Daisy,' he yelled, his voice a mixture of desperation and surprise. 'Daisy! What's wrong? Where are you going?'

I couldn't work out why he was confused. Didn't he know what had just happened was wrong?

'Please, sir. I need to go. I need to get home.'

'You need to stop and steady down, that's what you need to do.'

'What do you mean "steady down"? I can't steady down, not after that. Not after what just happened.'

He lifted his arms in surrender, his gaze rock solid, unblinking.

'I know it's taken you by surprise. I was hardly planning it myself, was I? It's not like I go around making a habit of it, you know.'

His words threw a new scarier doubt in my head. Until he said it, I'd never have thought it could have happened before with someone else. But now the seed was there and was taking root.

How many times had it happened before?

How many schools did he say he'd temped in?

Had it happened in every school he'd been to?

Fear must have been scratched into my eyes, as instantly he saw it, his face every inch the wounded party.

'Daisy, please. PLEASE! It's me, the same person you've been talking to these last few weeks. The *one* person, I think, that you've felt able to talk to lately.'

His eyes were imploring, although he'd finally stopped stepping towards me.

'I'm sorry if the kiss freaked you out. I don't know why I did it. It just happened. I felt like it was what you wanted, that you wanted me to do it. You did want me to do it, didn't you? I didn't get it wrong, did I?'

Thoughts swarmed round my head, scattering any sense that tried to form. He *was* the one person I'd talked to lately, and I *had* thought about him doing it, but now it had happened it felt wrong.

I tried to remember what I'd said before he'd leaned in, what exact words had fallen out of my mouth, but there was nothing except a fear that I must have told him to do it.

'What is it, Daisy? What are you thinking about? You can tell me.'

A snort of nervous, confused laughter erupted from my mouth, followed by the words, 'I don't even know your name.'

It sounded lame and juvenile, like some underage kid in a club who'd just copped off with a stranger for the first time.

He cast a glance over his shoulder, as if telling me was more dangerous than what he'd already done.

'It's Tom,' he said. 'Well, Thomas, but Tom, you know.'

There was a Tommy in our English class. The class he taught. He was three months to the day younger than me. I knew that because I'd got off with him last year on his birthday.

This memory shocked me. Reminded me of how wrong all this was. I should still have been thinking about lads like Tommy Grant or Rob Stearn, scheming about how to get together with them, not leading one of my teachers down some shady footpath. What sort of person was I to find myself here, to have made someone think this is what I wanted?

Peering past Mr Hobson, I could see the left turn that led me back to the road, towards our house and Dad, and all I could think about was getting there, closing the door and hiding behind Mum's sunburst until all this went away.

'Did you hear me? I said it's Tom.' His smile was still in place, but it was fading at the corners. 'Daisy? Are you all right? I'm losing you again . . .'

'No, it's fine, I'm fine. It's just . . . the time. It's getting on. Dad will be expecting me and that.'

The mention of Dad wiped the curve of his smile away, and as I tried to move a step closer to home, his hand instantly grabbed at mine.

'No, don't go yet.' It was an order, not a request, and the tone seemed to shock him a touch as he tried to grin once more. 'Not till we've sorted this out.'

'Sorted what out? There's nothing to sort out. It's fine, sir, really. It's my fault. I should just keep my mouth shut.'

'That's just it, though, isn't it?' There was a touch of panic in his voice, a new strength to his grip. 'What just happened back there . . . well, it needs to remain between us. If anyone finds out about it, well . . . I'll be in real trouble.'

I felt tears bubble at the corners of my eyes, at the depth of the situation I found myself in.

'I won't tell anyone, sir,' I sobbed. 'I promise. Why would I tell anyone? You were only here because of me, weren't you?'

'I know that, of course I do.' His free hand was tugging at his hair with a desperation matched by the strength of his grip. 'But look at you. You're upset. Who knows what you might say to your dad when you're upset like this. It's risky, Daisy, it's just too risky. For you as well as me.'

'What do you mean?' Tears were escaping down my cheeks. I was desperate now, scared by the threat in his words.

'Come on, Daisy. You must know what I mean. If you were to tell anyone about what went on here, the police would come after me. And they'd want to know all about you, about why you were spending so much time with me on your own. They'd start digging, they'd find out about you skipping school, because I'd have to tell them, and then they'd be asking a lot of questions about your dad too. You do realize parents can find themselves in court, in prison even, if their kids are caught absconding. You don't want that, do you? Neither of us does.'

A long raking sob left my mouth as I tried to rip my arm from his.

'You wouldn't tell them, would you? About the wagging off?' Horrific thoughts ran rampage. 'They'd get social services in. They'd take me away from him!'

He leaned in closer. 'And that's why we HAVE to keep this quiet, Daisy.' His voice dipped in volume, but the intensity was just as strong. 'If we keep this quiet, then we'll both be safe. Neither of us will be under pressure and neither of us will let things slip. Do you understand?'

I nodded, too terrified and out of my depth to do anything else. I felt his grip slacken slightly, but I daren't try and pull away, not yet.

'It will be fine, Daisy, really it will. Everything that's going on, it will pass in time.'

I nodded again, wiping a tear away as if I was pulling myself together, hoping he'd see it as time to finally let go.

'And if it doesn't, you can still talk to me. Knowing what I know now, I can help, can't I?'

With that he took out his handkerchief and pushed it into my hand, the one he was still holding tightly. With a smile and a final squeeze of his fingers, he let go, leaving me to stagger on, desperately trying to figure out just what had happened and what I could possibly do about it.

CHAPTER 12

The steaming spray hammered at my arm, taunting the cut as it washed it clean. I bit down on my lip and rested my forehead against the shower screen, waiting for the pain to pass.

I squeezed Hobson's hankie in my hand, watching as my fist turned red. I'd stared at the hankie the previous night for what seemed like hours. The house had been empty when I'd got home and I'd been unsure how to feel. The relief of not having to explain to Dad why I looked like I did sat alongside the terror of having to be on my own, waiting for the fear to descend.

Because of course it did descend and there seemed no point in putting off the inevitable. What other option did I have?

There was a fury to it all last night, an intensity that forced me to press harder, thinking the blades would have to go deeper to pull me back from the depths of the panic I was lost in.

And, as always, it worked.

But at a cost, since the blood refused to clot in the same way, escaping instead through the lint that I'd pressed against it. I had no idea how long it had continued, long enough for me to have no choice but to use Mr Hobson's hankie as my last line of defence.

The room fell silent once the pounding in my chest ceased, leaving my mind free to cast new self-doubts and accusations. How everything that had gone on by the river was my fault; how I'd managed to expose Dad through my truancy, putting his future and mine together at risk. I fought for answers, solutions, but got only the same repeating loop of thought.

That everything was screwed, out of control and my fault.

It was late by the time I dropped off, and it was one of those still nights that makes sleep fitful. The fact that I kept rolling on to my arm didn't help either, the sharp stabs of pain knifing me awake more times than I could bear.

Dad failed to wake me in the morning, though: further evidence that he was still rightly livid with me.

I'd just stepped out of the shower when I heard the front door slam and his car drive away, and felt a twinge of disappointment as another chance to put things right slipped by, right when I needed him most.

By the time I reached my wardrobe to find all of my long-sleeved shirts in the wash, I was ready to pull the duvet back over my head and write the day off before it began. In fact, if my phone hadn't buzzed impatiently at me, I would've done just that.

It was Dad, which was a surprise. He'd never been big on texting, and when he did send them, they were more like letters. In fact his message was so long it got split in two.

Sorry to miss you today of all days. Thought we could spend the afternoon together. Don't worry about school. I've told them you won't be in. Meet me on Grafton Street at 11.30.

Really looking forward to having some time with you.
Hoping we can talk a bit. Love you Dais, Dad x

It took me a sec to work out what he meant about today of all days, and it was another kick in the teeth when I clocked the date on my calendar: 3 July.

Mum's birthday.

I swear the realization started my arm bleeding again, and I felt my head spin at the prospect of restaunching it.

How had I managed to forget Mum's birthday?

I never had before. It was etched into my brain as firmly as my own.

Dad and me had a routine, a tradition I suppose, of buying each other a present, to cheer us up as well as thinking of her.

I prayed that he'd forgotten, like I had. Either that, or he'd decided not to bother as a way of punishing me.

I jammed a piece of toilet roll on to the weeping cut, gingerly eased my arm inside my dressing gown and made my way to the kitchen.

And there it was, on the table, a small gift-wrapped box with my name on the tag.

My instinct was to pick it up and hurl it at the wall, to prove to Dad that I was worthy of nothing, but the fear of upsetting him further stopped me.

Instead I read the inscription on the tag (*I thought you could use a replacement, follow your dreams, x*) before tearing the paper off.

It was a digital camera, one I'd mentioned to him months ago, with the ability to take film footage as well as photos.

He knew I wanted it, knew I wanted to start playing around properly, to mimic the films we'd watched for so many years.

My camcorder was old. Dad had picked it up on eBay in case it had just been a teenage whim. But him buying this? Well, it meant he believed in me, and wanted me to succeed.

And how had I repaid his faith?

I'd shouted, lied and hid everything that was important from him.

Wiping the tears off my cheeks, I put the camera back on the table and climbed the stairs to my room.

I had to find a way of putting this mess straight. And I had to make a start today. The only problem was, where on earth should I begin?

His shirt fitted me really badly, but I didn't care. If I wanted to try and grab him a present before meeting up, there was no time to buy any new clothes.

I'd looked for the oldest, softest one in his wardrobe, something that wouldn't rub against the plasters on my arm, and had settled on this old blue gingham thing.

It buried me.

I could have put a belt around my waist and worn it as a dress, but at least the sleeves hid everything, my hands included. I'd turned up the cuffs and gripped them inside my fists, and strangely I felt comforted by the whole thing.

Although Dad hadn't worn the shirt for months it still smelt of him, and as I waited for the bus I couldn't resist lifting the sleeve to my nose and breathing deeply.

By the time I got to town I was low on time and it quickly became clear that I wasn't going to find his gift. I'd headed straight to HMV and the DVD racks, but the usual ease I had in choosing him a film was replaced by acute panic. Despite knowing his collection off by heart, I couldn't settle on anything, started doubting my own memory, which in turn caused my forehead to sweat and my heart to palpitate. In the end, in fear of losing it right there in the middle of the world cinema section, I turned my back and headed speedily for the door.

Grafton Street was on the far side of the town centre, as far from the shopping centre as it was possible to be, and as I half-marched, half-stumbled towards it, my mind had time to fire a new round of accusations at me.

How on earth had I managed to forget Mum's birthday?

What sort of person was I to let such a thing happen?

Dad would be gutted when I turned up empty-handed, and what on earth was he going to say about me wearing his clothes?

The paranoia bubbled and spewed to every corner of my brain, forcing sweat to pour from my forehead and my limbs to ache.

I felt drained, empty of everything but the need to get to Grafton Street. If I was late for him as well as everything else, then it really would hammer home what a terrible daughter I was.

Turning on to Grafton Street, I held my breath, head flitting up and down the road until I was sure his car was nowhere to be seen. Once I knew the coast was clear, I exhaled quickly, bending double to my knees to force the tension out. But just as my hands came to rest, a horn sounded behind me, startling me upright and tense.

It was Dad, a smile glinting off the windscreen, more in hope than anything else.

Unfortunately the shock of the horn made me edgy, and instead of swallowing it down and launching into an apology, I marched straight up to his window and laid into him.

'What did you do that for? You scared me to bloody death, Dad. Have a word with yourself, will you?'

His smile dropped to the floor, replaced by a lined brow. I could see his best intentions evaporate, as my anger did the same thing, leaving behind a new depth of shame.

But instead of apologizing and throwing myself at him through the window for a hug, I marched round the car and climbed into the back seat. It was the most childish thing I could have done. What would it have taken to get in the passenger seat like a normal person?

But, as with everything at the moment, doing the right thing was beyond me. And the deeper I waded, the less able I was to turn anything around.

As we drove through the streets, the only sound was the weather forecaster on the radio warning of storms within the hour. I sat and hoped that somehow the rain might help clear the air.

CHAPTER 13

The parking sensor squealed as the bumper edged closer to the wall, echoing the tension that bounced around my body.

It had been an uneasy five minutes since I'd climbed into the car. As hard as I'd tried, I couldn't find a way to backtrack and apologize, so instead I sat there like a petulant kid, feeling Dad's eyes on me as he tried to work out who'd kidnapped the daughter he thought he had.

When we got out of the car, he noticed properly my odd wardrobe choice.

'I've not seen that shirt for a while. Looks ... er ... well, it looks better on you than me, that's for sure.'

I grabbed at my damaged arm, paranoid that he'd seen the real reason for me wearing it.

'Yeah, sorry. I'm a bit behind on the washing.'

Lame, my head told me, *that is so lame*.

'Not exactly ideal for this weather, though, is it? Look at you, you're dripping.' His hand reached for the sweat on my forehead, but I batted it away, grimacing at the sudden movement.

'No, it's fine. It's not the shirt. I've woken up with a bit of a temperature, that's all. Must be with end of term coming up. Bit knackered, I think.' I shuffled away from him, far enough for him to know not to touch.

'I didn't realize you had so few clothes, Daisy. If it's difficult keeping stuff clean, we could always go out and get some more.'

The thought of bleeding on clothes that weren't even mine freaked me out. 'There's no need, honest.'

'Well, all you have to do is ask. There's no need to be covering yourself in my rags in this heat.'

He chose to leave it there, and I could hear the cogs turning as he tried to find a new line of conversation.

We ambled down the street, my eyes rarely leaving the floor. The exertion of lifting my head seemed too much, and the sweat continued to pour off me, leaving me thirsty and leaden-limbed.

It wasn't until we arrived at our destination that I realized how weary I was, as I'd failed to notice we were at the Ritzy.

We'd done the same walk from the car park dozens of times in the past and I'd always felt this brilliant, growing excitement as the neon sign came into view.

Today, though, nothing but fear.

'I know we can't do a lot of talking while we're in there, but afterwards we can chat about whatever you like. You know, Mum and that.'

I didn't know where to start, or even if I could. I just wanted to crawl into a ball.

'Look,' he began, 'I know things have been a bit bumpy the last few weeks, and I know the bumps have all been down to me . . .'

I tried to interrupt, but for a man not used to talking about how he felt, he was suddenly on a roll.

'It's true I've been ignoring you and the stuff you need to know, so starting today, I'm going to change. I know I've got to, because it's not been fair. I'm sorry, Dais, really I am.'

It was so hard to stand there and listen to him talk like that, because it wasn't his way and because, in my head, he had nothing to apologize for. After all, I was the one who'd taken Mum away from him in the first place. I should've been apologizing to him.

I started to formulate the words in my head, but they were nowhere near my lips before he went on.

'So I know today is Mum's day, but in a way it's not. It's all about you. Whatever it is you want, or anything you need to know, today, it's yours. You understand?'

The words jarred in my ears. It wasn't what I deserved.

'You got the present, didn't you?' he asked eagerly. 'The thing I left on the kitchen table?'

I nodded, tears of shame pricking behind my eyes.

'Did you like it? It was the right one, wasn't it?' There was almost a pleading to his voice. Why was he trying so hard when I was the one at fault?

'I love it, Dad, but maybe you should take it back.'

He looked stunned. 'Take it back? Why would I do that?'

'It's not like it's my birthday or anything. And it must have cost a fortune.'

'Don't you be worrying about what it cost. You've wanted it for ages, and if it puts a smile back on your face it's got to be worth every penny.'

I forced a grin, the goofiest one I had left, but I had no idea if it looked even remotely genuine.

We paused by the entrance and I scanned the schedules to see what we were going to watch. But there was nothing on.

The earliest matinee didn't start until two thirty, leaving us a couple of hours early.

It didn't seem to bother Dad, though, who hadn't broken stride. Instead he stood at the door, holding it open in a weird theatrical pose that served only to make me feel more uncomfortable.

'What's going on?' I asked as I dragged my heels up the steps towards him. 'There's nothing on for ages. Don't you want to go and have a walk first or something?'

Could I really tell him? About the report or my arms or Hobson or any of it?

'Why would I want to go for a walk? Me and you are going to spend a couple of hours with some old friends instead.'

I stopped as I reached him, too nervous for some reason to walk inside.

'Go on,' he said, prodding me in the back. 'What are you waiting for?'

It was empty in the foyer, and pretty dark, and for a second I was on the path, beneath the bridge, with Mr Hobson in my ear instead of my dad.

It took another gentle push from behind to persuade me to go further, one push too many.

'Why are you shoving me like that?' There was a mixture of anger and fear in my voice, enough for Dad to pick up on.

'Whoa, sorry.' His eyes were wide with surprise, and he immediately removed his hand from the small of my back. 'It's just, well, I've never had to force you into a cinema before.'

'That's because you've never got me to bunk off before to a cinema where there's nothing showing. What's going on?' The sweat was really starting to pool on my face now, and I could feel my heart motor, sending shockwaves to my brain.

'There's nothing going on. Just be patient and trust me, will you?'

He led me through the empty foyer and up the stairs to the screens, leaving me none the wiser. He hadn't stopped for tickets (not that there was anyone in the box office). Instead he opened the double doors to the main auditorium and shepherded me inside.

It was empty and dark, save for the faint red glow on the screen. Not even a hum of music in the background to take the edge off the eeriness, which was messing increasingly with my head.

I felt Dad take my hand and steer me down the aisle to the front row, and there in the middle of it was a small table on which stood two large mugs of tea and a packet of Rich Tea biscuits.

'Take a pew,' he grinned, the yellow-white of his teeth guiding me to my seat.

I welcomed the sit-down to be honest, as the racing of my heart had started my legs shaking. I was on the edge of the fear now and hadn't a clue how to deal with it with anyone else around, especially Dad.

'I gave a lot of thought to what we could come and watch today,' he crowed, obviously proud of what he was about to unveil. 'But none of the new releases were really cutting it. In fact I decided there was only one film that was good enough for you today, so here it is.'

He lifted his head to the shadows at the back of the auditorium and waved quickly, before sitting next to me, his hand snaking into mine.

'I'm so sorry I've let you down,' he whispered, although I had no idea why. After all, we had the whole place to ourselves. 'I hope this begins to show you that I want to put everything right.'

I had no time to answer before the last of the lights disappeared, followed by a raucous fanfare as the studio logo swam into view. The second I saw the opening credit, I knew what he'd done, and the sheer kindness of it was enough for the fear to engulf me.

CHAPTER 14

There were many films that I really loved, but there was definitely only one that did the job whatever mood I was in. And that was *The Shawshank Redemption*.

Dad knew it too.

'I've been wanting to do this for ages, hire the whole place just for us. But it felt like if we were going to do it, it had to be the right film. So I had a word with the manager and he managed to track down a print. We got it imported from the States. Cost a few quid, but it was worth it, wasn't it?'

I heard the words but wished I hadn't.

It was so much more than I deserved.

For weeks I'd acted like a cow towards him: ignored and shouted at him, hid away and cut myself, thrown myself at one of my teachers, for God's sake.

I deserved to be screamed at, to be taken in hand and grounded. Not treated like his princess.

The seat turned into a radiator, forcing me to my feet too quickly, which led me to stumble across Dad's lap. He steadied me by grabbing my arm and I winced, backing away as soon as I found my balance.

I mumbled something, my brain failing to link up with

my mouth. I had to get out of there, to somewhere I could breathe.

I struggled towards the aisle, stumbling around the chairs, Dad's voice bouncing off the walls around me.

'Daisy? Daisy? Where are you going?'

I didn't answer, just ploughed through the doors and into the corridor, searching for the exit in a building that I knew like the back of my hand.

The doors crashed behind me and Dad tore around the corner, relief on his face as he saw me, slumped against the wall.

I turned away from him and flinched as his hands made contact with my back. He tried again, his body closer this time, and as he touched me, he made a gentle shushing sound, the sound that Hobson had made before kissing me.

My arm flung out instinctively, catching him bluntly on the shoulder, knocking him off balance.

'Don't touch me!' I yelled, surprised by the ferocity of my words. Then I repeated myself, quieter, but with the same desperation. 'Please, don't touch me. I can't do this. I can't.'

Dad was rooted to the spot. Too shocked, too scared to step closer. 'Can't do what, Daisy? Can't do what?'

'Any of this!' I gestured wildly at the walls.

'This what?' He was baffled, baffled and scared as he searched the ceiling for anything that would explain what I meant.

'You being nice to me. The film, the new camera, the apologies. You should be giving it to someone who deserves it, not me.'

He was trying frantically to catch and hold my gaze, but I wouldn't let him, no matter how hard he pleaded.

'Don't be silly, Dais. Of course you deserve it. You deserve all this and more! And who on earth am I going to give this to if not you?'

My mind was scrambling, incapable of taking any sense from his words. He had to hear the truth and he had to hear it now.

'You should be giving it to Mum, shouldn't you? You should've been giving all this to Mum for the last fourteen years.'

This silenced him for a moment, his mouth open as the words struggled to form on his lips.

'But she's gone, Daisy. I'd love us to be doing this all together, but I can't, because . . .'

'Because I killed her!' I cried, spitting the words out like poison. 'That's why she's not here. Because I took her away, that's why things are so screwed up.'

'What are you talking about? You're not making any sense.'

'I found the report, Dad, in the loft. The one from the hospital. It told me what I did, the trouble I caused and what it did to her. That's why you won't talk to me about her, isn't it? Because you blame me for what happened.'

'I don't know what you mean.'

'Stop PROTECTING me. That's why I'm in this mess now. That's why everything else has gone to pot.'

He took a single step forward, worry consuming him. 'Everything else, Daisy? What's everything else?'

I wished I could cram the words back into my mouth and

make them fall out in a different order. But it was too late, and I was too tired, too anxious to think of a way to backtrack. So I said nothing.

He repeated himself.

'Did you hear me, Daisy? What's everything else?'

'It doesn't matter. It's too late.'

'Of course it matters. All that stuff you just said to me. It's nonsense. All of it. You didn't kill Mum. What happened was an accident. It wasn't your fault. And if I can't talk to you about it that's not because of you, that's down to me. If anything, you being around helps me. You keep me sane. Do you understand me?'

I couldn't nod. He was kidding himself, protecting me as always.

'But I need to know what's going on. Why you're sweating like you are. What it is that's making you feel like this. Because whatever it is, we can deal with it together.'

My eyes closed as he spoke, hands covering my ears, to stop his words reaching my brain.

Whatever he said, I couldn't allow myself to believe it. Too much had gone on to allow him to be right. Everything that had happened was down to me.

His muffled words fought their way through my hands and I sensed him move closer. I pushed my palms harder to my ears and turned my shoulder against him, but it wasn't enough to put him off.

I felt his touch on my left arm as he wheeled me back towards him. But as his other hand made contact with my right arm, landing directly on top of my latest cut, I flinched, wrestling myself away instinctively.

I knew I'd given the game away. Knew it before I dared even open my eyes. The contact had been enough to knock the cut open and within seconds the blood had fought its way past the plaster, seeping through the fabric of his shirt.

Dad's face crumbled as he watched the pattern emerge on my arm.

'What's going on, Daisy? You're bleeding.' His calm voice was at odds with his expression.

'It's nothing,' I bluffed. 'I had an accident this morning. Banged myself on a nail when I was rushing out of the house.'

His hands flew to my arm, but I couldn't allow him to touch me, to see the extent of things, so I backed further away, until there was no more corridor left to play with.

'Let me see,' he whispered, his voice firm.

'It's nothing, Dad. It'll stop in a minute.'

'Well, if it's nothing, then let me see!'

'There's no need. Really, it's –'

'Daisy, you're scaring me!' he bellowed, jolting us both in surprise. 'You're sweating like you've got flu, you're ridiculously jumpy, and you're bleeding. Now if that nail was rusty it could be infected, so let me have a look!'

I tried to shuffle round him, but was trapped, and before I could stop him he was easing the shirtsleeve up my forearm, revealing my secret in all its hideous glory.

He aged a decade in that moment, as the little girl he thought he knew turned into someone he didn't understand. There was shock on his face, and anger, and he had no option but to aim it at me.

'Jesus Christ!' he cried, eyes flitting from my arm to my

face. 'What on earth have you done?' He rested my arm gently in his palm, the heat of his touch soothing the throbbing slightly. 'Who's done this to you? What happened?'

'Nobody did it to me.' I didn't know what else to say.

'Well, of course they did! You can't have done this on a nail. I mean look at it, there's a dozen cuts here. Who's done this? Was it a lad? Someone at school?'

'No, it's not like that, I promise.'

'Don't you DARE protect them. I want to know their name, and I want to know it now.'

'There's no names to tell, Dad. I promise.'

'Then how did it happen? There's not just one cut here. They're all over your bloody arm.'

'I did it, all right? It was me. I did it. I cut myself.'

'Don't be so ridiculous.' He was angry now, the volume in his voice reaching levels I'd never heard before. 'You don't just go around cutting yourself like this. Now tell me the truth!'

He was gripping my arm. Unintentionally, but with enough force to start the blood running off it and on to his fingers.

'I am telling you the truth. It was me who did it. I've been doing it for months. In my room.'

He took a small step back in horror, like I was contagious.

'Why are you saying this? Why would you do something like that?'

'I didn't want to do it. But I didn't know what else to do. I've been having these attacks, these panic attacks, and sometimes they take over so much that it's the only way that I can stop them.'

'By cutting yourself?' he yelled, his face incredulous. 'You actually did it on purpose?'

'I didn't want to. I just didn't know what else to do.'

'What sort of excuse is that?' The vein on his forehead was throbbing so hard I couldn't take my eyes off it. 'You should've come to me!' The words were catching in his throat. 'Why didn't you come to me?'

'I wanted to, honest, but I didn't know how to tell you. I didn't want you to be mad at –'

'Mad at you? Mad at you? Don't you think I would've been calmer if you'd told me and let me help, rather than finding out in the middle of a sodding cinema?'

'I'm sorry,' I took a step towards him, only for him to back away, hands held up in front of him, another barrier rising up between us. 'I'm so sorry. It's all my fault, all of it.'

'I just can't believe you've been doing this to yourself, for months, and I've not even noticed. Does anyone else know?'

Hobson flashed into my mind, his threats confusing me, the chance of taking Dad away still too big to comprehend.

Dad was impatient for an answer. 'Daisy? I said does anyone else know? Any of your friends at school?'

'No.'

'And what about anyone else?'

I paused for a second, a second too long.

'Well?'

'Well what?'

'Daisy, I need to know who knows about this. I want to know what's going on, and why they didn't tell me themselves! Who knows? Not one of your teachers?'

My face must have betrayed me, given him a flash of recognition to leap on.

'Which teacher, Daisy?'

'No one else knows, Dad, honest.'

'Don't lie to me. Not again.'

I was trapped, looking for somewhere to hide the truth.

'DAISY! Tell me who knows. NOW!'

'It only happened yesterday,' I sobbed. 'I wanted to tell you as soon as I got home, but you weren't in. And it's not his fault, it's mine. If I'd not asked him to keep me company, then it wouldn't have even happened . . .'

'What are you talking about? What wouldn't have happened?'

My mind was addled, unable to order the words in any intelligent way.

'He said if I told you, then he'd have to go to social services. Tell them about me skipping off school and how I was cutting myself. He said he didn't mean for it to happen. And he was right, I made him do it. I'd led him down there, hadn't I? He said kissing me was the last thing he'd expected to do . . .'

I thought the roof was going to blow off the cinema when Dad erupted.

'Hang on,' he yelled. 'A teacher . . . kissed you? Is that what you're saying to me?'

'Yes . . . well, he did, but it was my fault . . .'

He was on me in a flash, his hands gripping my arms, not knowing or caring if he was hurting me. 'What's his name?'

'It doesn't matter, it doesn't matter, it's my fault –'

'HIS NAME!'

He was pressing hard now, hurting me more than the scissors ever had, and I had no option but to whisper, 'Hobson. Mr Hobson.'

I hoped that once I'd said it the temperature in there would drop and that Dad would calm down, pull me into him and tell me it was all going to be OK.

But that didn't happen. Dad simply dropped my arms, turned quickly and marched towards the exit.

'Where are you going, Dad? DAD! Where are you going?'

I'll never forget the irony of what he said next. They were the last words I heard from him. They might have been the last ones he ever actually spoke. But he said them loud and clear, in the calmest voice imaginable.

'I'm going to kill him.'

But of course he wouldn't manage it. The only one capable of murder round here was me.

CHAPTER 15

The rain drummed urgently on the roof of the bus, threatening to puncture it at any moment.

We hadn't moved for ten minutes and the impatient vibrating of the engine buzzed through me, heightening my anxiety.

I had no idea how close Dad was to school by now. I'd hared after him as he sprinted from the cinema, but by the time I reached the car park he was already out of sight.

I knew he'd head straight for Mr Hobson, but had no idea how I was going to get there before him. I didn't have enough cash for a taxi and the heavens had opened, delivering the storm that the radio had promised.

It took the bus fifteen minutes to arrive and an awkward few more to leave as I rummaged in my bag for enough change to pay my way.

It didn't take long for me to realize that the mixture of heavy rain and some delay up ahead was going to scupper my chances even more, and so I sat and fretted about arriving at school as Hobson's body was lifted into an ambulance, with Dad being led, handcuffed, into a riot van.

I pinched at the skin on my wrist, the sharp twinges calming my heart, which was banging out of control. Why was it taking so long? When was the rain going to stop?

Craning my neck to look through the front window, I could see endless rows of cars, their windscreen wipers flicking irritably at the rain. We were going nowhere, and I could only hope that Dad was held up in it too.

At that moment I made a decision to get out and run for a while. If Dad *was* stuck, then there was a chance I could get to him and talk him down. It was worth a go, it had to be, so, turning the collar of his shirt up, I begged the driver to let me off before the next stop.

It was muggy and humid despite the rain, and it didn't take long for my lungs to feel starved of air, but I had no option other than to push on. The guilt I was feeling, in every part of my body, meant that I couldn't give up, not without trying my best.

My feet were sodden by the time I reached the edge of the bypass, and the blood-stained right sleeve of my shirt had been dyed a soggy pink. I saw the frustration of the drivers as they sat in their cars, hands wiping at their windows as they tried to work out what sort of idiot had caused such a tailback.

I'd been running for about ten minutes when I saw the glow ahead. I knew instantly it was the lights of a police car and I picked up the pace, fearing as I approached the root of the problem that my chances of finding Dad were fading. But as I got closer, my heart leapt as I clocked the back of Dad's car sat alongside the flashing light. I thudded on, desperate to reach him before he got past the crash.

This was the one chance I needed to put it all straight. If my legs carried me there, I promised myself, I wouldn't waste it.

I didn't notice anything strange about the car until I felt two arms wrap around my chest. Didn't see the strange angle it had stopped at, or the smoke rising from the bonnet, until the same arms lifted me off my feet, stopping my progress.

I wanted to turn round and see who had grabbed me, to scream and hit them and hurt them until they let me go. But I couldn't take my eyes off Dad's car, or what was left of it. As the arms carried me to the side of the road, I saw the wing of the car crumpled and buckled. I could see the space where the bonnet and windscreen should have been. But they weren't there any more. There was just a twisted mess of tyre marks, metal and shattered glass, joining seamlessly with the barrier in the central reservation.

I think I screamed at that point. At the policeman holding on to me, at the people that littered the scene – coppers, firemen, paramedics. I have no idea what I managed to say.

My eyes scanned the road, desperate for a sight of Dad, head bowed, smoking a fag, but there was nothing other than smoke and chaos.

It wasn't until a squad car to the right of the crash moved that I knew where Dad was. As it pulled away, I saw a gaggle of uniformed people huddled over a body, grabbing for equipment. I saw their hands pummel at his chest, their mouths cup his and their lips move, encouraging him to stay with them.

I fought and fought, but my captor held on, long enough

for me to see the crouching men by my father finally climb to their feet, shaking their heads.

One of them checked his watch, another scribbled something on a pad before walking away.

It was all I needed to know for sure.

I'd done it again. Just as I had with Mum.

Leaving me no option but to give in.

To the arms that were holding me and the darkness that offered some blessed relief.

CHAPTER 16

First, there was just light.

A sharp pinprick, burning through my eyelids.

Then nothing.

Next there were voices. Some I didn't recognize, others, like Donna's, that made me panic before they slipped away again.

Then there were people shuffling around me, gripping my wrists, writing on clipboards, stroking my head.

How long this went on for I had no idea. All I knew was that the noises and visions came and went as I drifted in and out. Whether they were real or part of my blissful sleep, I couldn't begin to know.

It wasn't until I woke to find Mr Hobson sat in the chair by my bed that I knew the dreaming was over.

I screamed, my voice rippling the curtains that stood sentry around my bed. I pulled my hands up to my eyes, rolling away from him.

He was on his feet instantly, shushing me urgently, before giving up and hammering on a red button by my bed.

After that there was a flurry of bodies, a glint of a needle, a struggle and a puncture before I slipped away inside myself again, happy at being rescued from him.

When it was time to open my eyes again, I did it slowly, fearful of his presence in the chair.

But it was empty and the room dark.

What became evident very quickly, however, was where I was.

Hospital.

The smell was unmistakable: a cloying antiseptic that seemed anything but clean.

It smelt of death.

My mind whirred.

Death meant Mum, which meant guilt, and secrets, which led to panic attacks.

Attacks led to scissors and more guilt. Which meant lying and further secrets.

And secrets? Well, I'd hoarded them for too long, and they merely led to death.

Dad's death.

The crash. The smoke. And the knowledge that I'd done it again.

The scream escaped without me realizing. Forced its way down the halls and roused a sleepy, irritable nurse.

'What sort of noise is that?' She grimaced, checking a drip that was invading my right wrist. 'Are you wanting to wake the entire ward?'

She talked to me like we knew each other, like it wasn't the first time I'd disrupted whatever it was she'd been up to.

I stared at her, daring to ask the question I already knew the answer to: where was my dad? But all that came out was a noise I didn't know I was capable of.

She warned me. Warned me what would happen if I kept making such a din.

But that was all I wanted to hear. As long as I knew the needle was on the way, then I was happy. It was all I needed to stop remembering what I'd done.

And if I had the needle often enough and quick enough, then maybe, eventually, hopefully, I wouldn't bother waking up.

CHAPTER 17

There were no tears when they finally admitted what I already knew about Dad. Maybe the contents of the needle had hardened me, but I looked the nurse full on as she told me. These were words I had to hear, and I breathed them in, along with the guilt that came with them.

It had taken them a few days to calm me down after I first woke up. At least that's what they told me. Time had ceased to matter. Whether I slept or woke, in daylight or in darkness, I was trapped in the same nightmare of my own making.

They tried to pity me, soothe me, stroke my hair and pat my hand, but I wouldn't let them near me. It was just too risky.

I wouldn't even let them tend to my arm, still weeping and throbbing because of what I'd done.

'I'll have to get the doctor,' one of them eventually told me, 'and he won't be as patient as me, I'll tell you that for nothing.'

The doctor left empty-handed as well, ears ringing at my protests.

They seemed to tire after that, leaving me to slip in and out of fitful sleep, returning only to collect untouched dinner trays, eyebrows raised as I fixed them with a terrified feral gaze.

Eventually, though, two women returned, one a doctor and the other a pen-pusher of some kind.

'I'm Evelyn,' the non-doctor said, smiling briskly. I noted her good sense in not trying to shake my hand or touch me in any way. 'Do you have a middle name, Daisy?'

I was confused by the simplicity of the question and what bearing it could possibly have. Unless she was a copper and was ready to arrest me.

I said nothing, gave nothing away.

She seemed comfortable with the silence, opening a folder in her lap, her pen scratching angrily on a page of densely typed paper.

'So, as I say, my name's Evelyn and I'm a social worker. Your social worker from this point on.'

For some reason I wanted to laugh. Social workers were for kids who got clobbered by their dads, not ones who killed them. I considered telling her this myself, but the white-coated woman didn't give me the chance.

'And I'm Alice.' There was a touch of irritation in her voice and instantly I worried what I'd done to upset her. 'I'm the psychiatrist on the ward. I'm sorry I haven't had time to come and see you properly until now.'

I tried to weigh up what I was dealing with: a shrink and a do-gooder, both of them capable of giving me exactly what I deserved, both of them with the power to lock me up in some way for what I'd done.

Evelyn spoke first. 'Daisy, we need to try and work out the next move for you. After you're discharged from here.

We need to know if you have relatives that we might be able to contact, anyone who might be able to act as your guardian.'

I pulled my legs up to my chest, feeling my cuts groan as I wrapped my arms around my knees. Even if there was someone, there was no way I was telling her. No way I was going to sign someone else up for the same fate as Mum and Dad.

'I understand this must be very difficult for you, my love –' I winced at Evelyn's term of affection (she spoke without a trace of emotion anywhere in her voice) – 'but at times like this, it's important to have family around you. And the quicker we can identify someone, the sooner we can move on.'

I didn't need to think about it. There was no one. Both Mum and Dad had been only children. Dad did inherit a step-brother after his father remarried, but there was a big age gap between them and they'd never been close. I'd only met him once, at Grandpa's funeral, and even then he'd not said a word to me. Dad reckoned he'd only pitched up in case there was something in it for him, and when there wasn't, we didn't hear from him again.

I saw the two women eyeing me as I sat silently. The social worker was getting angsty, her foot tapping out an urgent Morse code message on the polished floor.

It was obvious she didn't want to be here, that she wanted to tick her boxes and move on as smartly as she could, and I knew that my reluctance to answer was already starting to get on her wick.

The doctor obviously saw it too, as she took up the attack, her body language everything that Evelyn's wasn't.

'How are you coping with the anxiety you've been suffering, Daisy?' she asked, her voice completely calm.

I raised my eyebrows, wondering how she knew.

'The nurses have been very worried about you. About your levels of distress and inability to eat or drink. That's why you've been given a drip – is it bothering you?'

I shook my head.

'They're also concerned about your arm: that you haven't allowed them to change the dressing. When you were admitted there was a level of infection from where you cut yourself and if we don't keep on top of it your temperature will rise again.'

I shuffled on the bed, thinking of a way to hide my arm as well as the drip, realizing quickly as I squirmed that I felt more vulnerable than ever.

'Do you want to tell us how long you've been self-harming, Daisy?'

This was Evelyn again, her tone flat-lining as she failed to even look up from her paper. I wondered if she was putting a shopping list together as she spoke, as it seemed to be annoying Alice as well.

'Let's not worry about that for now. What's important is that we make you comfortable, and that a nurse gets that arm clean.' She ushered Evelyn to the back of the room, a gesture that revealed the pair's dislike for each other as plain as day.

What followed was an awkward dance, as a nurse tried to get close enough to clean me. At first I flatly refused to let her touch and, had it not been for Alice and her endless patient smile, the nurse would soon have been picking the instruments out of her forehead rather than using them to clean me up.

In the end we reached a compromise of me dressing my own arm, as they watched and prompted.

They prodded in other ways instead, nagging questions about how long this had been going on, what had happened for me to be so unhappy. I zoned them out, looking at the lines and gouges, remembering the panic associated with them, ashamed to realize that I deserved each and every one of them.

By the time I'd cleaned half of them, the three adults realized that they weren't going to get anything out of me today, and that was enough for Evelyn to make her excuses and leave.

'I'll be back in tomorrow, Daisy, once I've done some more research. I'm sure you must have some family you're not telling us about.' She forced a smile on to her face, cheeks groaning with the force of the effort.

The nurse didn't last much longer either. Content that I was germ-free, and after checking that every sharp implement she'd arrived with was back on her tray, she shuffled into the hall.

Which just left Alice, and although she was happy to sit in my silence, it was obvious she wanted information. And she wasn't going to get it. No matter the size of her death wish.

Instead, she told me the way things were.

'Daisy, you've been here for six days now, and aside from the infection in your arm, there's nothing physically wrong with you.'

I picked at the skin on the side of my thumb, my heart-rate picking up as I waited for the 'but'.

I didn't have to wait to hear it.

'Emotionally, though . . . well, that's a different matter. You've barely said two words to any of the staff here. The most we've got out of you was when your temperature was raging and you were delirious.'

'What did I say?' I didn't look at her as I asked the question.

'Daisy, it was so nonsensical it barely needs repeating. But it was enough, coupled with your self-harming and inability to connect with anyone, to know that we are going to have to make plans for you.'

I felt my insides splinter as the prospect of another night under strip lighting stretched out before me. 'I want to go home,' I moaned. 'Just let me go home.'

'To whom?' she asked. 'If you have any family, any friends we can contact, then for goodness' sake tell us about them. This is no place for you. No place at all.'

She paused before she went on, seeming to weigh up what she was about to say.

'And that's why you need to talk to us. Because if you don't, then the places you could end up in . . . Well, they make this ward look like the Hilton.'

She smiled sadly before pushing herself upright.

'Think about what I've said, won't you? Please?'

But I wasn't in the right place to listen. She was wrong, I thought. There could be nowhere worse in the world than here and now.

I was wrong.

On both scores.

CHAPTER 18

Dad wasn't coming back.

I'd replayed our final conversation over and over in my head, looping it around in the hope of finding a different ending, but it always played out the same. Dad was still angry, I was still scared and ultimately he was still dead. I tried to dream up alternatives, like deleted scenes on a DVD, but there was nothing, just the glaring empty truth that he'd gone.

Some of the time, the fear kept its distance, gnawing at my skin without getting into my veins, but there were times, mostly in the middle of the night, when sleep refused to come and rescue me, that it broke through the surface and pulsed through me, controlling my every thought and movement.

I pulled my room apart the first time it happened, desperate for a sharp edge to fight the panic with. But there was nothing. Cups were plastic, mirrors bolted to the wall and the nurses too careful to leave any weapon lying around.

Pacing the floor, I nipped and scratched at the skin on my arm and, when that failed, I worked at the scabs hidden beneath my dressing, tears of relief and embarrassment mixing as my heartbeat finally subsided.

I got a huge lecture off the nurse the next day, probably

because she had allowed it to happen on her shift, and I swear when she wrapped the last of the bandages on to my arm (she'd flat refused to let me do it), she applied about ten times more tape than she had the night before. I remember the disappointment as she brought out the tape. I'd been hoping for a safety pin that I could've hidden away.

The nurses were tiring of me – I could see that and couldn't blame them. There were people on the ward who were properly ill and needed their time. But instead they spent their hours slowly mummifying me.

I'd slept a little that morning, having been given some pills that they claimed would take the edge off the anxiety, and while they made me sleep, they didn't help me wake up. Rousing myself was difficult – my eyelids were leaden and mind fuggy.

I'd been dreaming about Dad. We were sitting together watching a film, and he was comforting me, stroking my hand gently, telling me everything was going to be all right.

It was perfect, so perfect that I forced my eyes open, desperate to see him clearly, to tell him how happy I was that he was back.

I couldn't see him properly at first, but he was definitely there beside my bed, his hand still gripping mine, stroking the back of it. I smiled for the first time in days, asking him to pass me the water on my table.

It tasted stale, like it hadn't been touched in days, and the metallic taste woke me properly, throwing Dad into focus.

And it wasn't him, no matter how hard I squinted.

Instead, there was Mr Hobson, face unshaven and clothes crumpled. It looked like he hadn't changed them in days.

Wrenching my hand from his, I pushed myself to the far side of the bed. I wanted to rub my eyes until he disappeared, but knew it would do no good. He was on his feet, shuffling around the bed, finger to his mouth, hushing me urgently.

Strange. I hadn't even realized I'd been making a noise.

'Oh my God, Daisy,' he whispered, the rims of his eyes a crimson red. 'I'm so sorry.'

I screamed again, hearing it clearly this time, feeling my eardrums burn at the volume.

It wasn't loud enough to make him run.

'I've not slept since I heard the news.' His appearance certainly backed that up. 'I wanted to come the second I heard, but the Head told everyone you weren't up to visitors.' He risked a tiny step towards me. I pushed my back further against the wall. 'But I had to keep coming to see you. Check you were OK.'

'What are you doing here?' My voice was shaky, like it belonged to an old woman. 'What do you want?'

'I don't want anything. I promise. I just had to see you, tell you that I'm sorry.'

'Well, you've said it now, so go. I can't do this. I can't talk to you again.'

He stayed where he was. The only movement towards the door was with his eyes, as he checked we were alone.

'Look, I promise I won't come again. I won't. I just needed to see you, needed to know that you weren't going to tell anyone about this, about us. What happened by the river.'

I crumbled at this point. He wasn't sorry, wasn't grieving for me or remorseful at what had happened. He just wanted to cover his back now he didn't have Dad to bribe me with.

The anger grew in me and I shook my head from side to side, trying to ease the pressure.

'Get out,' I mouthed, quietly at first. He took a step closer, straining to hear me, so I increased the volume, startling him, forcing him to shush me again, his arms outstretched and desperate.

'Please, Daisy,' he begged, and I saw tears starting to escape down his face. 'Please, I didn't mean for it to happen.'

But it was too much. I couldn't handle his feelings as well as my own and, as my shouting increased, I lashed out, arms bouncing off his shoulders as I tried to knock him clean out of the room.

Nurses streamed in to find me attacking him, raining blows on to his face and neck, whatever I could get to. They dived between us, ripping my hands away from him, restraining me against the headboard.

I didn't hear them telling me to calm down, because the blood pumping in my ears was deafening. All I could see was Mr Hobson transformed into the victim, as the nurses fussed around, worrying about the wounds on his face.

I struggled against them, trying to tell them that it was his fault, that he'd driven me to it. That he was the reason why Dad was dead, that he made me kill him, but they didn't listen. They hammered on the red button beside my bed and hung on until reinforcements arrived.

I was so angry, so off the scale, that I thought there wouldn't be enough syringes in the world to calm me down. But I was wrong, for as the plunger fell and the liquid crept up my arm, the world went into slow motion and I watched, powerless, as they led Hobson away. Then the lights faded to black.

CHAPTER 19

Everything moved quicker after Hobson's visit, especially the nurses. Having seen me in action they didn't want to spend much time in my presence. They were more used to ingrowing toenails and ruptured appendixes, and without an injection of danger money obviously thought it best to leave me alone. I tried not to let it bother me.

The only people who visited with any kind of regularity were Alice and Evelyn, my escapades spurring them into a frenzy of activity.

'Well, Daisy,' moaned Evelyn, 'I'm afraid I haven't been able to contact any relatives suitable to act as guardian. I did find a step-brother on your father's side –' my heart stopped as I remembered the surly man by my grandpa's grave – 'but he's in poor health himself and isn't capable of offering you the care you need.'

'So what does that mean?' Even though I knew it wasn't an option, I couldn't help but hope that they'd send me home.

'Well, you can't stay on the ward!' She sighed, as if she'd be happy to leave me here until I blew out the candles on my eighteenth. 'As much as we think this might be the best place for you right now.'

Alice jumped in, irked by her tone.

'What Evelyn means, Daisy, is that you're grieving, understandably so. And we need to find you a placement that will be sympathetic to this.'

A placement? What was she talking about? She made it sound more like work experience than somewhere that I could call home.

'We've discussed the possibility of a foster placement for you, with a family that has experience of young people in your position. Ideally we'd look for this to be a long-term option. We don't think it would be in your interests to be shunted around from one set of new parents to another.'

New parents? The thought bounced around the inside of my head in panic.

Were they winding me up? The one parent I'd had wasn't in the ground yet and they wanted me to accept the idea of him being replaced? And what about the woman they'd chosen to be my mum? What would I say to her? Would they expect me to like her, or love her even? I didn't want this. I couldn't cope with what it all meant.

The panic must have been jumping off my face, because Alice started to backtrack.

'That isn't what concerns us most, though. Our primary concern is your level of self-harm. You've found a way of worsening your injuries every night since arriving but haven't offered any insight into why. We'd be concerned about placing you within a fostering environment until we have a better steer on what you're feeling. You show symptoms of depression and anxiety, but at the same time you have these flash points, like the episode with your visitor.'

'The nurses were shocked at what went on,' interrupted Evelyn. 'Said it looked like you wanted to kill him.'

'Of course we know that's not true, but we're worried about you, about what's going on to provoke such an extreme reaction. Is there a problem with your teacher we should know about, or is it to do with your dad?'

Dad. I ached to see him. Couldn't believe that he wasn't about to walk through the door with a rollie tucked behind his ear. But every time I let that image settle it evaporated, replaced by the sight of the paramedics pounding his chest, of them walking sadly away. I couldn't tell them what had gone on – how could I? Sharing had done me no favours so far, had it?

We sat among the silence for a minute or two, Alice's eyes boring into me, reading every blink or tap of my foot.

'We really should talk about what happened with your teacher. Because even if you don't want to tell me about it, it said a lot about what I think is going on for you.'

'And what's that, then?'

'It's obvious that you've been under incredible pressure. What that pressure is down to we don't know, and it would definitely help if you told us.' She paused briefly, but I gave her nothing. 'But we feel that your self-harming, coupled with the agitation, delusions and bouts of aggression, suggests something known as a "stress psychosis".'

I stared at her blankly. She'd lost me.

'I'm sorry. I'm not meaning to confuse you. Or scare you either. Can I explain what I mean?'

I nodded, needing to know, whatever it cost me.

'Since your admission you've been distressed. And I'm

not surprised. Losing a parent is devastating for anyone at any time.'

I winced. Didn't want to think about Dad not coming back.

'But what is of more concern is this recurrent idea that what happened was due to you: that you caused the crash.'

Had I told her that? Not that I remembered.

'I know you haven't told us this directly. But there were times, especially in the first seventy-two hours, and then again after your visit yesterday, when you were so agitated, so convinced that it was all your doing, that we had no option but to sedate you. Do you remember this, Daisy?'

The needle I remembered. The rest of it was patchy, so I shook my head.

'You were very insistent. Adamant, in fact. Shouting it to anyone who would listen.' Her face was grave. 'We can see from your self-harming that you've not been coping with things, and when people self-harm it's often as a result of low self-esteem, which is then magnified each time they cut themselves. By the state of your arm, it's safe to say you've been feeling probably as low as you possibly could.'

She continued to search my face for signs that she was on the money.

'What we think is that your dad's crash was the final straw in a way. It made the guilt of what you've been doing to yourself unbearable, and as a result you've internalized what happened to your dad as being your fault. That you made the crash happen.'

As theories go it wasn't a bad one. But they didn't know what I knew. What I'd said to get Dad in the car.

But there was no point in saying anything. They'd made up their minds. If anything, I could only make it worse. Sit there and suck it up. That's what I had to do.

'Now, we could stay here for the next two hours, two days, two weeks, telling you that this had nothing to do with you. But we know that's not going to help. So, we're going to discharge you, today.'

This was Evelyn's cue. 'As we've said, it wouldn't be appropriate to put you in the care of a foster family . . .'

'Not yet,' Alice said, smiling.

'But we have managed to find you a placement at a therapeutic community, called Bellfield. It's not too far from here, on the east side of town, close to the sea.'

'It has a good reputation, Daisy.' The smile was back on Alice's face – she was excited for me, like Christmas had come early. 'It's a place that can help you. Help you understand what's happening and how to change things for the better. With their help, these thoughts of yours will pass.'

'Would I be there on my own?' I had visions of locked doors and pills served twice daily.

'What do you mean?'

'Would they keep me on my own? Locked up? What is this place? A loony bin or something?'

Alice shook her head.

'No, no, no. It's a therapeutic community. You'd be there with four or five others your age. Teens who've gone through events like yours, who are struggling to make sense of things.'

I didn't know whether to be pleased or terrified. Was the prospect of other kids less dangerous than being given new parents?

'Having others there will help you, just as your presence will help them.'

I doubted that somehow, but Alice was adamant.

'Seeing what the other kids are going through will help you get some perspective on your own issues. And there are therapists too, specialists on hand twenty-four hours a day, all of them there to help you turn the corner.'

It sounded like hell. The last thing I needed, or wanted, was people surrounding me, encouraging me to talk. What good would it do? Who would it bring back?

But I couldn't say that to them, so I blurted out the first thing that came into my head.

'What about my clothes?'

Evelyn seemed pleased that I'd asked, or rather looked smug with herself.

'Don't you be worrying about that. I've been out and bought some essentials to get you through the next couple of days. Until you feel strong enough to go home and collect some things.'

Home. I feared and longed for it at the same time.

'Oh, right, thanks.'

'I'll be back before you leave, Daisy,' said Alice, obviously relieved I hadn't caused a riot at the news. 'We upped the medication to help with your anxiety yesterday and you'll need a new prescription to take with you. It's not a long-term thing, mind, just until the specialists at Bellfield can assess you themselves.'

I nodded, hoping my eye contact would tell her that I was grateful. Somehow the words themselves wouldn't come.

*

Despite where I was heading, it was a relief to walk out of the hospital doors.

A breeze cut through the warm air and I tried a smile, which sat awkwardly on my face, before slipping to the floor.

It felt strange to be back in my own unwashed clothes again, but after looking at the essentials that Evelyn had bought, I had little option, and anyway anything was better than a hospital gown.

My jaw had dropped when I saw what she had brought with her. It was like she was dressing a doll. A couple of cheap supermarket T-shirts in pink and lilac, both emblazoned with a star on the front in sequins. Strangely, they didn't appeal. Especially as the sleeves barely reached my biceps, leaving my bandaged arm exposed for all to see. Dad's shirt felt far more comfortable, despite smelling of the ward rather than of him.

By the time we reached the car, I was tired, unable to stifle a yawn.

I had no real idea where this Bellfield place was. It was on the side of town that I didn't know that well, despite Dad taking me to the beaches over the years. I'd paid plenty of attention to the arcades and the tacky shops selling rock and sugared dummies, but little else. I never thought I'd end up living there, out of choice or otherwise.

Evelyn's car was a mess. The floor was littered with empty Coke cans and chocolate wrappers, and I couldn't help wondering if they were hers or had been left by some of the other kids she dealt with. I reckoned they must have been hers; she didn't strike me as the sort to sweeten kids up out of choice.

I flicked a wrapper off the seat and listened as she tried to put me at ease. She told me how great Bellfield was, that we'd been lucky to secure a placement there. She knew of kids who'd been waiting months for such an opportunity. Apparently my situation was different, though: having no other family threw waiting lists on their heads. I'd been bumped above them. I was a special case.

I shuddered at the idea. There was nothing special about what was going on. Nothing out of the ordinary about this tin-pot car, or the contents of the bag that I clutched in my hand, or even the conversation she was trying to make us have.

The last thing I wanted to do was seem special. When I got to this place, I had to be anything but. I needed to blend in, be dull, lifeless, the kid no one wanted to talk to.

If I could manage that, then everything would be fine. No one would get hurt.

CHAPTER 20

The two sides of the house didn't fit together. It was like running a double bill of *American Pie* and *Titanic*. It just didn't make sense.

The left-hand side was towering. Four storeys of old stone and turrets. I was no expert, but it must have been a hundred years old. It looked like someone had dumped the Addams Family's gaff by the sea.

The other half, though, was just plain ugly – two storeys of red brick and plastic windowframes. And although it must have been about seventy years newer, it looked shambolic, like the older bit was the only thing holding it up.

The house was at the end of a cul-de-sac, hidden behind a ramshackle fence, and as we drove through the gate I wondered if the people in the houses around about knew what, or who, they were living next to.

It was warm still, the smell of salt heavy in the air.

To the right of the main entrance, just before the old gave way to the new, there was a balcony with half a dozen people sat on it, and as I crunched up the gravel towards them, all eyes fell on me.

Evelyn looked the happiest I'd seen her, all teeth and

smiles. It looked like she might burst into a show tune at any time.

One of the figures, a guy, waved at her from the balcony. She smiled and blushed before noticing me looking at her. The smile disappeared. The blush, however, only got bigger.

The guy popped his mug down before hopping over the balcony, landing cleanly on the lawn. He skipped towards her, beaming.

'Now then, Evie,' he said. 'Been a long time.'

'It has,' she answered, clinging on to a remnant of the efficient Evelyn I knew. 'About a year, I think.'

'That all? Feels longer.'

She laughed quickly before clicking back into her default setting.

'So you must be Daisy, yeah?' The man smiled. His face was honest, open, straightforward. Just as Hobson's was.

I pulled my cuffs over my wrists, before ramming my hands into my pockets. It wasn't safe to talk to him. Not yet.

'My name's Eric. I'm one of the staff here. We've been looking forward to your arrival.' He beckoned to the crowd behind him.

There were more of them now, hiding in a haze of cigarette smoke and coffee fumes. They didn't look excited to see me, although I could guess which of them were staff.

All of them who a) weren't smoking and b) were waving like a bunch of loons.

The others, four of them from what I could see, were less effusive. One of them was sprawled across the balcony, one was texting furiously on the largest mobile phone I'd ever seen, while two girls were deep in animated conversation.

None of them waved, looked up or acknowledged me. It was like Evelyn was here on her own, like I was her shadow.

Eric didn't seem bothered by me not shaking his hand. He turned and beckoned me forward. 'Step this way. Come and meet the rest of the reprobates.'

The smiles from the adults got bigger as I walked closer, and as the sun glinted off their teeth, I thought I'd walked into the middle of an American sitcom. Somehow, though, their welcome was genuine, despite me putting on my best 'don't smile at me' face.

I was introduced to each of them in turn. The two women were Maya, thin with dreads, and Floss, a blonde who looked little older than me (but was definitely a member of staff). There was another guy as well, Sam, who was a bit older than Eric, probably early thirties and out of shape. He had a big smile but sad eyes, and looked like he hadn't slept properly in weeks. I knew the feeling.

'There's a few staff missing, who you'll meet later or tomorrow,' said Eric.

'Including Adebayo,' added Floss, 'who'll be your key worker.'

I had no idea what that meant. Was that different from Evelyn? Did it mean this other woman would be just as miserable and save her smiles for staff that she fancied?

I nodded and turned to look at the kids on the balcony.

One of the girls seemed more interested all of a sudden, but she wasn't happy about something. She'd looked gnarly since she heard Adebayo mentioned.

'Why's she got Ade as well as me?' she complained at Maya. 'You aren't key-working anyone since Patty left. Why don't you take her on? Why do I have to share everything?'

Maya tried to appease her with an arm round the shoulder, but was rebuffed.

'Don't touch me,' the girl crowed before storming away. 'I got rights, you know!'

The other kids howled like they'd heard it all before. They mimicked the girl's voice, leaving her to shout back, her volume not fading as she stormed away.

'Laugh it up, arseholes. I'll have you all later, believe me.' Then it went quiet.

'That's Naomi.' Eric sighed. 'She's the on-site psychologist.' He laughed at his own joke, but not as hard as Evelyn, who guffawed from behind her hand.

The two lads were Jimmy and Patrick, and I reckoned they were both older than me. Even though they were only probably sixteen or something, they both had faces that looked lived in, and in Jimmy's case trampled on.

He was rake thin, with long almost ape-like arms. The veins stood so proud on his forearms that you could almost see the blood pumping through them.

He shook my hand in some elaborate changing grip that drew laughter from the others, but he took no notice, just stared at me goggle-eyed before turning his attention to his phone. 'Listen, I've got to take this. We'll catch up later, yeah?' And he strode off, talking loudly into his massive handset. He must have had it on silent or something, because no one seemed to hear it ring.

Patrick didn't seem so keen to chat. He pulled himself up

off the wall at Maya's insistence, but didn't offer a hand, just some advice: 'Keep away from Jimmy. The boy's a loon of the highest order.'

This earned him a look from Maya, but he clearly didn't care. He just shrugged and drew heavily on his cigarette, which glowed red before disappearing before our eyes. He looked like he could smoke the whole thing in two drags, and seemed proud of the fact too.

He was overweight and scruffy, and I could smell him. His trainers were old and tatty, the soles flapping and riddled with holes. They looked like they hadn't left his feet in weeks.

Fortunately I didn't have time to think about it as something hit me full in the chest, almost knocking me off my feet. It wasn't until I regained my balance that I realized the other girl had done it. But she wasn't looking to start something, she was hugging me. Hard.

I didn't know what to do. I'd have shied away if I'd known. The last thing I needed was someone touching me, and if she knew what I was about, she'd have thought twice too. So I stood there as she squeezed like a hungry python, sending a look to Maya that hopefully said, 'Get her off me.'

It didn't take her long to get the message and she prised the girl away, who was grinning wildly, eyes shining with tears.

'I'm sorry,' she said. 'It's just we've all been excited about you arriving. We've been waiting hours to meet you.'

With that she snaked her arms around Maya and squeezed hard. Maya smiled and squeezed her back before gently easing out of her grasp.

'Well, Daisy's here now. But she might feel a bit nervous at first, so let's give her some space, yeah?'

The girl looked mortified. 'Sorry! Sorry, I'm sorry. I didn't think.' She shuffled forward towards me again, arms outstretched, and I did the same, away from her.

'Susie . . .' the carers chorused, and Susie stopped, her face falling in horror.

'It's all right,' Maya chimed. 'Don't worry about it. Just think, OK?'

Susie gurned, embarrassed, and sloped to the back of the balcony. She was small, five foot at the most, and as round as she was tall. She had wiry black hair like a horse's mane, which she'd pulled back into a tight ponytail. I'd always thought of myself as unfashionable, but next to her I felt like a cover-girl.

Susie reattached herself to Maya as I was introduced to a couple of other staff members, but by now there were too many names to remember, too many people looking at me, trying to work me out.

I suddenly felt knackered, aware of a growing tightness in my back, like I'd been sat badly in the car. Rubbing it with my hand made no difference, so I tried to shrug it off.

The others picked up on my sudden fatigue, with Floss taking my bag and leading me through the front door. It was a nice gesture, but her carrying my stuff hardly lightened the load. Two foul T-shirts, a three-pack of pants and a brand-new toothbrush wasn't exactly back-breaking.

'We'll do the grand tour later, Daisy. Once Ade arrives. She knows it better than any of us.' She led me through a long, wood-panelled hallway and up a flight of stairs flanked by an elaborate banister. It felt like I was in a country pile, but despite the grandness of certain things there was a shabbiness to it. The walls had been decorated recently and there was a whiff of paint in the air, but wherever I looked there were intervals of damage: stains on the walls, fraying carpet on every third step, odd bits of graffiti scratched into doors. Whoever owned the building loved it, but they obviously couldn't keep up with the people living in it.

As we hit the third floor, Floss turned off the staircase and through a heavy wooden door.

'Girls' landing,' she sang. 'Don't worry about remembering which floor you're on. If you end up by the lads' rooms, you'll soon know by the smell. It reeks up there. I don't know what's making it, but whatever it is, it can't be legal.'

She wasn't what I expected the staff to be like. None of them were so far. I'd imagined them to be serious, you know? I expected them to leave long gaps between sentences, to tease me into speaking so they could analyse my thoughts. But so far there was little difference between them and the rest of the kids. And in Floss's case only a few years as well.

We paced down the corridor until we got to a white door at the end. She slid in a key and pushed slowly.

The smell of paint invaded my nostrils, jolting me like smelling salts. It was too much for both of us. Floss crossed to the windows and battled with the latches as I took in the room.

There wasn't much to see. Just a medium-sized box, painted the most sterile white you could imagine. It was so numbing that it was almost impossible to see where the walls met. It was like walking into the middle of a snowstorm.

With a final grunt, Floss gave up on the window. 'Idiots must have painted them shut.'

'I'll have a go,' I whispered, gripping the handle on the window.

It didn't budge, even when I applied some shoulder to it. It wasn't until I pushed gently on the glass that I noticed the window was different.

It wasn't glass. It gave a little at the touch, wobbling away from me, before bending back into place. My forehead creased with confusion.

'What's going on with these things?' I asked.

'Sorry, Daisy. The decorators must have been blind or stupid. Or both.'

'No, I mean the windows. They're not glass.'

'Oh, that. None of these windows are. Or anywhere else in the house. They're all plastic. Reduces the temptation, you see.'

She wasn't making it any clearer.

'Temptation?'

'Let's face it, Daisy. Everyone living here has got things they're working through. And more often than not, working through them leads to a fair bit of anger. The last thing we need is that anger being taken out on the windows. Believe me, if we had glass in here, then we'd be living in one breezy house.'

There was no drama in her voice, just a matter-of-factness. From what I'd seen of her, I didn't reckon anything could get under her skin. Immediately I was envious of her.

'Listen, I'm going to go downstairs now and sort out the paperwork with Evelyn. Give you a bit of time to get used to your room. And don't worry, you hear? Once we get your stuff in place, it'll feel more like home, I promise.'

I tried to believe her, but failed miserably. Nothing about this said home. I was only on the other side of town, but I couldn't feel any further from my house.

Even if I ripped out the Plexiglass and replaced it with Mum's window, it still wouldn't be enough. Whichever way I looked at it, I was on my own.

The thought was exhausting and immediately all I wanted to do was sleep.

My bed was by the window furthest from the door and I moved towards it. I didn't fancy staring at the window at night, knowing I couldn't open or break it, and besides, I felt vulnerable being so far from the door. If someone was to get in, I wanted to be close by. To be able to kick it closed before they could get to me.

It was no big deal. I reckoned I had the energy to drag the frame a few metres, especially as all I planned to do after was collapse on top of it. But when I grabbed the headboard and pushed, it refused to give. It didn't look heavy, just a simple wooden base and slatted headboard, but for some reason it wasn't budging. I walked round to the other end to pull instead, but it made no difference. It dug its heels in like a stroppy kid.

What was going on? I dropped to my knees and lifted the duvet to find each of the legs bolted to the floor. One of the bolts was coming loose, like it had been wrestled one time too many, but the other three were showing no sign of letting go.

I let the duvet drop and pushed myself on to my feet.

First the window and now this? It was a room full of tricks, and I wondered what other surprises I couldn't see.

It raised the paranoia in me, forced my heart up into second then third gear. I paced towards the door, fearful of what else I'd find before I reached it.

As long as I got out of the room before I counted to five, I'd be fine, and my heart would slow.

The door slammed shut behind me. I hadn't even got to three.

CHAPTER 21

I tried to regain my composure as I walked down the stairs. Away from the stink of paint and prison furniture, I felt a bit more human, and would have been fine if I hadn't tripped over something lying across the bottom step.

Naomi. The lairy girl from outside.

I caught her arm with my foot, knocking a packet out of her hand, its contents spilling across the wooden floor.

'Jesus Christ,' she yelled, leaping to her feet. 'Watch where you're going, will you?'

'Sorry,' I moaned, dropping to my knees to collect what I'd spilt. Talk about a way to make friends. 'I didn't see you.'

'Yeah, it's hard, innit? Noticing people sat on a step . . .' Her words were thick with sarcasm and aggression. 'People often mistake me for a floorboard.'

I pointed my blushing cheeks towards the floor, lighting the area I had to search. As soon as I was down there, I knew what it was I was looking for, because I could smell it.

Tobacco. Instantly I was home with Dad and the speed of the thought knocked tears to my eyes. Grimacing, I pushed the memory away. The last thing I should do now was show emotion, to anyone, never mind Naomi, who was still sucking her teeth in disgust.

'Don't miss any of it. That was a full packet. If there's any missing or covered in crap, it'll cost you a new pouch.'

'It's fine,' I replied, relieved. 'There's only a bit on the floor.' I passed it up to her while still on my knees, not daring to look her in the eye.

Naomi exhaled dramatically. 'You were lucky. Others have had a slap for a lot less.'

Her cigarette papers had skidded across the polished floor too. I leapt to my feet and retrieved them for her. Braver this time, I dared to see how she was looking, whether a slap was on the way.

She didn't look especially angry. She had one of those faces that slope down naturally, so everything, even the most neutral expression, had something of a scowl about it. Even her hair was angry, a series of tight rolls falling past her shoulders.

She took the papers from me and fell back on to the step. There was no suggestion of a thank you, but she managed something that wasn't a threat.

'I don't know why I bother with these things. They ain't a patch on Marly Lights.'

She laid a cigarette paper on her lap and dropped a clump of tobacco on top of it. Her fingers shook slightly as she tried to spread it the length of the skin, her forehead creased with the exertion of not dropping it all over the floor again.

'Don't know why I bother with it. Struggling to get it rolled is worse than the cravings in the first place.'

A small laugh passed my lips. I couldn't help it. She was funny, so serious. More serious even than me.

'Yeah, yeah, laugh it up. If I wasn't paying for everything I busted up round here, I'd still be affording my Marlies, or at least Mayfairs. Anything except this . . .'

She chucked the tobacco and papers back across the floor, before slumping, head in hands. Collecting the pieces, I sat on the step beside her, silent as she was.

I don't know if I did it out of habit or to please her, but either way I couldn't help myself. It seemed like the natural thing to do. It was what I always did when I saw Dad's tobacco – I rolled it. And within a minute I was prodding her gently with my finger, a cigarette the best peace offering I could manage.

She looked confused, like she didn't recognize what I was holding, then the scowl softened long enough for her to say cheers.

'Nice work,' she breathed, taking the smoke in and holding it deep in her lungs. 'You a smoker, then?'

'Not exactly.' I didn't want to get on to the subject of Dad with anyone. Not yet, not ever.

'Well, you've got the tools. You can stick around. You're already coming in handy.'

I pulled a paper from the case and set about rolling another. I might as well make a pile for her to enjoy.

Not that it pleased her. 'Listen, if you want one, you ask, yeah? I'm up for looking after you if you help me out, but there is such a thing as manners, you know?'

I tried to answer back, tell her it wasn't for me, but she cut me off mid-sentence.

'Look, it's fine. I'll let you have it this time. But next time, you and me'll have words, you hear?'

The cigarette sat in my hand. I didn't know what to do with it. If I tried to tell her again that it was for her it would sound lame. I went to put it behind my ear like Dad used to do, but as I raised my hand to my head, she sparked a lighter in my face.

The flame danced in front of me long enough for her to get riled again.

'Come on. Don't be wasting my petrol as well.'

It didn't leave me with a lot of options. I put the cigarette in my mouth and leaned in towards the flame.

The smoke rolled around my mouth and I held it there, hoping it looked like I was doing it properly.

Naomi stared at me like I was a freak.

'What are you doing? It's not a cigar, you know.'

I smiled pathetically, before breathing in again, pulling the smoke into my lungs.

It hurt. Hurt as I drew it in and stung as I pushed it out. I blew as hard as I could, trying to get the smoke as far away as possible, as if it would limit the damage it was doing. I felt my face turn green as I tasted the heat in my throat.

'You all right?' She didn't exactly look concerned.

'Yeah, fine. I'm just not used to smoking without a filter.'

'You should've said. I've got some in my pocket. That'll teach you to nick my baccy without asking, eh?'

We sat in silence for a few minutes, but I could feel her eyes on me, checking me out, my clothes, my hair, my way of smoking. She wasn't exactly being subtle about it and it left me no choice but to keep puffing away. I was too scared to grind it out beneath my foot before it was all gone.

'So,' she barked, 'what are you in for?'

Her directness derailed me slightly, so I shrugged and blew smoke out, as if dismissing the question. Implying that the answer wasn't important.

But it obviously was to her.

'Well?'

'Don't know really. There's some stuff they've told me I need to work out.'

She sniggered. 'Duh, well, obviously. They gave that line to all of us. I mean, what stuff? What you in *for*?'

It was weird the way she spoke about the place, making it sound like prison, and for a second I thought I was talking to Morgan Freeman in *The Shawshank Redemption*. Except I couldn't see the same happy ending heading my way. Couldn't see Naomi taking me under her wing the way the characters do in the film. But I knew I had to say something that might put her off asking anything else. So I gave her the blunt truth.

'I'm here because my dad's dead.'

The words physically hurt and I knew if I'd said that to any of the kids at school then it would've been enough to make them back off. But this wasn't school and she wasn't a friend. Her interest had been pricked.

'Bummer. What happened?'

'Car crash.' Surely that was enough?

'So why aren't you home with your mum?'

Unbelievable.

'She's dead as well.'

'Brothers?'

I shook my head.

'Sisters? Uncles? Aunties?'

'Nope.'

She sucked her teeth again. 'Yep, that'll screw your head up good and proper.'

'Thanks for your encouragement!' This conversation wasn't doing anything for my confidence.

'No problem. And don't worry. By the sound of things you should fit in just fine. Everyone else is a fruitloop as well. Me included.'

With that she pushed herself up and ground the cigarette end under her foot. She didn't bother to pick it up as she walked away, though she did turn back to add, 'Oh, and no need to thank me for the smoke. I'll come see you later. You can roll me some more.'

The silence that followed was a relief, although for some ridiculous reason I didn't stub my fag out as well.

I sat and stared at it, thought about the ridiculousness of the whole conversation, and the fact that I'd ended up smoking at all. It tasted foul and stank as well, but I lifted it back to my mouth anyway. What harm was it going to do? The situation couldn't get any worse and, in some weird way, smoking made me feel closer to Dad.

So I sucked hard, feeling my lungs recoil at the shock, before exhaling and inhaling again.

Maybe this was all I was worth? And if that was the case, smoking suited me.

CHAPTER 22

It would be a lie if I said the rest of that first night was uneventful. Every second at Bellfield seemed to be full of some underlying drama or tension, whether it was just banter or something a lot more confrontational.

The truth was that I spent that first early evening in a zombie-like state. Whether it was the shock of being landed in this alien place or the exertion of leaving hospital, I wasn't sure. All I knew was that I felt disconnected from everything.

My body ached, the earlier stiffness in my back multiplying by the minute. It was getting so bad by the time we ate that it was difficult to sit down. I could feel the muscles around my spine spasm, like someone had shoved half a dozen golf balls down the neck of Dad's shirt. Each time I leaned back in the chair, a jolt of pain shot me upright.

It didn't go unnoticed. Naomi offered an expression of contempt before whispering something to Susie, who giggled and then looked embarrassed as she caught my eye.

Floss noticed it too.

'What's going on, Daisy?' she asked.

'Nothing,' I answered, trying to make light of it. 'Just a bit achy, that's all. Tired, I suppose.'

She didn't look convinced.

'Keep an eye on it, will you? And tell us if it gets worse.' She seemed concerned. 'Oh, and that reminds me, your meds. Evelyn said you were to take them before each meal.'

She pushed herself to her feet and paced out of the door, leaving me to people-watch.

The dining room was long and thin, more a canteen than anything homely, with huge metal shutters lining the right-hand side, which housed the kitchen. The shutters were down tonight as we were having takeaway in my honour, a celebration that caused a few ripples among the others.

'How come she gets to choose?' Patrick moaned. 'I've been here eight months and I've never chosen yet!'

'That's such bull,' barked Naomi. 'You chose that crappy fried chicken last week. Worst damn thing I've ever eaten. Was more like rat.'

'That wasn't me. That was Jim!'

All eyes turned to Jimmy, who was on another wavelength, tapping furiously on his oversized phone.

This seemed to diffuse things a bit, as Susie giggled again, while Naomi and Patrick rolled their eyes.

'Who you texting?' Patrick asked.

'Just a mate. Reckons he can get me a gig next week. Somewhere I can try out some new tunes.'

'Safe,' mocked Naomi. 'You can get us on the guest list. We'll look forward to it.' It was obvious she didn't believe a word of it.

'Won't be a problem. VIP passes the lot of you.' Jimmy smiled, without looking up.

This drew more eye rolls from the others, with Patrick looking particularly scathing.

The arrival of the pizzas seemed to signal the end of ribbing Jimmy, as the four of them descended on the boxes like vultures.

I waited until they'd scavenged what they needed before sliding a slice on to my plate, then picked at the salami and removed the chunks of pineapple. I might have been depressed, but I still knew fruit on pizza was sick and wrong.

Patrick was wolfing his down, destroying each slice like he smoked his cigarettes. It was as if he feared someone eating them off his plate before he did.

Jimmy, on the other hand, was secretive, taking his to the table at the far end of the canteen, sitting with his back to the rest of us, arms wrapped protectively round his plate.

'Never lets any of us see him eat,' Floss said, sighing as she returned with a cup holding two orange pills. 'Hasn't since the day he arrived.'

I looked at the pills, two orange spheres that I'd been taking since early in my hospital stay, and it struck me then that I didn't even know what they were called.

'You need some water?'

I shook my head and pointed at my cup, before tipping the pills to the back of my throat and washing them down with a grimace.

It didn't cause a stir with the others. In fact, after seeing me, Floss handed out other cups to Susie, Naomi and Patrick, but she went nowhere near Jimmy.

Susie washed hers down, thanking Floss enthusiastically. Patrick flat refused his, swiping the cup on to the floor, while Naomi tried to strike a bargain with hers.

'I'll take 'em as soon as you give me a proper knife and fork to eat with.' It was clear from her voice and Floss's body language that this was a common argument.

'Sweetie, you know the situation. We've been over it every night this week. Until we can trust you with the proper knives and know you're not going to smuggle them upstairs with you, then it's got to be the wooden ones.'

'Have you felt how blunt the proper knives are? I couldn't cut shit with them, even if I wanted to.'

'Then what were you doing with so many in your room? And why were they hidden in different places?' Floss's tone wasn't confrontational, just matter-of-fact, calm.

It didn't stop Patrick from sticking the boot in.

'You wanna be careful giving her the wooden ones anyway. Never mind *cutting* her arms, she'll give herself multiple splinter wounds with them bad boys.'

He guffawed loudly and looked to the others for support, but got none. Susie looked scared and hugged herself gently, while Jimmy was still on the far bench.

It was all Naomi needed to step up a gear, and she threw her chair backwards before launching herself over the table at Patrick.

'They're strong enough to cut you, you freak,' she yelled, as she thrust the fork towards him.

If she hadn't been so out of control it would've been funny. Patrick certainly thought it was, as he shuffled away from her, flicking slaps at her head as he danced.

'Come on, then. Cut me,' he taunted, pulling a face. 'Do your worst.'

Naomi let out a scream, a whole-hearted banshee wail that started at her feet and propelled her towards him.

I don't think Patrick expected her to make contact. He thought he was too quick. So when the fork pierced his skin before splintering, everything went into slow motion. His hand reached for his face, and as he saw the blood on his fingers everything speeded up again and he lunged at her, elbows raised. There was a crunch as Naomi's head went back, followed by a flurry of bodies as carers jumped in from all sides.

Amazingly, Naomi was still on her feet, insults pouring out of her mouth. Despite Maya and Floss hanging off her arms, she still tried to get at Patrick, goading him with every insult she had.

Patrick was no calmer himself, bucking and writhing as three male carers manoeuvred him to the floor. Even though all of them were bigger and older, they were struggling to contain him. Two of them pinned his arms down, resting their body weight on his shoulders, pushing his forehead into the floor, while Eric applied pressure to the small of his back. With an eye on his flailing legs, he talked gently to Patrick, his voice calm and even as he tried to bring him down.

'Think about it, Paddy. Think about what's happening, and try to breathe, you hear?'

It was unreal, unlike anything I'd seen, on screen or in reality, and I looked to the others, only to find them unmoved. Susie was shuffling around a little, but was still trying to eat her food, while Jimmy just strutted across the room, ditched his plate by the serving hatch and punched numbers into his phone.

That was it for me. I didn't feel capable of watching any more, so I slipped off my chair, felt my back holler in annoyance and limped towards the stairs, not knowing if anyone had even noticed I was gone.

CHAPTER 23

My heart was hammering as I closed my bedroom door. I leaned against it, almost in fear that the fight was going to follow me up the stairs and into my room.

My back was screaming at me now, forcing me to bend double. It was like my spine was an elastic band retracting from an extra long stretch. Every inch that I bent meant more pain, but I had no choice.

I slid down the door and on to the floor, my knees tucked into my chest, my neck starting to contort in the same way as my back.

My heart pummelled my ribs as my mind raced to make sense of it. What was going on? It wasn't a panic attack: this was physical. I felt like someone was standing over me, screwing me up into a ball.

I wanted Dad. Needed him and wanted to shout for help, but couldn't force enough air into my lungs. All I could do was use what breath I had to keep on top of the pain.

Biting cramps rushed through me, each one sending my neck and back into shapes alien to them. I kicked my leg against the door, hoping that the fight downstairs had stopped and someone would hear me, but doubted my efforts would be enough.

Fortunately it was.

At first I mistook the noise for an echo. Thought my kicking was reverberating down the long wooden hall. But the banging kept on going long after I had stopped. Then a voice followed. A voice I didn't recognize, but it didn't matter. It was the greatest voice I'd ever heard.

'Daisy? Can you open the door?'

I managed to twist my head enough to see the door handle straining, then felt the cold of the wood pushing against my back.

'Whatever it is against the door, you need to move it. We're worried about you and need to come in.'

There was an urgency to the voice, an unmistakable sense that whatever obstacle was between her and me, it wouldn't be enough to stop her.

'It's me,' I cried. 'I can't move.'

At that point I heard her shout a name I didn't know, plus a demand to get a doctor. She didn't know what state I was in, but was sharp enough to know it wasn't pretty.

'Daisy, I need you to try really hard to move away from the door. Just enough for me to squeeze through. Can you do that?'

I told her I could despite thinking otherwise. My upper body was completely cramped up now, my neck twisted into my left shoulder as a spasm ripped through it and down my spine. All I could do was swing my legs round, which I did until they hit the door. From there I pushed my legs straight and grimaced as I skidded forward, far enough away for the door to rocket open, a woman's face appearing around it.

I relaxed a touch when I saw her, mostly because she didn't look appalled at what she'd found. I don't know whether it was the relief of seeing someone that swayed me, but she was the most striking woman I had ever seen.

Her face was full and round, her skin a deep shining African brown, dark freckles breaking out across her nose.

As she saw the fear on my face, a long, easy smile stretched into view, a smile that told me, without saying a word, that everything was going to be fine now. That there was nothing I needed to fear.

Pulling herself through the gap in the door, she fell to her knees and cradled my head in her lap. I cried out at the exertion, but it was worth it. She laid her hand across my forehead, pressing gently, sucking the pain away and into her palm.

I forced my eyes up towards her, to be met by the same smile that had appeared at the door.

'Well, I didn't think we would meet like this. A handshake is more traditional, but this will do fine. It is great to meet you, Daisy. My name is Adebayo, but everyone calls me Ade.'

'I'm sorry,' I whispered, tears jumping from my eyes in both pain and relief.

'Now that is your first mistake. There is no need for sorry. Everything is fine and everything will soon be better. Just relax and trust Ade. Help is on the way.'

It had only been a week since Dad died, but in that time the thought of anyone touching me had seemed horrific. But here, on the cold wooden floor of my new room, being hugged by a complete stranger felt like nothing I'd ever experienced before. It felt like I was being saved.

CHAPTER 24

News of my collapse called an end to hostilities downstairs. In fact in the half-hour it took to get a doctor to me, I had visits from everyone on site. Even Jimmy got off his phone long enough to poke his head round the door. He wasn't being nosy or anything, he just told me to 'chill' before disappearing.

The others, however, would've sat on the bed and watched had Ade let them.

'This is not a reality programme,' she told Naomi and Susie. 'There is nothing for you to see and no way for you to help, so let us settle Daisy down, OK?'

Susie apologized repeatedly as she scampered through the door, while Naomi rolled her eyes and stomped away.

'Have I upset her?' I asked through clenched teeth.

'No, no, no. You must not worry about Naomi. Her nose is just a little out of joint with you arriving, that is all.'

There was something so calming about the way she spoke. There was a strong African accent through her words, but they rose and fell so gently that it was like listening to a ticking clock, somehow mesmeric.

The minutes passed slowly, each one bringing a new level of pain with it like an unwelcome present. Ade didn't move, despite her uncomfortable position, her hands stroking my hair gently. I allowed my eyes to close and dream that they belonged to Dad or, even better, Mum.

The serenity was broken by the arrival of the doctor, who looked less than impressed at being called out. She wore the look of a woman who'd been called here once too often.

She didn't give me much of a once-over, didn't even get down to floor level to prod me or see what hurt. She simply reached for her mobile phone and told Ade she was calling an ambulance.

'Quite why they discharged her so soon I don't know.'

She'd obviously been given the background on the way up the stairs.

'Are you not going to come down here and speak to this girl?'

It was the first time I'd heard ice in Ade's voice, but it was definitely there and the doctor heard it. What's more, she didn't like it.

'I don't think that will be necessary. I can see from her convulsions that she should be in hospital. This is not the place for her to be right now.'

Ade disagreed. 'Oh, I think this is the perfect place for her to be, as it is only hours since she arrived.'

The doctor looked around the room, the creases on her forehead telling us both what she thought of the place.

'If you are a doctor – and obviously you are, if you know better than me – then why did you bother calling me out?'

Ade let out a small giggle and shook her head slowly. 'Oh, I am not a doctor. Far from it. But I do know that I have read this girl's notes and I am wondering if that is the case with you.'

The doctor shoved a hand in her pocket as if searching for something. It was a tic that Ade also noticed.

'You will not find her file there. It is downstairs in the office, where I left it.'

'Look,' said the doctor, 'I'm not a psychologist. I'm a GP. I don't need to read a file to know that this girl is in enough pain to need my help. Now, are you going to let me do my job or not?'

'If that means you taking her back to hospital, then I am not. What I *will* let you do is give her the medication she needs to take these pains away.'

The doctor bristled, then set Ade a challenge.

'I suppose you can tell me exactly what I should be prescribing to her as well.'

'Of course, because I have read her file and know that for the past four days she has been taking haloperidol, an antipsychotic medication, and that she has not been given anything to guard against the side effects. That is why she is having these muscle spasms.'

The doctor took a step forward and looked closer than she had before. Ade didn't give her too much time before continuing.

'So I would imagine a small dose of Valium would allevi- ate these immediate problems, followed by a prescription for procyclidine to prevent the muscle contraction returning.'

The doctor got on her knees and tried to straighten my neck away from my shoulder. I shrieked as she did so and pushed my hand into Ade's.

'Can I see the medication she has been taking?' the doctor asked. She said this without looking Ade in the eye.

It didn't take Maya long to return with it, by which time the doctor had checked my pulse, blood pressure and tried to flex every limb in my body.

After looking at the label, she stood up and retrieved her bag from the door. She pulled out a small brown bottle, then scooted back to me. For the first time, it felt like she was actually looking at me.

'I *am* going to give you a relaxant, Daisy, because it is more than likely that these spasms you are experiencing are a result of your medication. Alongside this, you should stop taking your other tablets until a psychiatrist can look at how to balance them properly.' She smiled weakly, almost apologetically, before turning to Ade, her smile disappearing. 'But if the contortions do not ease within an hour, then we will have no option but to stabilize Daisy in hospital.'

She slid the tablets into Ade's hand before standing up and shooting me a final look. It was a mixture of sympathy and pity. 'Get yourself well, my dear,' she said, and then she left.

They didn't waste any time getting me to take the pills and I believed 100 per cent that they would work. After Ade's confidence in front of the doctor, how could I think anything else?

She stayed with me on the floor for about fifteen minutes until very gradually my neck began to straighten. It was like someone was slowly ironing the kinks out of my back and by the time the sensation reached the bottom of my spine I was in love with these drugs. I felt like a giant – like I could clean the cobwebs from the ceiling with a flick of my wrist.

The relief was so strong that I forgot everything else, what I'd done, who I'd lost, everything. I wanted to sing and dance and hug everyone in the building. The relief took me over.

Wedging my elbows into the floor, I pushed myself upright, relishing the return of my limbs. Ade straightened her legs as well, jiggling the blood through them after her own inactivity.

'Don't overdo it, Daisy,' she warned. 'The tablets will make you feel very tired.'

I didn't bother listening. I felt like I could climb a mountain or run a marathon. But the second I actually planted my feet on the floor I felt my balance waver, as my feet forgot how to hold me upright. I toppled backwards, but not far, as again Ade was there, wrapping her arms around me, pulling me across the room and on to the bed.

She yanked the shoes from my feet and pulled the duvet up to my chest.

My eyelids drooped as the drugs buzzed through every cell in my body. I managed a woozy smile and 'Thank you'. It was the best I could do.

The same girlish giggle came back from her, along with the shake of a head.

'No, no, no, Daisy,' she said. 'I should be thanking you.'

I had no idea what she was talking about, but was too tired to argue. Instead I let my head sink into the pillow.

Sleep came quickly, within moments. But I knew as it gripped me that Ade was still in the room, because I heard her voice. Where her voice stopped, though, and my dream started, I wasn't sure, because the last words I heard didn't make any sense at all.

'I should be thanking you, Daisy Houghton. You are my lucky charm.'

CHAPTER 25

It was a shock to wake up and find I'd slept for twelve hours. Pulling myself out of bed was a bit of an ordeal, but discovering that my limbs felt like they belonged to me again sugared the pill.

After finding the bathroom and changing my underwear, I pulled on Dad's shirt and headed towards the stairs.

There was music coming from two of the other rooms on the corridor, presumably Naomi's and Susie's. Behind one door I could hear the jangly guitar of some cheesy pop song, while from the other, the harsh bass line and whine of some rapper or other. It didn't take much to work out whose music belonged to whom.

As I yanked open the door that led to the stairwell, other music filtered in too, this time from the boys' floor, more beats, more bass, different tempos. I paused as the various sounds assaulted my ears. It was chaos, perfect chaos, which just about summed up my first day here entirely.

The stairs vibrated as I walked down them, but I was careful this time not to knock anyone flying as I went.

Thinking hard, I traced my steps back to the dining room.

Aside from a slice of pizza I hadn't eaten in ages and my stomach was telling me to sort it out.

Maya was nursing a cup of tea and a file at one of the benches, and she was only too happy to show me where everything lived. Three slices of toast and a bowl of Shreddies later, my stomach had just about forgiven me.

Maya didn't hassle me as I ate. She wasn't hungry for the inside track on what had gone on the night before. She just looked happy to see me on my feet, and returned to her reading.

By the time I'd stacked my plates in the dishwasher, Ade had appeared, a look of delight on her face to see me up.

'Now this is a good sign,' she said, beaming. 'And the first time I've seen you walk without falling over.'

My face flushed and I said nothing. She had been a stranger last night and I'd relied on her so heavily. It didn't feel right to do the same again today.

'Tell me, are you feeling well this morning?'

'Better.'

'OK, fine. Then we must busy ourselves. I will show you around properly before we meet with the doctor.'

I must have looked apprehensive, as she shook her head and told me not to worry, this was a different person, not the 'fool who could not even look us in the eye'.

It was a relief that she wasn't rushing me up to see the doctor straight away. In fact, it became clear that Ade didn't really rush to do anything, last night's rescue aside.

We spent the next half-hour dawdling around the site as she pointed out the different rooms. It was a maze, full of corridors and hidden spaces. The older part of the building housed all the bedrooms, lounge, kitchen and games room, while the newer, soulless part took care of the staff offices and education unit. Until then I hadn't a clue that I wouldn't be going back to school, and although sharing a classroom with Patrick or Naomi didn't appeal, it was certainly a better option than facing Donna or Hobson.

As we walked, Ade talked about last night, asking how long I had been experiencing the muscular pain, how the others had been with me, how I was feeling about being here at all. I knew she was digging, enticing me to give things away that would help her assess me, but she did it so gently and with so little fuss that it felt different from when Evelyn had done it. And even though I wasn't giving anything away, she accepted every word with a nod, before moving on to the next subject.

'No one will push you to talk about things, Daisy,' she explained. 'Our job is to help you find the answers yourself, if that is your choice. But at the same time I cannot imagine that you want to be here any longer than is necessary.' She lifted her eyebrows at me and I nodded in return. Of course I didn't.

'Then use this place well. Me, the staff, the others like Naomi, or even Jimmy. All of us can help you in some way. All of us can help you leave as quickly as you wish.'

'Where do people go? You know, once they leave here?'

'That depends on their age, on how effectively they engage with what we do at Bellfield. I will not lie to you, Daisy. For every young person that finds a foster placement, or moves into their own flat with our help, there are those who are, well, moved on involuntarily.'

'Do you mean prison?'

She looked sad at the thought. 'There have been occasions when a secure environment has become the only option, yes. And those are sad days for us all. What you must focus on, at all times, is the day you walk out of here to start a new life with a new family.'

The thought made me shiver, reminded me just how on my own I was. What if I didn't get the answers to what was going on, or they never found anyone willing to take a risk on me?

'Is it possible they'll let me move back home?' I asked. 'What if I didn't want a new family? Couldn't someone just drop in on me, check I was OK, that I hadn't set fire to anything?'

'Anything is possible in time, and you must not worry about what will happen to your house. Nothing will be done without your consent. But I must be honest, the arrangement you're after would be unusual, impossible even, in the short term. Small steps, my friend, starting with sorting out your meds.'

Our appointment with the doctor didn't last long: a quick fifteen minutes for him to reach the same conclusion that Ade had. He was kind enough, smilier than the woman the night before and certainly not as quick to judge either of us.

All it took, apparently, to stop the convulsions returning would be two other tablets a day, and although he tried to explain how they worked, I didn't want to listen. I just wanted him to be right.

We left his office in the new part of the building and returned to the sunshine.

Summer had arrived and, although I didn't feel I deserved to celebrate it, it did make me feel more alive. Anything was better than hospital.

Ade, however, was in no mood to sunbathe.

'Daisy, there are things we must do today.'

There was something about the statement I didn't like, so I approached it with trepidation.

'Like what?'

'Several things. Some happen here every day, but that is this afternoon. The first thing we must do isn't easy, but it is necessary.'

'What's that?'

'We must go to your home and collect some things. Things that will make you more comfortable. Like clothes. Your clothes.'

'Do we have to go?' I asked. I wasn't sure I could do it, not today.

But Ade was adamant, without being bossy. 'Oh yes, my friend. It must be today. One more day in that shirt and you will smell worse than the two boys put together.'

And that was the conversation over. There wasn't anything you *could* say after that.

CHAPTER 26

The house felt dark despite the sunshine, so much so that I flicked on the hall light as we entered. I turned back to the door and looked up to Mum's window, relieved to see the bulb warming up her sun. Maybe I should leave the light on as we left, to keep some life in the place even though none of us remained.

'This is a lovely house,' Ade said, stroking my arm. 'I have never seen a window quite like this before. Was it here when you moved in?'

I shook my head, told her my mum had made it.

'Then she was a rare talent, your mother. A little like you, eh?'

It didn't feel right her making comments like that. What was she basing it on? She knew nothing about me.

'I couldn't do anything like that.'

'Did she make other things? Maybe something we could bring with us?'

I shrugged. There was nothing else.

'Daisy, I know this is not an easy thing to do. So you must be in control. We can spend as little time here as you like, or as much. Maybe it would be best to gather your clothes so we can get moving quickly if you need to.'

Obediently, I climbed the stairs, leaving Ade in the kitchen. From the sounds she was making, it appeared she was emptying both the fridge and the bin.

There was a stale smell upstairs as well, like the air had given up moving around. I didn't bother opening any windows. What was the point?

Instead I headed for the airing cupboard, grabbing the biggest holdall I could find, before emptying the contents of my underwear drawer into it.

Next were various pairs of jeans from my wardrobe, and a couple of oversized hoodies, shapeless and too big, but perfect to hide in.

What I couldn't find, though, were shirts. Long-sleeved ones anyway. My mind flicked back to the day of the crash, and I remembered that I was wearing Dad's shirt because none of mine were clean. Raking through the washing basket only gave me a couple of options. It was obvious they weren't going to be enough.

I paused before entering Dad's room, knowing that everything in there had the potential to push me over the edge. But at the same time I had to do it. Inhaling deeply, as if about to push my way underwater, I opened the door and went in.

It wasn't in the worst state I'd ever seen. He'd managed to open the curtains that last morning, but there were small piles of clothes puddled in each corner of the room. A stale tobacco smell lingered – little wonder, given the overflowing ashtray on his bedside table. An ashtray and a half-empty bottle of spirits. It certainly wasn't the legacy he deserved to leave.

I fought hard to push the emotions back. This was something I had to do now: had to be strong, get things done on my own. There was no other way. I had no choice.

After rifling through his wardrobe, I found what I was looking for. I picked out half a dozen of his shirts – not his best work ones, and nothing with a short sleeve. But they were soft and lived-in, and would hide everything that needed to stay hidden.

I shoved them into the bag and went back to my room. Scanning the walls, I chose my favourite photos of me and Dad, peeling them from the wallpaper before dropping them on top of the shirts.

The bag wasn't heavy as I dragged it down the stairs, but it highlighted how little energy I had in my bones. Ade was in the lounge, eyeing the endless shelves of DVDs.

'I have never seen so many films in one place,' she said. 'Have you seen all of these?'

'Most of them, I suppose.'

'And which is your favourite?'

I shrugged again. It seemed to be my default setting and I felt instantly guilty for being so surly. In an attempt to redeem myself, I selected a handful of cases from the wall and handed them to Ade with a weak smile.

'I have not seen any of these,' she said, then sighed. 'Do you want to take them with you?'

'Yeah, that would be great.' Although I didn't feel I deserved to watch them.

She decided that I should take the TV and DVD player

from my room with me, that it was important to have as many of my things at Bellfield as possible.

I left her looking at the walls and when I returned five minutes later she was still in the same place.

'Tell me. What is on these?' She pointed at a row of unmarked VHS cases that looked clunky next to the DVDs.

'Home movies,' I replied. 'Dad was a sucker for filming everything.'

'And have you watched them?'

'No. Most of them were never transferred from video to DVD. Some of them are on super-eight reels as well. Dad had one of those cameras when he was at uni.'

We studied the shelves for a few moments, but I was starting to feel on edge. Ade knew it too.

'Do you have everything you need for now?' she asked.

'I think so.'

'Then we should be heading back. Don't worry. Nothing here will be moved and we can come back whenever you feel like it. This is still your home, Daisy. Eventually decisions will have to be made about what happens to it, but you will be involved, I promise you.'

As we headed for the front door, lead filling my boots, I hesitated before flicking the light switch off, and felt something give inside as the button moved beneath my finger. Ade put a consoling arm around my shoulder and ushered me back into the sunshine.

After tossing a large black sack into the bin, she led me to the car and then held up a second carrier bag.

'I also have this for you.'

I squinted into the sunlight. 'What is it?'

'Let's get moving and you can see for yourself.'

As the house disappeared from sight I turned my attention to the carrier, hoping there wasn't more bad news hiding in there.

Inside I saw a Ziploc bag on top of a box. I knew immediately what was inside the box. It was the camera Dad had bought me and the thought of it tore me in half. Part of me wanted to toss it out of the window, as it reminded me of how I'd behaved, but at the same time that seemed too easy. Maybe I deserved to have these reminders around me, in my face twenty-four/seven.

I lifted the smaller bag out and rotated it, scanning what was in there.

It was Dad's things, stuff he must have had in his pockets during the crash. I bit down on my lip, determined to keep both the emotion and the fear tucked away.

There was his wallet, rammed full of tatty receipts, Post-it notes and fifty quid in tens, plus car keys, hankie, a packet of tobacco, cigarette papers and, finally, the gold among the other stuff, his Zippo lighter.

I turned it over in my hands, remembering how he loved it, how he always knew where it was, how he'd panic when he momentarily mislaid it. It was his treasured gift from Mum, something of her that he could always carry with him. And now . . . well, it was mine, and I knew I'd treat it the same way Dad had.

My hand shook slightly as I reached for the hankie and my heart rate escalated as I panicked at the prospect of flipping out in the confines of the car.

Ade saw my agitation in a flash, and without a word

opened the window on my side, allowing a soft breeze to hit my cheek.

It helped but wasn't enough, so I grabbed the packet of tobacco from the bag and started to roll a cigarette. It wasn't easy with my hands shaking, but the concentration it took calmed me slightly, forcing my mind elsewhere, away from the fear. The problem was, once it was rolled, the panic would return, so without thinking I rammed the cigarette in my mouth and sparked up the Zippo.

The smoke burned, but with less intensity than yesterday, and after the first couple of frantic drags, the sourness of the taste decreased. It might have been helping me, but Ade wasn't quite so impressed.

'I didn't know you were a smoker.' She frowned, glancing at me in a way that said, 'You're not, are you?' Then she added, 'I can see that this morning was difficult, but smoking is not the answer. And it's not making my car smell good either!'

I shrugged. There was no way I was putting the cigarette out, not if it kept everything at bay.

'It is fine this time,' she said, 'but next time we will stop if you need to smoke, OK?'

'Fine.'

I was in no rush, so I puffed on, before throwing the butt from the car and leaning my head towards the open window. My mouth tasted dreadful, but I didn't care. If it helped, then it was good enough for now.

CHAPTER 27

It was well past two in the afternoon when we got back to Bellfield and I was whacked. Carrying my bag was all I could manage, so it was a relief when Ade grabbed the TV and DVD player. She paced on in front of me while I stumbled behind, wishing my room was on the ground floor.

As we reached the balcony I could see Patrick sat on it, swinging his legs and drawing heavily on his fag. He eyed the stash that Ade was carrying, his eyes narrowing as I approached.

'Film nights in your room, then, yeah?'

He didn't say it in a particularly sleazy way, but I felt my shoulders tense at the suggestion. There was no way he was watching anything with me.

Ade saw this and took it as an opportunity to give me a warning of my own.

'You must not worry too much about Paddy,' she said, her eyes holding a look I hadn't seen before. 'Like everyone here, he is vulnerable, and has lots of things to work through. It would be best to keep your room as your own private space.' Her face softened a little, not wanting to freak me out. 'We are here to make you feel safe. You understand that, don't you?'

I nodded, but I wasn't worried by Patrick. He wouldn't be setting foot in our corridor, not without a fight.

My room looked less of a shell with stuff in it, but homely it wasn't. Ade promised me some money to buy a duvet cover and throws, anything to cheer it up, but there seemed little point. Whenever I looked at the plastic windows I'd know I wasn't home.

By the time I'd hung up my clothes I was ready to collapse, but Ade had other ideas.

'No, no, no,' she chivvied, 'this is no time for sleep.'

I rolled on to my bed, cocooning myself in the duvet. 'Just ten minutes.'

But she wouldn't have it.

'Daisy, it will soon be three o'clock.'

'So?'

'So that means we have to be downstairs in the lounge.'

'Why?'

'Because every day at three we all meet.'

I pulled my head from the duvet. I didn't like the sound of this.

'Who's we?'

'Everyone. All the others, and whoever is on shift.'

'I don't get it.'

'We will both get it if we are not downstairs in two minutes. Come on!'

And without any warning she yanked the duvet from my back and pulled me to my feet. For a second I thought she was going to give me a fireman's lift down the stairs, but she settled instead for prodding me down them.

We were the last people into the lounge, but by no means

the most miserable there. Naomi and Patrick were sat at opposite ends of the room, wearing the biggest scowls imaginable.

There were four settees in there, saggy old four-seaters, and they had been arranged to form a large square about the size of a boxing ring. I wondered if they'd been set up like that so Naomi and Patrick could go at each other again. I shuddered at the thought.

Jimmy and Susie sat together on one settee, oblivious to the tension simmering between the other two. Jimmy was drumming his fingers against his knees, head bobbing and mouth singing a tune that only he could hear. Susie sat and gazed at him, her own head nodding, trying to pick up the rhythm he was creating.

Not wanting to be too close to any of them, I perched on the arm of the fourth settee. Ade flopped on to the cushion beside me.

No one was talking, not even the two staff members already there, who smiled at me without saying a word. We were obviously waiting for someone or something, but I had no idea what.

After another minute the door opened and a woman strolled in. At first I thought she'd taken a wrong turn, as she wasn't dressed for this place. She was decked out in a power suit, all lapels and sharp creases.

Everyone sat forward, mouths falling open. And then Jimmy let out a long, slow wolf-whistle, dissolving a lot of the tension hanging in the air.

'What's this, Bex?' Patrick shouted. 'No one told me they changed the date of Halloween!'

Naturally, Naomi took exception to what he said and

hurled a cushion in his direction. 'Shut up, dickhead. Everything's a joke to you, isn't it?'

From there it was just another couple of insults until they were both on their feet, pacing towards each other, two carers apiece hanging off their arms.

What was it with this place? I couldn't keep up with it or handle how volatile it constantly seemed to be.

Breathing deeply, I retrieved the tobacco from my pocket and busied my hands.

The chaos didn't last long, as the new woman strode into the middle of the room, wedging herself between the pair of them. She was smaller by some distance, but there was an air about her, and with a single word and a pointed finger she put them firmly back in their boxes.

Her face was stern but not threatening, and as soon as peace was restored she softened, especially when her gaze landed on me.

'Brilliant,' she beamed as she pulled off her jacket, tossing it carelessly on the back of a settee. 'Right, everyone, so sorry I'm late. Yet another meeting. I'm guessing I'm probably the only one to have not met her yet, but this is our new resident, Daisy Houghton.'

There were smiles and greetings from everyone, which made me feel self-conscious, picking nervously at the tobacco peeking out of my cigarette.

'We're delighted to have you here,' she went on. 'My name's Bex and I'm apparently in charge of this place.'

Patrick of course saw this as the perfect opportunity for more insults, but everyone seemed to ignore him and Bex continued.

'You're probably wondering why everyone is here, and in part it's to welcome you, but it's also part of our daily routine. Monday to Friday, three o'clock, come hell or high water, we get together in here. We call it our "community meeting". Sometimes we don't talk much, sometimes we don't shut up for forty-five minutes, but whichever it is, it has to happen. I suppose what I'm saying, Daisy, is that many things are optional here, but community meeting isn't. And if you choose not to come then we'll just come to you.'

'They bloody do as well,' moaned Naomi. 'Everyone's teacups are still in my room from last week.'

'And strangely enough you've been here every day since,' laughed Ade, sticking her tongue out at her.

'Daisy, I don't want to put you on the spot,' said Bex, 'but is there anything you wanted to say by way of introduction?'

I crinkled my nose and shook my head. Why would I do that? Did she think I was proud to be here?

She seemed fine with that. Patrick wasn't, though.

'She's been a barrel of laughs since she arrived,' he moaned. 'Serious case of verbal diarrhoea, this one.'

Bex saw this as the perfect opportunity to turn her attention elsewhere, much to my relief.

'That's no problem, Daisy. Take all the time you need, and know that everyone, staff or resident, is here to help you.' She turned to Patrick. 'So, Paddy. As you're so keen to talk today, maybe you can guide us through what went on last night?'

His chest swelled with pride, seeming to take pleasure in

being the centre of attention. 'What?' he crowed. 'What's a few glasses of vodka between friends?'

'Oh, I didn't know about the vodka. I . . . er –' and she looked to the rest of the staff in mock-surprise – 'I don't think any of us knew you'd been drinking, but we'll be sure to have the vodka from your room straight after this.'

Patrick blushed a deep angry red.

'What I'm talking about was what went on during dinner last night. Anyone care to fill me in?'

There was a rush of voices as Naomi, Patrick and even Susie all raced to get their points across. It was like listening to a bunch of pre-schoolers fighting for teacher's attention.

Bex, to her credit, was patient with them, listening to their wildly varying stories, not smiling or laughing at the ridiculous lines they were coming out with. Floss and Ade weren't quite so controlled, Floss hiding her face behind a cushion as Naomi wailed about how she'd been disrespected. You couldn't see her face, but you could make out her shoulders shaking with laughter.

Once the witness statements had been made, Bex wasted no time in setting everyone straight, and although her words were direct, there was no sense of anger in any of them.

'It sounds to me like everyone forgot the basic rule about what we're trying to achieve here. It's all about respecting people. Naomi, you know why you were given wooden cutlery – it's something we've discussed here time and again. We can't allow you to take knives from the kitchen and hurt yourself with them. We care about you too much to let that happen.'

Naomi stared at her, unblinking, but the way she sucked her teeth, her head tilted slightly to one side, showed she didn't want to hear it.

Bex turned to Patrick, who was sat back, arms spread across the width of the settee. He was trying to look brave, but on his own on the four-seater he just looked lonely.

'And as for you, Paddy . . . well, you need to consider your part in this too. Do you not think it would've been respectful to keep out of Naomi's conversations? Don't you think it might be difficult for her to see her privileges taken away? The last thing she needs is you crowing about it.' She flicked her eyes between the two of them, before looking at the five of us in turn.

'Daisy arriving is an important moment for us as a group, so let's use it, shall we? Let's focus these next few days and weeks on showing each other some respect. Try and help each other, not rip each other's eyes out, yeah?'

There was a begrudging 'yeah' from the two of them, plus a more enthusiastic response from Susie, who looked less interested in Jimmy now and seemed more interested in hugging Bex.

Nothing further was said about the incident. In fact, as Bex took a seat next to Patrick, squeezing his hand warmly in the process, the tone of the meeting seemed to turn on its head and the next fifteen minutes were spent discussing the summer holidays that lay ahead.

It was so frantic, the pace at which things changed. Only minutes after the heated conversation ended, both Naomi and Patrick were getting excited about a trip that Maya was planning for the next week. And by the end of the meeting they had the whole of their holiday mapped out, with most of it being spent together.

It was head-spinning stuff. Stuff you couldn't have made up. Not if you expected people outside the walls to believe it was true.

CHAPTER 28

No one was disappointed to see the end of the meeting and as we left the lounge I half-expected to hear Naomi and Patrick renew hostilities. But the ceasefire seemed to be holding firm for now.

Eric, though, wasn't feeling quite so friendly towards Patrick.

'So, Paddy, do you want to tell me where the vodka is in your room? You do know we're going to have to take it, don't you?'

It was Naomi who answered for him.

'Why can't you lot just leave it alone for once?' she spat. 'It's the way you treat us that makes us need a drink in the first place!'

Eric ignored her, his gaze still on Patrick, who didn't look in the least bit concerned.

'You can look for as long as you want. You'll never find it.'

'Are you giving us permission, then? Do you want to come and watch us do it?'

'Nah, just make sure you leave the place tidy. I had the maid in earlier in the week and she's worked wonders with it.'

Eric rolled his eyes and turned away. He'd obviously heard Patrick's patter before.

'Oh, if you get chance,' barked Patrick, 'there's some socks that need pairing as well.' He waited a few seconds until Eric turned the corner, before uttering, 'Dickhead.'

Naomi thought it was brilliant, slapping Patrick on the shoulder before turning to me. 'We're going for a smoke,' she said. 'Fancy coming and working your magic for us?'

The thought of sitting in my room didn't appeal, and as Jimmy and Susie seemed to be following them as well, I agreed, falling in behind as we headed towards the balcony.

It was still sunny out and the balcony offered some shade and a slight breeze.

The others slumped on the wicker chairs that littered the area and although there was space next to Patrick – this seemed to be a bit of a theme – I leaned against the wooden beam. It may not have been comfy, but it felt a lot safer.

'Such a waste of forty-five minutes,' Naomi moaned as she tossed her tobacco towards me. 'Do the honours, will you?'

I smiled weakly and pulled a cigarette paper from the packet.

'Oh, and do one for Paddy as well, will you?'

'Cheers, mate.'

I couldn't work out the allegiances but tried to look uninterested. As long as I blended in, everything would be fine. They'd leave me alone and vice versa.

I bashed a couple of rollies together in smart time and handed them over. They turned them round, looking at them from different angles, before giving me approving nods.

'Told you she was handy, didn't I?' Naomi cooed, proud that she'd been the one to discover this 'talent' I had.

'Aye, not bad. Just as well, I suppose, cos she doesn't seem to be much use for anything else.'

It was another typical Patrick comment, but it was one that didn't slide away, as for some reason Susie took exception to it.

'And what would you know, Paddy?' she asked. 'Daisy's only been here a day and you reckon you know all about her. It's rubbish, that is.'

I was grateful for her support and if I wasn't trying to blend into the background I'd have spared her a smile. It must've taken guts to say anything at all, especially when she was nearly a foot smaller than him, her voice a mousy squeak against his growl.

'I've seen enough like her to know she's no different. Give her a couple of months and she'll get shipped on just like Patty did. Sad cow.'

My face burned. I had no idea who Patty was or what had happened to her. I didn't even know if the sad cow was me or her. But I told myself not to listen, choosing to roll and light a cigarette of my own.

'Nice Zippo,' said Jimmy. 'Used to have one myself but gave it to a lass.'

'Groupie, was she?' Naomi asked, her voice full of sarcasm.

That didn't seem to register with Jimmy though. 'Not really. I didn't get off with her or nothing. She was just this girl who started hanging around after gigs. She appeared wherever we were playing.'

'You sure it wasn't your mum?' Naomi found herself hilarious. 'You do realize there are rules against calling your mum a groupie, don't you?'

Patrick saw this as his chance to weigh in as well. 'Was this before or after you met Simon Cowell, Jim? I can never keep up with the timeline on this. Had you signed the deal by then? Or was this before you went platinum?'

Jimmy switched off. He didn't look angry or embarrassed. Instead he got to his feet and pulled his mobile from his pocket. After staring at the screen for a moment, he looked at the others and pointed to his phone.

'Yeah, yeah –' Patrick nodded – 'we know. You need to take this. Go for your life, kidda. After all, it could be your manager again. World tour this time, who knows.'

'Europe first,' beamed Jimmy, no trace of a joke in his voice, and he planted one of his long arms on the balustrade before vaulting to the grass below, pressing the phone to his ear and talking loudly.

'That boy is an absolute friggin' loon,' barked Patrick. 'I swear it's getting worse not better. He's taking calls from that "manager" of his every day now.'

'He's not hurting anyone, is he?' whispered Susie.

'Hurts my bloody ears, he does. Forever drumming on tables and going on about life on the road. He needs to be careful they don't ship him out of here for somewhere more serious. They lock others up for a lot less – the sort of places they don't let you out of. Not until they've taken a chunk of your brain away first.'

Susie looked over at Jimmy, her face so washed with concern that I had to chip in too.

'It can't be complete fantasy, though, can it?' My voice sounded brave and certain, more so than I actually felt. 'I mean, he's on the phone to someone, isn't he?'

Naomi laughed. 'Did you hear the phone ring?'

'Well, no, but he's probably got it on vibrate or something.'

She shook her head, looking at me like I was as nutty as him. 'Daisy, Daisy, Daisy, you have a lot to learn. Firstly, that phone of his is at least ten years old. There's no way he could even send a text on it, never mind set it to silent.'

'And secondly,' interrupted Patrick, 'and probably more importantly, there's no frigging battery on the back of it.'

He had barely got his words out before collapsing into a fit of laughter. Naomi joined in as they high-fived each other, finding new words to describe just how crazy Jimmy was.

I turned to Susie as they howled. 'Is that right?' I asked. 'His phone does work, doesn't it?'

She shook her head sadly. 'Never has from what we can see. He left it in the lounge once and there's a gap where the battery would fit.'

I exhaled slowly and looked over to Jimmy, who was in the garden, phone still clamped to his ear. Whoever it was talking to him, he believed it entirely, and obviously loved them as well, as I could still see the beam of his smile as he chatted away.

A cheer from Patrick brought my attention back. He'd whipped a plastic bottle from underneath his jumper and I knew he was far too excited for the contents to be just water.

'You know I said they'd never find the vodka?' he bragged. 'Here's why! I put it all in here.'

You'd have thought he'd invented the wheel, not learned how to pour liquid from one container to another, and after a long swig from the bottle, he passed it on to Naomi, who did the same.

She wiped her lips with the back of her hand and paused, gesturing to Patrick to see if she should pass it on to me.

His mouth curled into a frown before thinking better of it. 'Yeah, why not? Let's see if she's a better drinker than she is a talker, eh?'

Naomi thrust the bottle into my hand and told me to knock myself out. For a second the devil in me took over, wondering how much cooler it would be just to pour the vodka on to the ground, or better still to take a mouthful before spraying it all over him, anything to pay him back for the way he spoke to me and to the others.

Unfortunately, I wasn't that brave. Instead I took the bottle to my lips and swigged hard, hoping that whatever was in there would take the edge off things and make the day pass that bit quicker.

It wasn't the worst thing I'd tasted, no worse than the watered-down beer I'd drunk at so many parties.

'Easy, will you?' Patrick moaned, lurching forward to snatch the bottle from me. 'No need to take it all, you greedy cow.'

I held my hands up in mock surprise, ignoring the heaving of my stomach. I wanted to tell him to make his mind up. Did he want me to be one of them or not?

'I'm hardly going to get trashed on this now, am I?' he moaned. 'Not on this thimbleful.'

'Won't they know you've been drinking anyway? Smell it on your breath?'

Naomi shook her head in despair. 'You've got a lot to learn, you have. That's why you should only do vodka. Gin or whisky you have to hide with chewy afterwards, but vodka, they can hardly smell it. You won't even need a Polo to put them off the scent.'

Whether it was true or not I had no idea, but they believed it. It seemed to be one of their rules, their ways of surviving life here, and as they rambled on, imparting other scams to keep the carers at bay, I sat back, listened and rolled myself another fag. Whether it was true or not, once you had a bit of vodka inside you, it was certainly entertaining.

CHAPTER 29

They might have been volatile and erratic, but both Naomi and Patrick seemed to have life at Bellfield mastered, and for the next few days their methods suited me fine.

The education unit in the new part of the building was closed for the summer, so with no lessons to attend the days were long and lazy.

I did everything I could to minimize the amount of time I spent up and about, and was helped in no small part by the medication they continued to feed me.

The side-effect pills seemed to have kicked in, because there was no repeat of the weird spasms, but as for the other meds? Well, they knocked me on my arse.

Mornings were the most difficult. I seemed to wake up each day in the middle of the most horrific fog, a clinging heavy cloud that immersed me, messing with the simplest of thought processes. It was then that the anxiety gripped hardest. Although the new-paint smell was dying (thanks to a number of industrial-strength incense sticks), the daily realization that Dad had gone was too much to deal with, and was followed quickly by a sharp dose of finger pointing and guilt.

For at least the first half-hour of every day, I'd lie there, waiting for the panic to creep up and grab me. It'd niggle and tease, threatening to bite whenever it chose, but strangely, despite the constant threat, it never quite did. I put this down to the pills. I was sure it had nothing to do with me.

By the time I was showered and hidden inside another of Dad's shirts, it would be mid to late morning, but however long I lingered I was always the first one to rise. The carers were so pleased to see me I thought they were in danger of breaking into a Mexican wave. The really bored ones even made me breakfast, or at least a cup of tea while I battled with the toaster.

It was always lunchtime before all five of us were up, and we'd gather in the lounge, waiting to hear what was planned for the afternoon. With the sun wilting everything in sight, this meant late afternoons on the beach, and although we were hardly talking about the tropics – this was England, after all – it was still fine by me.

One thing I did notice pretty quickly was how the staff tried to make life as comfy for us as they could. If the beach was the plan, then we didn't go armed with a manky sandwich and a bottle of water; it would be full-on cool boxes of stuff, or a disposable barbecue and kebabs on skewers. The weird bit, though, was that the other kids didn't even bat an eyelid: the five-star treatment was what they expected.

It was odd, unnatural, as although I didn't know where Naomi or the others came from, I couldn't believe they'd had it half as cushy there.

I'd asked Naomi if we were always treated like this and she was delighted to tell me we were.

'Bloody awesome, innit?' she crowed. 'Being a loon has its advantages, that's for sure.'

'But where does the money come from?'

'Don't give a monkey's, long as it doesn't run out while I'm here.'

Surprisingly, it was Susie who filled in the gaps. She might have been over-emotional, but if you wanted the low-down on anything, she was the girl to go to.

'It's fund-raising that pays for this stuff. That's why Bex is always dressed up. She's constantly talking to investors and councillors and stuff.'

'Can't be easy to convince people to put money in this place, though?'

'Yeah, but Bex is a legend,' interrupted Naomi. 'She's one of us.'

'What do you mean?'

'Grew up in care, didn't she? She was a proper raver back in her day, into all sorts of stuff, but she ended up in a place like this over in Manchester and they sorted her out.'

It seemed hard to believe, but I wasn't going to argue with her about it.

'That's why none of us mess with her. The rest of the staff know knack all, it's all just learned out of books with them, but Bex is different. She understands, get me?'

'Is that why we don't see much of her, then?'

'Completely. She's out there pressing flesh or whatever they do at these fancy places. Funny handshakes and all that, whatever she has to do to give us the good things . . .'

Bex wasn't the only one we didn't see much of. In the

week that followed my arrival, I'd seen practically nothing of Ade, and didn't know what to think about it.

Part of me was relieved, as our early conversations had hinted that she wanted to get into what had gone on before the crash, but at the same time I felt somehow calmer when she was about.

I certainly didn't feel the need to neck as much vodka when she was on shift.

There was never a shortage of the stuff, and there were enough quiet rooms tucked away for us to hide in and get quietly wrecked.

I tried to limit myself to evening drinking. After all, I couldn't hide it half as well as Patrick or Naomi did. It didn't bother them what time they got laced into it, and if they had too much they just went to bed for a couple of hours before starting again, but I waited for the night shift to start, when the carers were all in the staffroom, handing over, and I knew I wasn't going to get busted.

With the anti-fear pills on prescription and the vodka flowing, the first week or so ambled by in a haze. There were flare-ups of course, when the stash of booze was rumbled or Naomi was found smuggling knives from the kitchen drawer, but I discovered a way of being on the edge of all the skirmishes, never in the middle of them.

All right, I might have had a swig of vodka, but the bottle was never found in my room, and if the fear gripped hard enough to leave me desperate, I worked over the old scars on my arm, leaving the cutlery drawer alone.

It was working, I suppose. I was neither comfortable nor happy, but I *was* drunk and high. All the stuff that had gone on was locked up safely inside and no one here had the tools to get at it.

At least, that's what I thought. But the honeymoon was almost over.

CHAPTER 30

I stared at the walking boots through sleep-sticky eyes, hoping they were an apparition.

'Did you say they were for me?' I wheezed, tobacco sitting heavily in my throat.

'Who else are they going to be for?' Ade laughed. 'I'm wearing mine already.'

She was as well, a pair of brown leather clodhoppers that looked as battered as Paddy's trainers.

'Good for you,' I moaned, shoving my face back into the pillow.

'Are you cross at me for not being here the last few days?'

I was, but I didn't tell her of course, defaulting instead to a shrug and a yawn. Another day might have passed, but I still wasn't used to the way the pills were making me feel, or the vodka for that matter.

'It is ten o'clock and the sun is waiting for us.'

I groaned. I wasn't planning on being up for at least another hour. And as for being out in the sun . . . well, she could forget about it.

Except she wouldn't. Instead she embarked on a series of annoying little ploys designed to raise me from my pit. First the duvet disappeared, then the pillow, then I was peppered with drops of water from the glass by my bed. By the time she embarked on a tuneless rendition of some hideous African song, I feared my ears would start bleeding and I leapt into action.

'All right, all right, I'm up. Give me time to have a shower, will you? I do have rights, you know.'

She chuckled long and low. 'Oh, my Lord. Only one week here and you are already sounding like Naomi. It is definitely time we had a day out, just you and me. Half an hour and I'll be back here banging on the door. Get your best walking legs on and those boots fastened, yes?'

I nodded, too shocked that I'd sounded like Naomi to do anything else. Then, picking up my towel, I headed for the shower, hoping I could wash any other traces of her clean away.

We left Bellfield armed with breakfast. Ade was adamant about starting before the others woke, probably out of fear that they'd persuade me to sack the walk off in favour of lounging on the balcony, rolling their fags for them.

Strangely, that felt like the better option, but with Ade in unstoppable mode I was swept along and before I knew it I was on the coast road, with a banana in one hand and a slice of toast in the other. Ade even carried my mug of tea for me, still steaming and thick with sugar.

'You will need the energy, believe me,' she said, grinning. 'Today will be different from your other days at Bellfield.'

I immediately felt the need for a cigarette. The lazy days had suited me fine, and something told me the rug was about to be yanked from beneath my boots, which were already rubbing on my heels.

'So, you have been settling in well?' she asked.

'Suppose so,' I muttered, not quite knowing how to sum up my first week. 'It's been . . . interesting.'

'Oh yes. Days are never dull here. You are always guaranteed drama in one way or another.'

She left a pause before setting off down a fork in the road. The sea appeared in front of us, a huge strip of blue stretching as far as my eyes would reach. Funny how the sun made everything look different, better. In this light we could've been anywhere, the Med or the Caribbean, as for once the sea actually looked clean.

'Daisy, I feel I have let you down a little in your first week. I'm sorry that I haven't been here to settle you in and show you the ropes.'

Her apology seemed odd to me. I had no idea what she was saying sorry for. After all, she was the one who'd found me on the floor and sorted out my meds. Without her, that cow of a doctor would've had me back in a hospital gown, probably in the psych ward the nurses had gossiped about outside my door.

'Don't worry about it. The others have shown me how it all works.'

'Ah yes, the others. By this I presume you mean Paddy and Naomi?'

I nodded, knowing what was coming.

'And they can show you many things, but I'm not sure, if you are to use Bellfield properly, that they will be your best teachers.'

'Oh, right.'

'Daisy, what you must understand is that all of the residents here have huge potential. They would not be living with us if they didn't. But Naomi, Jimmy, all of them, have lived through things that they shouldn't have, seen things that people twice their age, of any age in fact, should not have seen. As a result, they are struggling to make sense of their lives, and at times they use crutches to get them through the day.'

I had no idea where this was going and, from the look on her face, she knew it.

'I'm sorry, I'm tripping over my words. I am talking about drink, Daisy, and other temptations that will be put before you. I'm not stupid and I know you're not either, so I will just say this. Drink will certainly make days move more quickly. It will make you feel braver and stronger and able to fight the world. But it will not answer your questions and it will not help you move from Bellfield more quickly. We love you being here, but nothing would give us greater pleasure than waving you off, knowing you have the answers you need to move on.'

Her words were sensible and honest, but they were also bloody annoying. It was exactly what Naomi had warned me against. That the staff had read all the books, absorbed all the jargon they needed to. But Ade didn't have a clue what was going on with me, didn't realize that the things she wanted me to answer were best left buried, for everyone's sake.

Nothing else was said for a few minutes, leaving me to force down my breakfast and slurp my tea. It was a worthwhile distraction.

It wasn't until we actually reached the coast that Ade moved the conversation on to a subject that we both found even more difficult.

'We need to talk about your dad, Daisy.'

I exhaled slowly, feeling the need for a smoke intensify. 'What is there to say? He's dead.' I felt my insides weep at the truth, the matter-of-factness of what I'd said.

'And it's been over two weeks now. We need to think about how to say goodbye to him.'

'What do you mean?' Was I being thick again, or was she talking in a different language?

'A funeral, Daisy. Or some kind of service.'

'I don't want one.'

She looked surprised at both the speed and the nature of my answer.

'Are you sure?'

'Positive.' I wasn't interested in even entertaining the possibility. 'He hated religion. Couldn't stand setting foot in a church. He used to moan that he felt like a hypocrite going to funerals or weddings, so he certainly wouldn't want other people to have to do the same on his account.'

Before I realized what I was doing, there was a half-made rollie in my fingers. As I licked the seam I thought about what I'd said. It was true, all of it. He always got edgy before any kind of religious ceremony, but it wasn't the only reason I was so against it.

It was the thought of being confronted with what I'd done. Of being surrounded by people who at first would want to hug me and take away the pain. I couldn't bear the fact that, as the ceremony went on, they'd eventually wise up to what had happened and how I'd set the wheels in motion. By the time his coffin slipped away behind the velvet curtains, they'd be whispering conspiratorially. By the time the smoke poured from the chimney, they'd be wanting the same punishment for me.

It was too much to consider, even if it was what I deserved.

'I know it must be a difficult thing to face, and you don't need to decide now. Take some time. It would be such a good idea, both for you and for other people. Your dad's friends, for example . . .'

'I don't give a toss about other people!' The words came out louder and angrier than I intended, taking us both by surprise. 'I don't see anyone queuing up to commiserate, do you? Don't remember them banging down the door when I was in hospital, so why should I give a monkey's about making life easier for them?'

It was true, all of it. But I wasn't disappointed by their lack of concern. I don't think I could've handled their sympathy, and didn't trust myself or feel deserving enough to have people look out for me. I just hoped I'd said it with enough conviction to make Ade back down.

It seemed I had. She didn't look cross or disappointed. In fact, her acceptance of what I'd said agitated me more than her.

'I understand. And there are options we can take that leave it open for you.'

'Like what?'

'We can arrange with social services for your dad to be cremated. Tell his friends that you aren't strong enough to cope with a service. They may choose to mark it in some way themselves, and we can keep his ashes safe until you feel ready.'

I shivered at the thought of an urn by my bed, a constant reminder with potential for the others to abuse, use it as an ashtray or steal it in revenge for not rolling them a fag. It was all too much. I wanted to get pissed, roll into a ball and forget about it.

'Please don't worry, Daisy. All these things for you to consider after such a short amount of time, when you are still feeling so raw . . . It will get easier, I promise. You must trust me. It really will.'

Rubbing Dad's lighter with his sleeve, I flicked the lid and sparked up my cigarette, feeling the smoke nip at my lungs.

I wanted to believe her, really I did. But I didn't trust her. Not yet. Not when I couldn't even trust myself.

CHAPTER 31

We arrived back to applause and ironic cheers from the balcony.

Ade shrugged it off with a wide beam and a wave, with me limping behind, cursing my blisters. The others loved it when they saw the state of me, with the ribbing starting as soon as I was in earshot.

'You're just jealous,' shouted Ade, trying to defend me. 'We've covered miles this morning and I bet you've only just got up!'

'Too right,' jeered Patrick, holding his mug aloft. 'We've been up long enough for a few brews, though.'

I sneered at him, wondering if it was just tea in his mug. I wouldn't put such an early start past him.

Ade strolled into the house, vowing to return with teas of our own, leaving me to collapse on the wicker settee. It didn't matter that the only space was next to Patrick. I was too tired and sore to care.

Gingerly I unlaced my boots and peeled the socks off my feet, expecting to see great swathes of skin come away at the same time, but aside from a couple of angry blisters, I was just about intact.

'Have fun, then?' asked Naomi, without looking in my direction. She was trying and failing in spectacular fashion to roll a fag, but there was an edge to her voice that suggested she didn't want to look at me anyway.

'Oh aye, buckets of the stuff. Love exercise, me. Especially in this heat.'

'Should've said no, then, shouldn't you? You wouldn't catch me being dragged out by Ade like that.'

There was such bitterness in her voice that I wondered if she'd ever been asked. Maybe that was the problem.

Groaning, I leaned forward and took the cigarette paper from her, hoping the offer would cheer her up a bit, and although she still couldn't look me in the eye, she managed a grudging thanks when I passed a fag back to her.

'How long were you walking, then?' Susie asked.

I hadn't a clue. It felt like forever, but that could've been a mixture of lack of exercise and the awkwardness of the whole situation.

Conversation hadn't exactly flowed after the funeral discussion and I'd spent a good amount of time cursing myself for being so aggressive.

I'd tried to chat, but every time I said anything, the focus soon shifted back to me and from there I just clammed up. There was nothing to say, so in the end we both said nothing.

It didn't seem to bother Ade in the slightest, the silence or my grouchiness. She simply ambled along, taking everything in, humming to herself. It would have cheered me up in itself, had her happiness not seemed so alien to me.

Even when she returned with two cups of tea, a sheen of

perspiration coating her face, the grin was still intact, and she made small talk with the others, Naomi in particular, before excusing herself to go and do some paperwork. If she had to go and write about her conversations with me, then she wouldn't be wasting much ink, that was for sure.

By the end of the day, I'd stopped thinking about the awkwardness of the walk, despite the stiffness in my legs.

With the help of a sneaky swig of vodka or two, I'd put it to the back of my mind. In fact, come the next morning I'd convinced myself it had been an attempt that had gone so badly she wouldn't dare repeat it. Once again, though, when it came to Ade I was wrong, as by eleven o'clock we were back on the coast road, the sun on our backs and plasters on our heels.

She'd had to work a lot harder to convince me a second time, promising not to walk me as far or for as long. What she didn't promise, however, was not to pester me with more questions, and when we stopped for our first water break after half an hour she started her offensive.

'I had a phone call with the psychiatrist from the hospital yesterday. Alice. Do you remember her?'

I nodded. She'd been kind enough, but as the one who'd prescribed the dodgy pills, my memories of her were slightly tainted.

'She was asking after you, how you are doing.'

'And what did you tell her?'

'I told her you were still at the start of your journey, but that I was sure you would get there.'

I wanted to sneer. All this talk of journeys and potential,

it was just guff, as the others had said, a way for them to justify their jobs.

'She filled in a lot of gaps for me too, Daisy. Told me more about the anxiety attacks you had while you were there. That you were very distressed, that you talked a lot about how everything was your fault.'

As my fingers reached for tobacco, I hoped my silence would tell her everything she needed to know and she'd back off.

It did nothing of the sort.

'It's not unusual to feel guilt when someone close to you dies, you know? It makes you think about things you should have done differently, things that perhaps you shouldn't have said. Do you know what I mean?'

I jerked my head slightly as I lit my fag, not wanting to encourage her.

'What is really important is that you don't allow these thoughts to settle. You must not give them the time of day, or allow them to replay over and over in your mind. It will do you no good to do this, Daisy, believe me.'

I exhaled hard, seeing if I could force the waves back with my smoke. Anything not to engage with Ade. She was getting too close.

'All this will take time, but it will take a lot longer if you choose to ignore it. Every day I'm happy to walk with you. Every day I will ask you how you are feeling, if there is anything I can do to help you make sense of whatever is in your head. But I cannot make you talk. This has to be up to you.'

'I don't see the point in talking.' I wasn't angry, just bored and frustrated with the conversation. 'What good will it do me? What's done is done. I can't take it back. Talking won't uncrash the car, will it?'

'Of course, no. As much as we all wish it would. But talking about it may allow you to understand it differently, realize that perhaps it wasn't your fault.'

Emotions built up in my throat and I sucked hard on my rollie, trying to burn them away. I wished things were that simple, but I knew, *really knew*, that they couldn't possibly be.

'Can you tell me one thing, Daisy? For today, just one thing. In fact, it does not even have to be said. Just a nod or a shake is all I need. Just tell me this. Do you really think that you are responsible for your dad's crash?'

'I know I am.'

She looked impressed that she'd dragged more than a gesture out of me. So much so that she shuffled closer, draping her arm around my shoulders.

'Then we have work to do, because I know that it is not true. I have seen that you are many things, Daisy Houghton, but a killer you are not. And I promise we will break this belief down. That one day you will wake up and this thought, this belief you have, will seem so ridiculous, so laughable, that it will just crumble away in your mind. Do you believe me?'

I wanted to believe her, more than anything. But I believed in my own powers more. After all, it wasn't just Dad who'd succumbed to them, was it?

At the same time, I could hear Patrick's and Naomi's voices too, reminding me that only Bex really understood us. Ade was calm and reassuring, but she was so together and at ease with everything that I didn't see how she could possibly help me.

And so I answered honestly.

'I don't believe you, no.'

Her arm didn't move from around me. If anything the hug got tighter and warmer, increasing my guilt.

'OK, fine. I'll just have to work harder, then, won't I?' She smiled again. 'We both will. Come on.'

And before I could flick my cigarette over the edge of the cliff, we were back on our feet, eating up the coastal path, Ade with a new sense of purpose and me with a new sense of dread.

CHAPTER 32

What followed was the longest and most one-sided game imaginable. Imagine Roger Federer playing tennis against a surly, uninterested teenager and you'll get a sense of how pointless it was.

Ade would spend hours, days, lobbing me ways of dealing with my shit and I'd watch them bounce at my feet and ignore them as they fell off the cliff. I didn't even have the decency to whack them straight back at her as hard as I possibly could.

I had to give it to Ade, she had patience and staying power, and a smile that refused to be wiped from her face. But it wasn't enough. I couldn't let her, or anyone else, in. It was just too dangerous.

I think her tenacity exhausted me as well. I was so tired of her prompting and probing, no matter how subtly, that I forgot how much I'd warmed to her early on, how without her I would have been back in hospital, perhaps in the psychiatric ward. I had a massive downer on her that drove me even closer to cigarettes and secret vodka. That was the only game I was interested in playing and I was getting pretty good at it too.

Not as good as the others, granted – even Susie, all five foot of her, could handle more booze than me – but that didn't matter. It gave me the respite that neither Ade nor any of the other carers could.

I got more careless about it as well, less secretive about what I was doing, and was rumbled with booze in my room a couple of times, earning myself a dressing-down at community meeting in front of everyone. Not that the others cared. It was a run-of-the-mill occurrence and if anything it let me earn my stripes, prove that I was one of them, someone they didn't have to share their secrets with, just whatever drink they'd got their hands on that day.

Naomi could still be icy, especially when she had to share Ade with me, and I never understood why, if she thought Ade was so useless, she got lairy in the first place. What I didn't ever do was ask her. I'd learned from day one that it was unwise to question her on anything, not if you liked the way your faced looked.

I'd been at Bellfield for nearly two months before she trusted me enough to include me in one of her little plans, the plan that meant getting drunk somewhere other than on site.

She and Paddy did it every now and then, disappearing for long enough to put the frighteners on the staff, who'd be dispersed in force, sometimes alongside the police, to bring them home.

Why she'd suddenly decided it was my turn eluded me, but I didn't argue. I had the devil in me and was up for whatever she had in mind.

'Eric's taking us all to the pleasure mile tonight,' she'd whispered, 'but he's taking us with one of the students, which should give us chance to slip away for a bit. You up for it?'

The mile was always so packed with tourists in summer

that I knew it was worth a go, and although Eric was on the ball, the students they sent in to observe us were pretty gormless. It certainly shouldn't be difficult to do a bunk from under their gaze.

'Why not? I've got a few quid left.' I flashed her a pocketful of shrapnel.

'That'll keep us in ciggies for the night.' There was a serious look on her face and I felt my chances of joining her dip. 'But to be honest, Daisy, we aren't going to need much dosh tonight. Not if you listen to what I tell you.'

'Even better,' I replied.

It felt good to be asked. All we had to do now was while away the hours until the minibus left and find a way of avoiding Ade in the process.

There was a buzz in the minibus as we rolled through the gates. Paddy had taken control of the music and had Jay-Z pounding through the speakers. I had no idea what he was rapping about, but the bass was low and heavy and shook through my bones, adding to my sense of excitement about the night ahead. Naomi had spent the afternoon reminding me of the need to be cool and to tell no one of what we had planned. If any member of staff got wind of it, they'd cancel the trip and we'd end up grounded for the foreseeable future. That was all I needed to know, and I spent a large chunk of the afternoon in my room, thinking it the safest option.

It was heaving as we approached the mile, which was little wonder given the warmth of the evening, and although the queues slowed the minibus to a crawl, it couldn't dilute our excitement. In fact, it added to the euphoric expression on Naomi's face. She looked so joyous that I was tempted to tell her to wind it in a bit. She was never usually so happy and was in danger of giving the game away.

'This is perfect,' she whispered. 'With it being so busy it'll be easier for us to slip away. Plus it'll buy us some time as well, make it more difficult for them to find us quickly.'

I nodded keenly, liking the sound of it more by the minute.

After another half-hour we managed to get parked, then, after a brief lecture from Eric, we piled out of the van.

'Listen, people,' he'd trilled. 'It's not often we give this much leeway, so do yourselves proud, stick together and keep safe, you hear me?'

There'd been nods and varying levels of agreement, Naomi kicking up slightly at the prospect of having to trawl around with the likes of Susie (you had to give it to her, the girl could act when she needed to).

'But most importantly, have a wicked time,' shouted Eric, and he led us on to the seafront and the gaudy lights of the pleasure mile.

It'd been ages since Dad had brought me here, and longer still since I'd been at night. It could have been the mood I was in, but everywhere I looked I saw the potential to go mad, to lose myself in the mayhem. It wouldn't be dark for another hour, but already the flashing neon and strobes from the fairground rides were taking over, invading and seducing me. I was never usually one for the roller coasters, but tonight I wanted to sample them all, suck every bit of adrenalin from every ride possible, to show Naomi I could match her each step of the way. Because if I could, then I knew there would be no room for all the other shit clogging up my brain.

We bounced along the seafront, pausing to grab money from Eric that we fed to the hungry machines. We rode motorbikes and cars, gunning them through exotic locations. We fired rounds of ammo in the most dangerous hotspots on earth, not caring about the hostages we took or the damage that rained down around us. The pound coins seemed to be endless and, apart from the odd one we pocketed to bolster our tobacco fund, we spent them greedily, as quickly as Eric could find them.

Everyone seemed to be high on the atmosphere. I'd never seen Paddy so entranced. He found one shoot-'em-up in the busiest arcade and didn't move for the next half-hour. In fact, he didn't even blink in that time, and I stood for a while just watching the drama unfold through the reflections in his eyes.

There were no arguments or snide comments between any of us, no simmering battles with the staff, just a collective high at being lost on the seafront.

It was almost a disappointment when Naomi pulled me to one side and said it was time to slide away.

'Can't we wait a bit longer?' I'd pleaded, like a kid being told it was time to go home.

'Nope, has to be now. It'll be dark in twenty minutes and Eric'll keep sharper tabs on us then. So here's the drill. In a sec I'll spin away. Two minutes after that and NO longer –' she fixed me with a death stare – 'you do the same. Just duck away and meet me by the old lighthouse, got it?'

I lifted my gaze above her head, fixing my eyes on our rendezvous point.

'That one?' I asked.

'Of course that one,' she hissed. 'Don't give the bleeding

game away now, you idiot. Just chill out and soon as you see me go start counting, yeah?'

I nodded and watched her amble to the edge of the group, her eyes falling on a slot machine that took her fancy.

Suddenly I felt nervous, anticipation nibbling at my guts. I felt more alive than I had in months, almost drunk without a drop touching my lips. My eyes flicked around the others, to see if anyone had wind of what we were up to, but there wasn't a sniff from any of them. Eric was in the middle of a two-player game with the student, while Susie, Jim and Paddy were sat side by side on motorbikes, eating up the roads of Monte Carlo.

I turned back to Naomi, feeling the need to tell her how much fun I was having, but she was gone, apart from the tight curls of her ponytail surfing through the crowd. I checked my watch, realizing there wasn't a second hand for me to follow, and immediately felt self-conscious, like I had the word 'guilt' tattooed across my forehead.

I couldn't take my eyes off Eric, despite knowing he'd see through me as soon as he glanced my way, and instinctively I knew I couldn't wait any longer. It had probably only been ten seconds instead of two minutes, but it didn't matter, it was now or never, and without hesitation I tucked my hands into my pockets, lowered my gaze and sidestepped into the crowds around me, allowing them to swallow me up. In seconds the top of Eric's head disappeared, and as soon as it did I felt a smile engulf my face. I'd done it, exactly as Naomi had told me to, and now the fun could begin.

CHAPTER 33

The pair of us were beaming as we trotted away, and although I chanced the odd paranoid look over my shoulder, there were too many people camouflaging our tracks for me to have anything to worry about. We were off the lead and were sniffing out the booze as quickly as we could. Or at least Naomi was. She knew exactly where we were heading and wasted no time in getting us there.

I stood and stared at the sign that hung above a set of elaborate metal gates. It read 'IRNWRX', forcing me to close one eye and squint at it hard, hoping blurred vision might help me make sense of what it meant.

'Ah, the Ironworks.' Naomi sighed with a hint of nostalgia. 'The finest and cheapest boozer on the north-east coast.'

I looked at the building again. Everything about it said cheap, but not only because the booze was on special offer; it looked downright nasty. The sort of place you didn't want to be seen in after dark. Yet here we were, ducking through the gates and heading towards the beer garden.

It was rammed in there, the men in identikit checked shirts and jeans, the women in their flimsy, web-thin dresses. There was more substance to their make-up than their clothes, and it made me grin to think of them rushing to the bogs every ten minutes, trowels in hand, ready to smear another layer on.

Spotting a particularly busy spot in the far corner, Naomi grabbed me by the wrist and pulled me behind her.

'Perfect,' she said, grinning. 'Free bar over there by the looks of things.'

She was right too, but not in the way I'd imagined. There was no buff barman clutching outrageous cocktails, or even a beer fridge left lazily unlocked for us to raid. Instead there was a table by the fire exit covered in drinks, with no one claiming them.

Naomi was on them in a flash, grabbing a pint glass that was about half full, decanting the dregs of another on top. It wasn't quite what I had in mind, but it was free, and I didn't want to piss Naomi off yet. The last thing I needed was to be left on my own in a place like this. Following her lead, I mixed a few lagers together, avoiding any that looked like they'd been there too long.

She was sharp and certainly no novice when it came to this sort of thing. Although she looked a good couple of years older than me, with her tight curls falling past her shoulders, it would've been a stretch to convince the bouncers we belonged here. So after grabbing her drink, she led us into the midst of a crowd, nestling behind a couple of particularly big bruisers. You could've hidden a sumo wrestler behind them, so we reckoned we were safe.

It didn't take me long to put the second-hand-ness of the drinks out of my head. Despite the few quid we'd pilfered from Eric, the change in my pocket wouldn't have gone far, and even if we had sweet-talked someone into getting us something from the bar, that just increased the risk of being rumbled.

And when you thought about it in those terms, we were happy with what we'd found.

Naomi certainly was, caning the first pint in super-quick time, then ducking back to the table and returning with a bottle of Sol that still had the slice of lime in the top.

'What a find,' she crowed. 'Nectar of the friggin' gods, this.' And with a salute to the heavens she tipped half of it down her neck in one gulp, before burping loudly.

That simple action summed up the next hour. It was loud, lewd and increasingly out of control, and I loved every second of it. For the first time in weeks I let myself go (with some help from the dregs thrust into my hand), and with the drink taking her over too, Naomi finally let her guard fall. It was the first time since I met her that I didn't feel in danger of a slap.

She was savage in the way she pulled the other drinkers apart, the women in particular. She gave some of the hardest-faced ones a backstory – the number of babies they'd spawned, by as many different dads; she knew how many of them were in care and how many of them had pushed kids out by our age. There were moments when she said it all too loudly, like she wanted one of them to hear, but in our excitable state it just added to the adrenalin rush.

On it went, until the sun had long gone, although I could feel its warmth in my cheeks. We'd lost count of the number of glasses we'd lifted – 'minesweeping' she called it – and Naomi had got braver as time went on, daring to distract lads from their pints before waving me behind them. While she chatted, I dived in, liberating a glass or two before retreating to the far end of the garden. After a couple more minutes of chitchat she would excuse herself and wobble back towards me, her grin as lopsided as her steps. It was seamless, like we'd been doing it years, not hours. Unfortunately, it was such a stellar performance that eventually we ended up with a small audience.

I noticed them first. Naomi was glazing over, little wonder given the amount she'd packed away, but there were four of them huddled together, all shaved heads and bumfluff. They were older than us, but I doubted they were eighteen. Maybe they had fake IDs on them. Whoever they were, they were paying us plenty of attention, going as far as a little round of applause after our final sweep.

Naomi spun to look at them, her beer goggles turning them into something they weren't, and before I could stop her she lifted her glass and beckoned to them.

They were over in a flash, clinking glasses and offering us fags, which Naomi accepted greedily. I waved the offer away and rolled my own, taking time to try and clear my head, assess what they were after.

Naomi was in her element, lapping up their compliments and offers of more drinks, pressing herself close to each of them in turn, so close you couldn't have squeezed a credit card between them. She may not have known any of their names yet, but they were quickly becoming friends.

I tried to let it all wash over me and accept they were here for the same reasons as us, to get slaughtered, but unlike Naomi I kept my guard a little higher and my hips further away from theirs.

Now our two had become six, it was becoming difficult to stay anonymous. A couple of the lads had quick tongues, loud ones too, and once the jokes started we stood out more than we should have. If we'd had any sense we might have called it quits and moved on, but now that the drinks were free and fresh from the bar . . . well, we got greedy. And pissed.

Naomi was the first one to start weaving, and though it was funny to us, it started to rankle with those around us. At first it was just raised eyebrows, which soon escalated into snide comments. But it was once she started dancing – a mixture of pogoing and grinding that involved treading on toes and spilling drinks – that the trouble started. A couple of groups told her to watch herself before backing away to safer ground, but one woman, who seemed to have got dressed in the late 1980s and forgotten to change, wasn't quite as forgiving. To be fair to her, she was now wearing the drink that she'd been holding, thanks to Naomi, and it was enough for her to walk forward and have words.

'Oi, you bloody idiot. Look what you've done!'

Naomi forced her eyes to focus before cutting the woman down with one swift sentence.

'Sorry, love,' she slurred. 'I didn't get you dressed tonight, so don't blame me for what you're wearing.'

Our new friends howled their approval, and Naomi turned to take their applause, turning her back to the woman momentarily, long enough for her to grab Naomi by the hair.

What followed happened in a flash, even with our senses slowed by the drink. As the woman yanked on her curls,

Naomi swung instinctively, her arm arcing wildly. Her fist slammed into the woman's cheek. She folded instantly. As her friends poured round her, trying to restore her to her feet, I grabbed Naomi by the arm and spun her towards the exit. We were getting out of there while we could still walk.

Unfortunately, the lads we'd just befriended chose to come with us.

CHAPTER 34

Naomi might have been wrecked, but she managed a swagger as we headed back along the seafront.

'That's the secret, you see,' she slurred. 'When someone grabs you, you have to go at 'em fast. The last thing they're expecting when they've got you by the hair is for you to swing back.'

The lads all nodded, hanging on her every drunken word, but it was my attention she wanted.

'You'll remember that, won't you, Daisy?'

She grabbed on to my arm and I smiled weakly.

'I said you'll remember that, won't you? Cos you know what the problem with you is, don't you?'

I wondered where she was going to start, so said nothing.

'Too bleedin' soft. I could see that from the second you arrived. If you want to survive you have to toughen up. You feel me?'

There was a weird pleading in her eyes, no doubt the effect of the minesweeping, and it wasn't worth doing anything except agreeing.

'You two flatmates, then?' one of the lads asked.

I think his name was Ryan. He hadn't paid me much

attention, had spent most of the past half-hour making Naomi laugh by whispering in her ear. Either that or he'd had his tongue in it.

I had no idea how to answer his question but Naomi happily played along.

'Bezzy mates, me and Daisy,' she yelled. 'Known each other ages. Practically sisters, aren't we?'

'Couldn't be closer,' I said, smiling. Funny how alcohol blurred everything.

'Is your flat near here, then?' one of the others asked. 'I reckon you must owe us a drink after the ones we shouted you back there.'

I saw Naomi's eyes spin as she fought for an answer.

'We live in town,' I butted in. 'So unless you fancy a twenty-quid cab, then I reckon we'll have to call it a night.'

'No need for that,' said a grinning Ryan, attaching himself to Naomi's hip. 'My gaff's only a couple of minutes away and I reckon I've still got some sauce in the fridge if you're up for it.'

I was ready to step in and make our excuses, but Naomi got in first, her stride picking up at the talk of more drinks.

'Sorted. We're up for owt, aren't we, Dais?'

'That's what we like to hear,' said Ryan, the excitement bubbling in his voice.

I reckon if they'd been any more sober they'd have carried us. Anything to get us there before we came to our senses.

It was clear to me what they were after, and they weren't all disgusting-looking, just drunk and leery. Whatever their intentions, they weren't lying about living nearby, as within minutes we were being led up the stairs of a crumbly old terraced house.

After wrestling with a second lock, we were inside Ryan's flat, which was a typical boy's pad. He obviously wasn't short of a bob or two, or his parents had forked out to set him up. There were gadgets everywhere: laptops, flat-screen telly, Blu-ray player, and the largest DVD collection I'd ever seen. Well, the second largest after Dad's. I pushed the thought of him away before it sobered me up.

I was drawn to the films while the others piled into the kitchen, returning with bottles of beer and crisps. While the lads looked ecstatic, Naomi had a piercing expression on her face, handing me a beer with one hand and gripping my wrist a little too hard with the other.

'Stop looking like such a goon, will you?' she spat.

'What do you mean?'

'Look at this place. There's amazing shit everywhere and a fridge rammed full of beer. And you head to the films. You're not in Blockbuster, you idiot.'

'Well, what do you want me to do?'

'Just look cool, will you? Otherwise they'll kick us out.'

I doubted that somehow. I didn't get the sense that they often persuaded girls past the front door.

They collapsed on to the sofas and Ryan fiddled with a remote control, looking smug when his iPod dock roared into life. Reluctantly, I pulled myself from the films and fell on to a beanbag, wondering how long it would take for Naomi to get bored.

A beer and a half later we were still slumped in the same

place, although I seemed to have re-found my beer goggles and was having a decent time.

All right, they weren't exactly boy band material, but they weren't arseholes or anything, and Ryan certainly knew how to stock a fridge with booze, as it didn't stop coming, along with the laughs.

Naomi sat at the centre of it all, and even though she was struggling to speak, the lads still hung on every word she managed. But there was no doubt who was in pole position there. Maybe it was because we were in his flat, but it soon became evident that Naomi was off limits to anyone but Ryan. So much so that two of the others started paying me a bit of attention, offering me fags or another beer. Everything a pissed girl could want.

I should've been wiser to it, I know, but my head was mashed and I barely seemed able to take a breath without another beer landing in front of me.

It got worse when one of the empties was plonked on the table and spin the bottle began. Every time it teetered to a stop, it seemed to be pointing at me, leaving me no option but to drink, the lads cheering as the lager frothed up my nose and eventually down my throat.

I've no idea how many bottles I drained in the process; all I knew was that I was having fun. The kind of fun that you can't say no to, and it was such a relief to be out of control and enjoying it, rather than feeling the need to cut myself, that I didn't stop, even when I found myself stumbling down the hall in search of the toilet or anything I could throw up in.

*

The porcelain was cold on my cheek. My leg was thrown over the side of the bath and when I tried to stand it buckled beneath me. It had clearly been sleeping as deeply as I had.

I focused on my watch. It was nearly two in the morning, so I must have been out for at least . . . I couldn't work it out, and didn't want to either. I just wanted my bed, even if it was bolted to the floor.

Stamping the blood back into my limbs, I dragged myself out of the bathroom and into the small kitchen. I turned on the cold water, twisted my head and slurped straight from the tap, hoping it would revive me, sober me up, do something that took away the traces of death in my skull. Oh my God. If I felt this bad now, how was I going to feel in the morning? Or face Eric and the others to explain why we'd done a runner?

The need to be at Bellfield overwhelmed me and I hoped desperately that Naomi felt the same. And if I couldn't persuade her? Well, I just hoped I had enough change in my pocket for a taxi, or at worst a night bus.

Swallowing a fresh wave of bile, I pushed my head round the door into the lounge. Although the lights were low, I could see Naomi slouched on the settee, with Ryan leaning over her.

I groaned. If she copped off with him there would be no chance of getting her out. I thought about heading straight for the door, but then I looked again and realized that she wasn't kissing him. She was asleep and Ryan was doing everything he could to wake her up.

He tried a number of tactics. Kissing her, licking her ear

(I felt the bile rise again), pinching her arm gently, then harder and harder, until he was practically giving her a Chinese burn. Each time she remained unresponsive I could see his temper flare a little more, until he turned to his mates and told two of them to grab an arm each.

'Unbelievable,' he snapped. 'She's absolutely sparko.'

'What do you want us to do? Chuck her out?'

Ryan looked horrified. 'You're joking, aren't you? After the amount of legwork I've put in? Get her down the corridor and into my room.'

Two of them laughed and made encouraging noises, while the other looked edgy: a door had been opened that he didn't like. I knew the feeling.

I toyed with the idea of bursting in, and turned back to the kitchen, looking for something hefty or sharp I could wield. But there was nothing – no rolling pins or sharp knives, just a pizza slicer blunted through overuse. There was no way I could do anything to help her. Even if one of them had got cold feet, it would still be me against three of them. I had no chance, even if I ran in there and puked all over them.

Instead I stood, chewing the inside of my lip as they hoisted her to her feet. The decent one tried to butt in again, telling them he didn't like it, but Ryan fronted up to him, eyes flaring, lighting up the room.

'Look, you prick. If you don't like it, just leave, will you?'

'But look at her, Ry. She's had enough. She's hammered.'

'And?' he spat. 'She was half-cut when she chose to come here and she's hardly daft, is she? You don't go back to a lad's house unless you're up for it, do you?'

'But she's asleep, mate.'

Ryan let out a short laugh and patted the lad's cheeks with both hands. 'Don't worry, old son. She won't be for long. Believe me.' He turned to the other two. 'Come on, fellas. You know where to go.' And he followed them as they lumped Naomi through another door that presumably led to his room.

I freaked out. I didn't know what to do. I didn't want to leave, knowing that if I did she was in big trouble, but at the same time what could I do?

I swore repeatedly in my head until it came to me: my phone. I yanked it out of my pocket, fumbled with the keylock and hammered 999.

'Come on, come on,' I mouthed, waiting for a connection.

I needed a pee, needed to sleep, needed to hear someone was on the way. But none of these things were possible. I had no signal, not even enough to get an emergency call away.

I peered back into the lounge, hoping to spot a landline, but saw only the scared lad on the sofa, his head in his hands. Even if he had morals, was he really going to let me phone the police when he was sat there letting Ryan do God knows what to Naomi? I couldn't take the risk.

I had to get past him to the door. If I could get down the stairs and out, then I could phone the cops, flag down a car, do anything to keep Naomi safe.

I slipped off my shoes. They might not have been heels or anything, but they could have made a noise that I just couldn't risk. I picked my way across the wooden floorboards, pausing in terror each time he moved or threatened to stand. He obviously didn't know what to do for the best and so, fortunately for me, stayed where he was, allowing me to creep through the door and on to the stairs.

I increased my pace, not caring if I made more noise now. I was only a dozen steps from the outside world. I tripped on the last few stairs, my elbows slamming against the front door, making a noise loud enough to wake the dead. I hoped it was loud enough to raise Naomi. Hoped it gave her the chance to fight Ryan off. If anyone could do it, it was her. She normally had enough anger to fight off a dozen lads and if the booze hadn't washed it all away, then she still had a chance.

I fumbled with the latch, threw the door open and hared up the path, not bothering to shut it behind me. It would save the police a job when they arrived.

Hidden behind a car at the end of the street I paused for breath and stared again at my phone.

'SHIT.' Still no signal.

I scanned the street frantically, finally spotting a phone box on the main road.

I chanced a glance back towards the house, sucked in a final deep breath and ran as fast as I could towards the phone box.

I had to make the call and I had to make it quick.

CHAPTER 35

As much as I wanted to make sure the police turned up, the coward in me made me do the swiftest runner imaginable.

The call had only taken a minute, long enough to tell them about a teenage girl in trouble with four lads. I didn't have to mention the word rape for them to understand what I saying, that they had to put their foot down and arrive sharpish. It was only when they asked for my name that I knew it was time to go, and as soon as I slammed the receiver down, the guilt started to pick away at my brain.

Why hadn't I told them my name? What did I have to be ashamed of?

Apart from leaving a drunken friend at the mercy of a group of tanked-up lads.

From there my mind went mad, twisting the whole night until everything that had gone on was my fault. If I'd said no to Naomi in the first place we'd already be home and safe. If I'd begged her to leave the seafront straight after the pub, then I wouldn't be trudging back on my own, wishing I'd stuck around and searched harder for something to take Ryan on with. How could I have just left her like that?

My senses played tricks on me, hearing sirens when I was

on the quietest roads. Even when I finally flagged down a night bus I was still seeing the lights of police cars glinting off the windows.

When I walked through the gates of Bellfield I actually saw a squad car, but this one had no flashing lights; it sat empty in the car park. The only life I could see was from the balcony as always, a mixture of lamplight, cigarette smoke and weary, anxious faces.

It was Ade who broke away from the rest, climbing over the balcony and rushing to me in large strides. It was the fastest I'd ever seen her move since that first night. She folded me into her, threatening to push my stomach over the edge again, her voice a mixture of anger and relief.

'Where on earth have you been?' she cried.

'With Naomi.'

'We guessed that. But the police called to say they picked Naomi up half an hour ago. They didn't know anything about another girl. We thought something awful had happened.'

I didn't care about me, only that I hadn't struck again.

'Where is she? Is she here?'

'She's at the hospital with Bex, getting checked over.'

'But she's OK, isn't she?'

'You know Naomi, she is indestructible. But if the police hadn't arrived when they did it could've been very different.'

I said nothing.

'We were lucky someone called them. If they hadn't . . . well, I do not want to think about it.' She held me by both shoulders. 'You don't know who made that call, do you?'

I shrugged her away and shook my head firmly. I wanted

no praise for any of this. I should never have left her in the first place.

Plodding slowly to the balcony, I looked for a friendly face, but I could see only Eric – fear, anger and exhaustion scratched deep into his features.

I wanted to apologize, but couldn't say the words with enough feeling to put right what I'd done. Instead I lowered my head and looked at Patrick, who sucked hard on his cigarette and turned away. Even Jimmy and Susie found it hard to look my way, although Susie couldn't resist squeezing my arm briefly. Both of them were saying the same thing.

How could you leave her like you did? We stick together. Always.

They were only thinking what I already knew. I'd broken the rules.

Without a word, I pushed through the doors and climbed the stairs to my room. Every step was a mountain.

Sleep eluded me despite my best efforts. The onset of a raging hangover didn't help and neither did the fear slowly casting its cloak over me. In my desperation I found the remnants of a bottle of spirits hidden at the back of my wardrobe, gunning it as fast as I could, hoping it would just push unconsciousness that bit nearer.

It didn't work, and instead I paced the floor, listening to doors slam around the house. With every bang I listened for Naomi, knowing that I'd hear her, her trademark wail taking issue with someone or something, regardless of how much trouble she was in. She didn't return, but the panic attacks did, ripping through me with a force that I hadn't felt while protected by the medication. Maybe the alcohol had lessened its effect, or perhaps I was just getting what I deserved. Either way it was impossible to fend off, and by the time the first rays of sun forced their way through the curtains, I was sprawled on my bed, my duvet clutched to my arm, the nail scissors I'd taped to the underside of my pants drawer lying used beside me.

I passed out eventually, once my pulse had calmed, and must have slept deeply, because I didn't hear anyone coming through my door. In fact, I didn't know about anything until Naomi's hands were round my neck.

God knows what she must have thought when she found me bloodied, but it didn't put her off straddling me, her knees pinning my shoulders to the mattress.

'You bitch!' she yelled. 'You grassed me up, didn't you?'

I would have shaken my head had she not been throttling me, so had to settle for a muffled, 'To who?'

'You know who! The rozzers, that's who.'

I tried to deny it, not knowing if coming clean would serve me any better than lying.

'Well, who else did, eh? You're a lying sack of shit. I know it was you. It had to be.'

Her eyes were glinting red, the devil forcing its way through her hands, which were squeezing me harder and tighter.

'Now you need to listen to me, cos I won't say this again. Don't you ever, EVER, disrespect me again. I can look after myself. I've been doing it all my life so I don't need you wading in trying to be my mother. You hear me?'

I nodded quickly, forcing my neck to move against her

grip, desperate for her to let go, which she did, before towering over me.

She looked at my arm, then gazed down at her clothes, scowling at the sight of my blood smeared on them.

'Now look what you've done, you skanky cow. If you're going to cut yourself have the decency to clean it up, will you?'

I pulled the duvet back over me, but the damage was done. In that instant she knew what I was about and it didn't matter that she cut herself too. This was ammo. It was all she needed to make life difficult for me.

'That's the last time I take you drinking,' she said, a sneer on her face. 'I'll tell you what you are. I've seen your type before. You're a Jonah. Everything you touch turns to shit. So keep away from me and keep your mouth shut. I don't need your bad luck anywhere near me. You got it?'

Tears stung as I nodded. She had it spot on. I needed to get out of here, quickly, before I brought everyone and everything crashing down with me.

CHAPTER 36

There was something mesmerizing about the waves, the way they broke against the rocks. Nothing put them off or distracted them, each of them approached the shore with the same intention and the same result as the one before.

I looked on, wishing that everything could be the same for me, that I could attack everything with the same simplicity, the same belief that I was going to succeed rather than wreck everything around me.

I focused on nothing but the sea, hoping I'd discover the answer there. I wasn't going to find it through the others, not through Naomi or Patrick, Ade or even Bex. I had to try and figure it out myself, but I had no idea where to even start.

The tide had started to ebb when I heard someone approaching from behind and I leapt to my feet, fearful of another throttling. My shoulders sagged with relief to see it was only Ade, the usual hopeful grin plastered on her face.

I hoped there wasn't a lecture on the way. I didn't know how much of it I'd be able to take without running away or flinging myself off the edge.

I was surprised, then, when she stopped a few metres

short of me, yanked the rucksack off her back and eased herself on to the grass.

'Are you thirsty?' she asked, brandishing a bottle of water.

I nodded, dehydrated enough not to throw it back in her face.

'I see Naomi came to visit you this morning.' It was a statement, not a question, and I hadn't a clue how she knew. So I asked her.

'It's not a question of mind-reading. I've been with her long enough to know that if she has a problem with you she will always try and sort it out quickly.' She paused as I rubbed at my neck. 'Plus I can see her fingermarks on your throat. I hope she did not hurt you.'

I blushed, not realizing she'd left me a reminder at how much I'd let her down.

'I'm all right. She only gave me what I deserved.'

Ade sighed deeply. 'Ah, there you go again.'

'Eh?' I was confused. 'I don't get you.'

'Always so quick to blame yourself.' Her eyes bored a hole in me. 'So tell me, what did you do that was so wrong?'

'Don't matter now, does it? Too late to take it back.'

'Yes, that's true. But sometimes saying it out loud lets you see it in a different way.'

She was starting to get on my wick. I knew what she was doing. I'd heard it before and I wasn't biting.

'It doesn't matter, Daisy. On this occasion, you don't even need to tell me. Because I know what you did. We all do. That is why the others were off with you last night. That's why, to the rest of us, you are something of a hero.'

I couldn't believe she was calling me that. It summed up

216

everything that was wrong with her. Ever since we met she'd got it wrong. She'd called me a lucky charm, told me I was talented like my mum, and now I was a hero? It was too much.

'What are you talking about? How can grassing Naomi up make me a hero? Because of me, she's in trouble with the police, Eric's not speaking to either of us and she nearly strangled me to death!'

Ade was on her feet as quickly as me.

'Because of you, my friend, Naomi was able to come home last night. Because of you, the police found her partially clothed. Because of you, the boy she was with was not able to have sex with her while she slept.' She cocked her head on one side. 'See what I mean about saying things out loud? Tell me now that you shouldn't have made that call. I dare you.'

I wanted to scream at her. I hated the logic she was trying to spew when she had no idea about me.

'If I hadn't agreed to go back with her to that flat, then there wouldn't have been any need to call the police in the first place, would there?'

This seemed to amuse her even more, her shoulders jiggling as she spoke. 'Oh, Daisy. You have not got to grips with Naomi at all, have you? If you had refused to join her, she would have gone anyway. She would have drunk more quickly, passed out earlier and been raped by the time you got home. I'm not saying that you didn't make a mistake. It wasn't the best idea to leave the others like you did, or to drink your bodyweight in left-over lager . . .'

I winced, knowing now she'd had the low-down from Naomi.

'. . . but you have not damaged anyone. Far from it. Because of you, Naomi did not get hurt.'

My head throbbed with anger. I could feel it surging through my body, through every muscle, into each of my knuckles. In that moment I really did want to let rip at her.

'What is it with you?' I yelled. 'Are you some kind of mystic or something? All I ever hear from you is what I'm not capable of, when you know nothing about me.'

It felt good to get it out, so I let myself go.

'All right, so you've read my files and you've seen the state of my arms. You've talked to your poncey shrink mates and between you you've got me pigeon-holed. Worked out what label I've got round my neck. Well, I'll tell you. Whatever label you wrote out, it's wrong. You haven't got a clue what I've done or what I'm capable of. But if you keep pushing me, I'll tell you. I'll tell you it all, then you'll get hurt too! At least then I'll have you off my back.'

I stomped past her, knocking her shoulder with mine before slumping on to a rock, my hands shaking as I knocked a cigarette together.

'Wow,' she said, following me. 'I had no idea that you were so powerful.'

What was she talking about? See? She had it wrong again. I wasn't powerful at all. Everything I did hurt someone, but she didn't get it and continued to goad me.

'Do you honestly think that your words have the power to hurt me?' It was alien for her to talk to me without a smile on her face. 'This is what you are saying, isn't it? That if you tell me what happened before the crash, then the same thing that happened to your dad will happen to me?'

I nodded, smoke billowing out of my mouth.

'Well, let me tell you something. There is nothing you can say that will hurt me. There is nothing you can say that will surprise, shock, disgust me or make me walk away from you. Because whatever you think you have done, I have done worse.'

I was the one who wanted to laugh now. Was she for real? She ambled around every day, smiling and joking and jollying us all along. She was a bloody cheerleader. She couldn't hurt anyone if she tried. So I told her that, in those exact words.

'A cheerleader?' She looked at me with wide eyes. 'Are you kidding me?'

'No, I'm not. Look, I'm grateful that you found me that first night, and that you kept me out of hospital, but you don't know how I feel. How could you? You're nothing like me.'

'Is that right? So tell me, if I was more like you, if I was as powerful as you, would you tell me what was going on in your head?'

This was a non-conversation. We were so different, on such different levels, that there was no harm in saying yes.

So I did. Which pleased her immensely.

'Then this is a breakthrough.' She grinned and unbuttoned the cuff of her sleeve. And in that instant everything changed.

CHAPTER 37

Hangovers had the potential to stop me thinking clearly. I'd learned that pretty quickly after arriving at Bellfield. It fact, they stopped me thinking at all. That was part of the reason I drank so much.

But as I sat on the edge of the cliff I really regretted getting tanked the night before, because I couldn't believe what I was looking at.

It was like I'd been sucked into a twilight zone movie or something, as there was Ade sat beside me, her arm naked to the sun, her dark brown skin littered with line upon line: the same lines that decorated my own.

I was so shocked that part of me wanted to laugh. It was absurd.

But I didn't. Instead I reached out slowly and rested my hand on her forearm, surprised when she didn't flinch or pull away.

There was the same smile, the same warmth, but a very different Ade now, which brought problems of its own, as immediately I felt the guilt in me swell, remembering how I'd spoken to her, how I'd insisted she couldn't have a clue about what I was feeling.

I wanted to say sorry but knew it wouldn't come anywhere close to covering it. I hoped my hand on her arm might say more.

'I haven't shown you this to make you feel ashamed,' she said brightly, 'so you can get rid of that thought right now, do you hear me?'

My face flushed at the accuracy of her words.

'I didn't mean to make you show me,' I stuttered. 'You must think I'm a right cow.'

'No, not a cow. A mule maybe, or something else that's just as stubborn, but not a cow.'

I lifted my hand from her forearm, feeling the warmth in my fingers, and looked again at her scars. There was a horrible symmetry to them, a preciseness to the intervals at which they fell, to the length of each line. They were old too, a lighter brown and raised from the rest of her skin, but obviously wounds that had long since healed.

'Don't think too much about what to say,' she sighed. 'I haven't shown you to shock or make you feel guilty. To be honest, I didn't know what else to do.'

'Am I the only one who knows, then?'

I didn't like the idea of another secret, of the mischief I could do as a result, but she shook the comment off with a wave of her hand.

'No, there are others back there who know. Floss and Eric, all of the staff in fact, some old residents too.'

'But Naomi? Or Paddy?'

'No, I don't think they've noticed.' She looked like she had to give it some thought. 'None of them have infuriated me like you. Hard to believe, I know.'

She bumped me with her shoulder, trying to knock some of the tension out of the situation.

I had questions bubbling away in my head, but couldn't work out if I'd asked too much of her already, or whether in fact she expected something back from me. You know, I'll show you mine if you show me yours . . .

It was a relief when she carried on talking.

'I have watched you these last two months, all of us have, and it has been torture. We've seen you carry this load around, some days so heavy that it is making you shorter before our eyes. All of us have seen it and we've all looked for the tap that we can turn to let it out. But at the same time we've seen that you weren't ready, for whatever reason.'

She looked serious for a second before relaxing again, the trademark smile sliding back into position.

'Me showing you this doesn't change anything either. There's no contract now, no expectation for you to tell me everything or even anything. I just had to make you see that you aren't alone in feeling powerful. That other people feel guilt too.'

'Who do you think you hurt, then?' I couldn't help asking the question. Hoped she didn't mind answering it.

'Right now?' she asked.

I nodded.

'Nobody.' Her answer was emphatic. 'Ask me again tonight, or tomorrow morning, I may have a very different answer for you.'

I didn't understand and my frown told her so.

'It depends how logical I am feeling, and that changes

with how tired I am or whether I got drunk the night before. All these things affect just how powerful I am.'

My head ached with the riddles. All I wanted was a straight answer, but they didn't seem to apply to me any more.

'So when you're tired or hungover, who did you hurt?'

'It's always the same person, always my brother.'

'Where is he, then? Does he live around here?'

'Oh no. He isn't anywhere. He died in Nigeria twenty-two years ago.'

I exhaled deeply, felt my lungs scratching, demanding a cigarette.

'Is that why you moved here, because of what happened to him?'

'I was already here. I'd been here five years when he died.'

'But I thought you said you'd hurt him.'

'I thought I'd killed him.'

'But how could you when you were on the other side of the world?'

Her smile got wider despite the gravity of what she was saying. 'I never said it made sense.' She bumped my shoulder again. 'You of all people should understand that, shouldn't you?'

I nodded, adjusting my position to face her, hoping she'd take it as a sign to go on. 'I lived in Nigeria until I was fifteen years old, with my parents and brother. My parents both had jobs, good jobs in factories. OK, they weren't doctors or teachers, but my father was responsible for other men who worked there. We were a lot luckier than others, you know?'

I didn't know, didn't know the first thing about Nigeria,

couldn't have pointed it out on a map, but that didn't matter. I just wanted her to keep talking.

'I didn't realize how lucky we were, so instead of being grateful I made life impossible for everyone.'

'Really?' I couldn't imagine Ade making things difficult for anyone.

'I took advantage of our situation. Instead of going to school, I took every opportunity to skip off. Couldn't understand what they could teach me that I couldn't learn from my friends at the market. I met new people there, most of them older than me, and they filled me up with stories, about how school did them no favours, how they earned a good enough living without it. I listened to them, was seduced by what they told me, and started working for them, delivering things to other people.'

'You mean dodgy stuff?' It all sounded so unlikely. 'Like what?'

'There were many things. Alcohol. Drugs. Money itself. There were other things too, things that I'm too ashamed to say out loud. I didn't realize at the time what I was involved with. I was naive. Stupid.'

My mind boggled at the potential.

'They convinced me to start hiding packages too. Said that they would pay me well if I could stash them overnight. So I did. Until my father found one of them in my room.'

'What was in it?'

For the first time in her story her eyes left me, falling to her arm, which she rubbed gently with her hand.

'It was a gun. A pistol. I didn't realize, because it was

wrapped up in rags so I couldn't feel the shape of it. But I should have realized. As soon as I saw it, I knew these people, my friends, had played me well.'

CHAPTER 38

I couldn't believe it, but there was no doubt it was true. The pain in her eyes told me that.

'My parents flipped out, as you'd expect. There'd been no warning that I was involved with anything like this, despite being a little rebellious.'

'So what did they do?'

'They panicked. Thought the only solution to my behaviour was to send me away.'

'So you all moved?'

'No, that was never an option. If we moved to a new town it would mean my parents giving up their jobs, their home. They weren't educated people, so there was no guarantee they would find jobs that paid the same. They had to stay where they were. It was me that had to move.'

'And that's when you came to England?'

She nodded, her gaze and thoughts elsewhere.

'At the expense of my brother.'

'Why? Had he been in trouble as well?'

'Oh no. Johnny was a saint compared to me. And he was sharp. Had a brain in his head that he wanted to use. We would joke about where it came from, that they must have dropped him as a child to knock such sense into him. He was my parents' great hope, the one who would make something of himself.'

'So why were they planning to send him here?'

'For school. University eventually. Whatever he needed to give him his education. My father had a relative here, a cousin who had not been blessed with children. His wife was so depressed about it that he agreed to give Johnny a home, in the hope that she would treat him as her own. But when I got into trouble, they persuaded them, somehow, to take me instead.'

'Was your brother annoyed?'

'He had no anger in him. It wasn't his way. And he was only ten years old. He didn't want to leave my parents. Why would he?'

'But you did?'

'It didn't matter what I wanted. I'd lost any choice when I brought that package into their house. As soon as they'd persuaded my father's cousin, I was off, before I could bring more shame on them.'

It was hard for her to tell me all this. There were no tears, but the light that usually shone from her eyes seemed to dim as she told me about life in a new country. How the cousin who took her in tried hard to make her feel welcome, but it quickly became clear that his wife didn't feel the same. Taking on a ten-year-old genius was one thing, but a surly fifteen-year-old?

They didn't know the extent of the trouble Ade had found herself in back home, but at the same time they saw her as damaged goods, as a child they didn't want to claim as their own.

'I did not blame them,' Ade said, painting something resembling a smile back on her face. 'Now or then. They took me in with the best intentions, but I didn't make it easy for them. I refused to fit in, dodged school in the same way that I did at home, threw any attempts that they made back in their faces.'

'Did you feel like going back home, then?'

'With what? My parents had spent their savings sending me over here. I could not ask them to pay for me to return when I was behaving like I was. I had to at least pretend I was doing well, if only to make it easier for my brother.'

'Why, what had happened to him?'

'What my parents feared would happen. He became aware of what was going on around him, saw the poverty people were living in, the way so many struggled to feed or clothe themselves. It pricked something in him, troubled him so much that he started to ignore his studies, became more interested in protesting instead. He joined a group of people who wanted to challenge what was going on, people who wanted to turn things on their head. He was only fifteen, but he was sharp, intelligent. When he spoke they didn't see a child. When he spoke they listened.'

'There's nothing wrong with that, though, is there? I mean, people are allowed opinions, aren't they?'

'Of course, but not when they don't keep them to themselves. This was Nigeria twenty years ago. Put your head above the parapet and you put yourself in the firing line.'

I felt uncomfortable, fearing where this was going, hoping that I was wrong.

'He was only fifteen years old when he found himself in the middle of a march, and for years I felt, *knew*, that if it wasn't for me he wouldn't have been there. He would have been tucked away in a comprehensive school in England edging nearer to becoming a doctor or lawyer. While he was being battered with truncheons by the police, I was sat on a bench drinking cheap alcohol with people who knew nothing about me and cared even less.'

She stood up, shaking the blood back into her legs.

'Shall we walk?' she asked. 'I make more sense when I'm on the move.'

I nodded, lifting her rucksack off the ground, throwing it on to my back.

'Things fell apart when I heard the news. I don't know what hurt more, hearing it second-hand through my new mother or the fact that I couldn't go home for the funeral. My parents didn't say I wasn't welcome, but they made no attempt to arrange my return, and in my head I took that as the sign that I was on my own.'

'That must have hurt, to not be with them.'

'It did, but in my head it was a problem of my own making. If I had not been so headstrong and foolish, then none of it would have happened. Or at the very worst it would have been me on the end of the truncheons, not Johnny. The guilt got inside me, took up my every moment until I was convinced that I should be punished more than he had been. I have no idea why you self-harm, Daisy, but for me it was punishment, a weekly reminder of the shame

I'd brought on our family, and what I had caused them to lose. It almost pleased me that, when the pain disappeared, I still had the scars as a reminder.'

It was strange to hear her reasons, so different from my own and so controlled in how she chose to do it. I thought about her scars and the preciseness of them, which, after hearing her story, somehow made sense. It was punishment, not panic that made her do it, and suddenly I was scared, terrified that whatever worked to stop her cutting wouldn't apply to me, that I'd be doing it as long as the panic attacks kept coming.

We walked for a while, enough time for me to roll a cigarette and focus my thumping heart.

'Is it a long time since you cut yourself?'

It seemed like a safe question to ask. She was so together now, after all.

'Fifteen years,' she answered, glowing with pride.

'And you're never close to doing it again?'

'Sometimes, of course. It took me a long time to get here, a lot of talking to realize that I wasn't holding the truncheon that broke my brother's skull. I will not go back now. I've reclaimed what happened, turned how I felt around, and now I look at it differently from how I did. Instead of wasting my life mourning him, losing him drives me now. It makes me get up every day.'

I felt deflated at the prospect of a long process ahead of me, wanted almost to pick holes in her recovery.

'But you'll always have the scars, won't you? Don't they just remind you every day?'

'For a long time they did, but not any more. I'm reclaiming them as well, one by one.'

I looked at her, confused, which made her break stride and roll her sleeve up to the very top of her arm.

'Every year, on the date of my brother's death, I congratulate myself for not hurting myself any more, or for being responsible for his death. Every year, on 6 May, I reclaim one more line, to remind myself that I am still here.' She giggled, a reaction completely at odds with the conversation. 'My friends tell me I'm mad, that I've just found a different way to hurt myself. But I think they're wrong. This isn't killing me now. It's reminding me that I've beaten it, that I'm still alive.'

With that she let her hand slide down to her waist, exposing the full length of her arm.

The scars continued above the elbow with the same precision and regularity, until they were halfway to her shoulder. There everything changed.

Instead of the dull puckered skin that made up each scar, there were bursts of blue ink, a series of tattooed lines, each one interrupted only once, where it spiked upwards before falling back into a perfect flat-line. The effect was mesmerizing, repeated again and again all the way to the very top scar. It looked like a gigantic heartbeat and I stood staring, as if watching a monitoring machine in an intensive care ward.

My jaw fell open. There was nothing to say. Nothing that could do it justice. So I did nothing, except wipe the stray tear that fell down my face.

CHAPTER 39

If this were Hollywood, there'd have been stirring music at this point, or a montage scene of me and Ade talking intently in different locations, fighting off all the crap in my head.

I've seen the films, know the scripts by heart.

It wasn't like that, of course. Hearing and seeing her story didn't make my guilt go away, but it did shift something. It gave me a sense of perspective, of hope maybe, although I was none the wiser as to how her story could actually help. I fought hard to hold on to the positives: that we had this in common, that we would find a way to connect. I'd doubted her for long enough and she'd trusted in me. That had to be worth something, especially with everything else back at Bellfield taking a nosedive.

The repercussions from our night out rumbled on. Not with Eric, who'd got over it after an apology, but with Naomi and Patrick. The speed at which they forgave each other after their fights didn't extend to me, and aside from an occasional dig in the ribs or choice insult, it was like I was invisible.

That would have been fine had we not been living under the same roof, and besides, I'd relied on them for buying my tobacco and smuggling in the spirits.

It was almost a relief when September rolled around and classes began. At least it gave the days some focus, allowed six hours to pass without craving the company of cheap vodka.

It was a strange experience going to school without leaving the gates, a bit like being home-schooled, I supposed. Our teacher was hardly troubled in terms of pupil numbers, as it was basically two of us, me and Susie, plus Jimmy, who pitched up every now and again, taking a guitar secretively next door before huddling over it, his fingers lumbering over the fret board. As with his phone calls, he seemed to be in a world of his own making. We couldn't hear what he was playing, he always plugged a pair of headphones into the amp, but I couldn't imagine it was tuneful. When he was in there, doing his thing, I'd keep an eye out for the others, in the hope that I could save him from more grief.

Susie had quite a thing for him and spent chunks of every day telling me just how wonderful he was.

'Have you ever met anyone like him?' she cooed on one occasion.

That was an easy one to answer. 'Nope.' At least I didn't have to lie.

'It kills me when I see the others rip it out of him. He's such an easy target.'

'He doesn't really help himself, though, does he? All that business with the mobile phone. People kind of notice stuff like that.'

'He's not hurting anyone with it. It's just his way of coping. I just wish they knew how talented he was.'

I was confused. 'You think all the music stuff's true, then? All the gigs and groupies, that's for real?'

'Absolutely. Don't you?'

I tried to think of a way of saying it tactfully, of not puncturing her dreams. 'Er, it's hard to say. I've never heard him sing or play anything. You?'

She looked a bit sheepish. 'Not really. I thought I heard him once through the ceiling, got Naomi in to listen to it and everything. But she just pissed herself laughing and punched me. Told me it was the radio, that it was Coldplay or someone.'

'And was it?'

'Was it what?'

'Coldplay?' Boy, this was hard work.

She shrugged. 'Dunno. I'm no expert. I wanted it to be Jimmy. That's enough for me. I don't know why it's not enough for them either.'

Conversations like this were draining to say the least, despite how much I liked her, and it was almost a relief to try and concentrate on some schoolwork.

Time outside of lessons belonged to Ade. Ever since our talk on the cliffs, I'd feared there would be some kind of expectation to spill my own story, and the thought consumed me, haunting my every moment with her.

We walked each day after school, along the rocks that were becoming familiar, our place in a way. I'd never seen her heading there with Naomi and I was scared that she was spending so much time with me at her expense. The last thing I needed was another reason for Naomi to go ballistic.

It didn't concern Ade, who brushed my fears away quickly.

'At some point you are going to have to start putting yourself first and stop worrying about the others, Naomi especially.'

I shot her a look. I doubted she'd been pinned to the bed by Naomi lately.

'I know that she is unpredictable, but that does not mean you should feel like a victim around her. Living in fear is hardly going to help you get better, is it?'

'And walking a marathon every day is?' It was petulant, and I cringed as soon as the words formed, but I couldn't stop them coming out.

'Not in isolation, no. But we are going to bring a weapon walking with us every day, something that will gradually wear down these thoughts of yours.'

'Oh aye, and what weapon's that, then?'

'Logic.'

I stopped walking and stared at her. Was she having a laugh?

'I'll bring the logic if you bring some trust.' There was a tinge of impatience to her voice. 'If you can't manage that, Daisy, then this time will be wasted. I don't mind spending my time with you – in fact, I can't think of a better way to pass my shifts, because I can see how confused you are, and I know, with some trust, that we can beat whatever is ruling you at the moment. But without trust?' She paused, her brow furrowed. 'Then you can forget it. You might as well go back to the house and wait for Naomi to slap you again. Is that what you want?'

I shook my head slowly. Of course I didn't.

'Then we start here and now.' She swung the rucksack off her back and unzipped it carefully, pulling a clunky-looking box and lead out from inside.

It was a Walkman, an oversized hunk of plastic that she must have had since the 1980s. It was older than me, almost heavier too as she thrust it into my hands.

'What are we going to do with this?' I turned it over in my hands, wanting to heap further scorn on her idea.

'You are going to speak into it. This wonderful-looking thing is going to train your mind, teach it to dismiss all the untrue thoughts that are in your head.'

'You are kidding me?' Apart from playing tinny-sounding music, I didn't see what use it was going to be.

'No, I'm not kidding. I know it looks unlikely, but this machine played a big part in me finally dismissing the belief that I killed my brother.'

I didn't get it and told her so, politely this time.

'Bear with me. It will become clearer, I promise.' She beckoned me to sit next to her. 'The one thing I know about you is what the doctors told me. That you feel you are responsible for your dad dying. Is that correct?'

I nodded.

'Despite not being in the car when he crashed. Yes?'

Another nod.

'Even though you were nowhere near the bypass when the accident happened?'

'It was still my fault.' I believed it too. Stronger than ever.

'My argument to you is the same as my therapist's with me. Your thoughts are wrong. They are empty and without substance. How could *you* cause a car crash that you were nowhere near? Or how could I kill my brother from another continent? Do you understand what I'm getting at? These thoughts of yours, or thoughts of mine, they are illogical and we shouldn't waste our time entertaining them.'

I could see what she was saying, what she was trying to

236

do. But she didn't know the full story, did she? Didn't know my track record.

'What I'm going to show you is how to make your mind dismiss these thoughts. How to recognize, with the help of logic, that they are not true, that they don't belong to you. As soon as you truly understand and believe this, they will simply crumble away and you will have your mind back.'

She'd told me this before, given me the pep talk, and as brilliant as it sounded, I still didn't see how a cassette player was going to get me there.

'So what do I need to do?'

'You need to start wearing these thoughts down. To make your brain so tired and bored of hearing them, it will start to see them for what they are. So that in time it will start to reject them for the nonsense that they are.'

She took the Walkman back and plugged the lead in, before passing me the other end of it, a small microphone covered in black felt.

'Find yourself a quiet spot, here on the bench or by the cliff, wherever you feel most comfortable. When you are ready, press the red button and start to repeat the same sentence into it: "I killed my dad. It was my fault."'

I felt my stomach tighten.

'The tape is twenty minutes long, so you are going to have to repeat that statement until one side is full. If you need to have a break that is fine. Just hit stop, take a few breaths and start again.' She stroked my back and leaned into me reassuringly. 'I know this is a lot to ask, but I promise, a hundred per cent, that it will help.'

I didn't want to do it. Didn't know if I physically could,

but I forced myself to think of the alternatives, of letting the thoughts rule me, of being at Bellfield around Naomi until they kicked me out at the age of eighteen. Slowly I pulled myself to my feet, studied the machine's buttons and ambled to a bench by the edge of the cliff.

It took me a few moments to steady myself, to persuade my finger to stop shaking and apply enough force to the red button, but eventually I managed it.

'I killed my mum and dad. It was my fault.'

It was slow work at first and I had to pause on a couple of occasions to centre myself, but I did it. After about ten minutes, the words seemed to mean less. It was still me saying them, obviously, but they didn't have the same power, the same meaning, which gave me hope in itself.

Throughout the twenty minutes, Ade was there, twenty metres behind me, her eyes meeting mine each time I needed them without ever invading my space, and I took strength that she'd sat there at some point, recording her own fears just as I was doing. In the end I found a rhythm and a dead-pan tone to my voice that made me comfortable enough to fill the tape, the click of the red button cutting me off mid-sentence. I only hoped that when these thoughts finally left me, it would be just as sudden.

Coiling the microphone lead around my fingers, I climbed to my feet and breathed out deeply to sea. All right, I'd only spoken into a tape for twenty minutes, but I'd never have entertained the idea at the start of the day. It had to be worth something, and as Ade's arms snaked around my shoulders, pulling my head next to hers, I had no doubt, no doubt at all, that I'd made a start.

CHAPTER 40

The Walkman became my constant companion. No one knew what I was listening to. That prospect was unbearable, as was the potential for them clocking the Walkman itself. It was hidden inside a cord bag that Ade had given me. In fact, I'd hidden it in a carrier inside the bag, not that I was paranoid or anything.

I didn't keep anything else in there. Tobacco and lighter lived in my shirt pocket, as I didn't want to give anyone an excuse to go rooting around and find what I was hiding. If I was to follow Ade's plan, then it had to be done with the utmost secrecy. Even when I had the tape of my voice playing through my buds, I did it at a volume that the others couldn't clock. I could see it was confusing them, see Naomi straining to hear what I was listening to. They must have known it wasn't music, as there was no bass leaking out. Mind you, they thought so little of me it wouldn't have been a surprise to them to find I walked round listening to the shipping forecast.

I played the tape a lot, more than the twice daily Ade had suggested. Becoming the Bellfield leper had focused my mind, made me think about what Ade had said when I arrived, about the day I walked out, the potential for a family beyond what I'd lost.

I can't lie: the thought of foster parents still petrified me, made me play out images of a wicked stepfamily who'd punish me in the way I deserved. But the Walkman had given me the bravery to confide in Ade about everything, and if she found my fears ridiculous, then she didn't show it.

'Every time you find these thoughts invading your head, I want you to challenge them, to face them full on and say, "Where is the evidence that I am responsible for what happened? Where is the evidence that any new family will do anything but love me?"'

I stared at her. It was a look she was starting to recognize.

'You are making that face again!' She smiled. 'Remember the trust. What I'm asking you to do is simple. Every time the thought comes, you simply ask it how you caused the crash. Did you pull the steering wheel while he was driving? Did you stamp on a pedal by mistake? The answer to all these questions will be no, and as with the tape, if you tell your brain this often enough, eventually it will tire of the thoughts and dismiss them as soon as they arrive.'

'Is this what you did too?'

'Absolutely. It takes time and commitment, but it will work.'

I must have sagged at the mention of time, as she saw my disappointment.

'What is it?'

'I don't know. It's just . . . all these things you're giving me to do. I believe in them, I do. At least I want to . . .'

All I could think about were the things I hadn't told her,

about Mum and Mr Hobson, the other problems I'd created. Did these things change what she was asking me to do? I didn't know and was too scared to ask, or tell her about them.

'. . . but why does everything have to be so complicated? Why does everything have to take time?'

'Believe me, I wish there was a wand I could wave, or a pill that would make it all go away. But it doesn't work like that. You can self-medicate, hide inside a bottle of spirits, but that won't take the problems away, it will only mask them until the bottle is empty. Alcohol isn't powerful, your mind is. These strategies I'm giving you, these are the only things you need to beat these thoughts. Once you understand what you are doing, once you truly believe that you are in control, then these thoughts –' she paused, looking at me more deeply than ever before – 'won't be yours any more. You have my word.'

So started Groundhog Day. An endless round of lessons, Walkman sessions and, whenever the weather allowed, walks along the cliff tops. In fact, as autumn rolled in, Ade made it clear that falling temperatures and falling rain weren't going to stop us from our daily outing, and on the whole I didn't complain.

Maybe it was the training she was putting my brain through, or the absence of vodka wrecking my defences, but whatever the reason I felt like I was winning. All right, there were times when the anxiety would bite harder than others, hours when I had to fight dirtier than usual to stave off the fear, but these times were getting shorter, less sustained.

Ade was delighted. She took great pleasure in getting me to grade the day's fear levels out of ten, beaming when the number was lower than the day before, supportive when I was overwhelmed and struggling. There didn't seem to be anything that her smile couldn't cure. I swear there were days in October when it parted the clouds.

The routine of the walks was working too, something about the rhythm that we found in our strides that focused our minds. Although I knew why we were walking, that eventually I'd tell her more about the inside of my head, it didn't bother me in the same way it had before. I was easier in her company, not so paranoid. I believed that if something did fall out of my mouth, then she'd probably heard or felt it before.

And man had she lived. In the days when she'd been at her worst, addled with guilt and cut to pieces, she'd trusted all the wrong people, people who'd got her higher instead of talking her down. And she'd stayed with these people for so long, lived with them in squats for such prolonged periods of time, that I found it almost impossible to believe she'd found her way back.

This alone gave me a new sense of belief, although I felt guilty about it. She'd hit rock bottom and stayed there for years. It was only a few months since Dad died and she was giving me the skills she'd waited so long for. It was up to me now to not mess up the chance she'd given me.

I suppose it was this feeling that led me to share a little more, to let her in on why I cut myself, to explain that I didn't do it out of guilt like her, that it was simply my last line of defence against the panic attacks.

This didn't shock her of course. It pleased her. Gave her 'another piece of the jigsaw', told her that we simply had to identify what was bringing the fear on. If we could identify that, then we were halfway there.

The prospect of turning another corner pleased and distracted me. In the hours when I wasn't plugged into Walkman torture, or questioning every dumb thought that flashed into my head, I was on my own, trying to work out a way of telling her the other stuff, the stuff she hadn't given me the tools to cure.

I was so distracted, it was like the others didn't exist. Even Susie and Jimmy, who still spoke to me, became peripheral. As for the other two, I'd become used to avoiding their snide comments and, bit by bit, they seemed to be ignoring me too. It was almost blissful, like the earlier kickings had never happened.

Which is why, when the next one came, it hurt like hell.

CHAPTER 41

Community meetings had become routine. I understood what they were meant to achieve, but to be honest they didn't really affect me.

All right, I'd had a few rockets in the early weeks for sneaky drinking, and after me and Naomi did our runner, but recently? Nothing. And as a result I'd started going in with my guard down, which was my big mistake.

It was the Friday before half-term when I took my seat on the settee next to Ade and glanced over at Naomi, expecting to see her usual look of irritation. She'd had a right face on her lately about the amount of time Ade had been spending with me, but had aimed it at Ade and Bex rather than at me.

But today there was no such look. Instead she perched on the arm of the settee, next to Paddy as always, a look of satisfaction on her face. It wasn't a mood I associated with her, and that should have made me wary. Instead I settled back, ready to drift through the next forty-five minutes.

We started in the normal way, with pleas for people to tidy up the kitchen after using it, and Bex berating Paddy and Naomi for not attending lessons, nothing that raised the temperature. Not until Bex asked if there was anything anyone wanted to share. Usually this meant a succession of shrugs and a few minutes of awkward silence, so I focused on the floor, identifying everyone in the circle by the shoes on their feet.

It was only when a cassette landed by my trainer that my focus was broken.

I knew what was on the tape as soon as I saw it. My voice, my horrible truth.

I didn't know what to do. Was it better to leap up and grab it, or ignore it, hoping it wasn't what I thought it was? But to be honest I knew it had to be mine. Why would anyone else have something that belonged in the 1980s?

Glancing up, I saw a look of bemusement on everyone's faces. Well, everyone but Ade, whose cheeks seemed to be flushing like mine.

'Naomi?' Bex asked. 'Was it you who threw that?'

Naomi looked smug, yet was working hard to appear serious. 'Yep.'

'Er, what are you doing with a tape? I mean, where did you get it?'

'I found it,' she crowed. 'On the girls' corridor. Glad I did too.'

My face burned at her lie. There was no way she found it in the hallway. It had been hanging around my neck not two hours before, and there was no way I would have been that careless over something I was so ashamed of. I'd taken to hiding it, the Walkman and all, in the very bottom of my wardrobe, under a pile of washing. I didn't think anyone would be desperate enough to root through that to find it. But as I looked at Naomi and she held my gaze, eyes narrowing momentarily, I knew I was wrong and that I was in for a proper hiding.

'I thought it was weird to find a tape. I mean, I didn't really know what it was till I found this on the landing as well.' She brandished the Walkman from behind the cushion, her face scrunched in mock confusion.

If I wasn't bricking it so much I would've been on top of her, beating the lie out of her, but of course I did nothing, except to swear repeatedly in my head.

'To be honest, I nearly binned it,' she went on, loving every minute, 'but then I reckoned it might have meant something to someone, what with it being so old and that, so I took it to Paddy to see if he knew who it belonged to.'

My heart crashed through another level, knowing if Patrick was involved the pain was about to intensify.

'I'd never seen it either, but reckoned we could work it out if we listened to the tape. We thought if we heard what was on it we'd know straight away who it belonged to.'

He'd got to his feet while talking and shuffled clumsily over to the tape. He picked it up and wandered round inside the circle, brandishing it like a detective with a piece of evidence. I knew where this was going, understood the humiliation that was heading towards me, and in that moment something snapped. I launched myself at Patrick, my hands grappling for the cassette.

He wasn't the quickest of movers, and I managed to latch on to the tape, my other hand grappling round his shoulder. He spun in surprise but I clung grimly on, ripping the cassette from his hand before slumping to the floor.

All hell broke loose. Within seconds Naomi was on top of

me, yanking my hair. She obviously thought I was going to trash the tape before they could expose me, and with my scalp shrieking in pain I was distracted enough for Patrick to prise the tape from my hand, bending my fingers back in the process.

There was a flurry of bodies above me and a commotion as the carers pulled them both to opposite ends of the room, but unusually there was no resistance from either of them. They simply lifted their arms in mock surprise, telling them to calm down, that all they wanted was the tape.

'What's going on, Bex?' Naomi cried. 'Why didn't anyone tell us who we were living with?'

'I don't know what you mean,' she answered, 'but I won't have violence in this meeting, do you hear me?'

'Violence?' Naomi asked, incredulous. 'If you want to talk about violence, let's talk about what we heard on the tape. We can't believe that you'd put the rest of us at risk like this.'

Bex shook her head, clearly confused. 'Naomi, what on earth are you going on about?'

'Her,' she said, pointing at me. 'Myra bloody Hindley over there. I mean, I know we've all got previous, but we never expected to be living with a bloody killer!'

It was a tumbleweed moment. A clichéd scene from a crappy film when every head in the room turns and focuses on you in slow motion.

A look of satisfaction oozed across Naomi's face as she snapped everyone back to normal speed.

'So when were you going to tell us, then? When were you going to let us in on the magic? Didn't you reckon we had a right to know who we were living with? Jesus, this place is sick. Sick!'

Bex looked ready to explode but Ade got in first.

'Naomi, you have stepped over the line. You've no right to attack anyone like this. If you really had concerns, you should have shared them with us outside the meeting, in private. Not humiliate Daisy in front of the whole community.'

'Yeah, yeah, that's right. She's your little project, isn't she? What is it, Ade, never worked with a serial killer before, eh? Reckoned it would look good on your CV? Well, it explains why you've kicked me to the kerb, doesn't it? I can't compare with that psycho, can I?'

Ade was on her feet, fires burning in her eyes. 'I don't know what you heard on that tape, what conclusions you've drawn from it, but you have no right to –'

'To what?' Naomi screamed. 'No right to be concerned about living with someone who killed their parents? I don't know what it's like where you're from, Ade, but here we tend to take those sorts of things seriously.'

The mention of home seemed to wind Ade, enough to give Bex the space to jump in.

'You can quit with that sort of talk, you hear me? There's no place for that here. None of us want to hear it.'

'Then what *do* you want to hear? Ever since I've got here you've given us the big one about sharing, about how we can help each other, how it can sort things out for us. Well, forgive me, but how does that work if we can't talk about something as important as this? How could you keep this from us?'

'We haven't kept anything from you,' Bex implored. 'No one has a clue what you're talking about.'

'I'm talking about what we heard on the tape. What *Daisy* was saying into it. Not just once either. Over and over again.

We had to turn it off in the end cos it was freaking us out.'

'It would have freaked you out too if you'd heard it,' piped up Patrick. 'I mean, who brags about killing their folks?'

'This is a right load of shit,' shouted Jimmy suddenly. It was so rare for him to engage in anything that the force of his words jolted me. 'You two have had it in for her for weeks. I ain't buying it. It's all bollocks.'

This delighted Naomi all the more and she leaned forward, pointing at me. 'Why don't you ask her, then, Jim? Ask her if it's true. See what she says.'

She paused, head cocked mockingly. 'Well, go on, Daisy. Deny it. Go on. Do it. DO IT!'

I couldn't say anything. My tongue had stuck to the roof of my mouth and, even if I managed to prise it down, what could I say? It was my voice on the tape, my thoughts, even if there was less force in them than the day they were recorded.

'That's enough!' cried Bex, releasing me from the silence. 'Naomi, I want you and Paddy in my office now. The rest of you can have some free time. We're finishing early.'

Naomi and Patrick looked at each other and smiled. It must have taken some effort for them not to high-five each other. Instead they walked towards the door, pausing by me as they went.

'See how difficult life is if you keep stuff from us?' Naomi spat. 'Don't do it again, eh? Otherwise things really will get tough.'

They left quite a scene in their wake. There was Susie close to tears, Jimmy confused and arguing with Eric, and me, shell-shocked, wondering where on earth I went from here.

CHAPTER 42

My face was wind-whipped by the time I reached home, despite the scarf I'd tied around my face. I'd been aiming for a Lawrence of Arabia look, something to ward off the elements, but had failed miserably.

My cheeks and fingers, the only things left exposed, throbbed with cold, but I didn't bother clapping my hands or retying the scarf. It was a bit late for that. I was entering into the completely numb phase, which seemed like a more bearable option.

I'd never walked so far before, had never had reason to. I hadn't meant to today, but as I walked my mind refused to settle, so I kept on going, hoping the answers lay ahead of me. By the time I knew where I was, it was dark, I was hungry, and I was stood at the end of the path to my house, hands trembling on the gate.

'Shit,' I whispered, patting down my pockets. I'd been in such a rush to get away from Bellfield that I hadn't thought to pick up my house keys. All that had mattered was scarpering before Ade caught up with me.

I kicked the gate, knowing the only way to get warm was to break in and I was hardly an expert. It was dark and cold enough for the street to be deserted, so I put my head to my chest and shuffled up the path, sneaking down the side of the house and into the back garden.

I knew none of the windows would be open – Ade had checked all that stuff last time we came. I also knew that Dad had fitted locks on the dining-room and kitchen windows, which left only the small one in the downstairs loo. Dad had never bothered to put a lock on it, so although it seemed an unlikely option I knew it was the only one open to me. I picked up a hefty stone from the rockery and stood before the glass.

Nerves were pricking now and I glanced around again, clocking the lights shining from the house behind ours. If I was going to do this, I was going to have to muffle the sound as the glass broke. Off came my scarf, which I wrapped clumsily around the rock. I'd seen it in *Ocean's Eleven* or something and hoped it wasn't another bit of Hollywood nonsense.

The window gave easily under the stone, but not quietly, and I cringed as the shards fell to the floor, shattering against the tiles. Knocking the remaining glass out as best I could, I hoisted myself up on the window ledge and squeezed my head and shoulders through.

It was tight, too tight. I remembered getting through it a few years ago when I'd locked myself out after school, but that was different. I was half a metre shorter then and the window had been open, not grinning at me like now, with sharp glass teeth.

Breathing in, I twisted until eventually my stomach was through, leaving just the width of my hips to pass. With a final, furious wriggle and bend of the knee I was in. I crashed to the floor, body landing to one side of the toilet, my right arm sinking straight into the middle of the pan, submerged in stagnant water.

It was a shock, more so than the sliver of glass that punctured the palm of my left hand. It wasn't until I'd dried my arm that I even realized I'd cut myself. It stung like buggery, in some ways worse than any of my self-inflicted cuts. At least I'd done them out of choice. Well, sort of.

I may have been inside, but it made no difference to the temperature. In fact, it felt damper inside than out. Darker too. I bundled along the corridor, knocking pans to the floor as I clattered against the kitchen wall. I swore at myself, annoyed. I'd walked around this house all my life, often in the dark, yet suddenly I had no clue where anything was. The lights had been disconnected, thanks no doubt to some do-gooder social worker, and all the radiators were refrigerator-cold too.

The walk had left me ravenous, so I rifled through the cupboards for food. It was slim pickings, but I was beyond caring, so a half-eaten packet of Ryvitas and a tin of black olives seemed heavenly at the time, even if the crispbreads were soft.

Chucking my bounty on the coffee table, I slumped on the sofa, legs pulled beneath me, and rolled a cigarette. I felt a twinge of guilt for a moment as I lit it, wondering if Dad might appear at the edge of the darkness, bollocking me for damaging my lungs.

It had taken a couple of hours to get here, but now I was inside I had no idea what to do or how long I should stay. Not that it mattered, being here beat being ritually humiliated by Naomi.

It was so cold in the room I got up and stamped around, refamiliarizing myself with the DVDs on the shelves, trying to remember the last time I'd actually concentrated on a film from start to finish. It was depressing to realize that it must have been months ago, when there was juice in the sockets.

That should've been my cue to call Bellfield and get someone to pick me up, but I couldn't face the lecture about bunking off again, so I bundled a load of scrunched-up paper and kindling into the fireplace, setting it off with Dad's Zippo. If I was going to stay and wallow in the dark, at least I could be warm doing it.

The fire cheered me up. It threw some light on to the walls, reminding me of the pictures hanging there. It was such a relief to be away from the shatterproof windows of the unit that I found myself slowly nodding off.

It was that blissful type of sleep you don't ever want to end, so when it was interrupted by a key in the front door I was irritated beyond belief. I suppose I should've been scared rather than annoyed – after all, it was probably the police checking for squatters – but even when a flashlight slid across the wall and into my eyes, I wasn't tempted to run. This was *my* house, even if I'd had to tumble into a toilet to force my way in.

'Who's that?' I barked, eyes shielded from the light.

'It's me,' sang a familiar voice. Ade's. 'You know, you really have to quit this running-off business. It costs me a fortune in petrol money.'

'Then stop following me.'

'You know I can't do that. It would please Naomi too much.'

I felt my back stiffen at her name, paranoid for a second that she was lurking behind Ade, ready to finish me off.

'Did it take you long to work out where I was?'

'Well, I tried the cliffs first,' she said, sitting beside me, 'but it was so windy I guessed you weren't angry enough to stay there long. Once I'd checked you hadn't blown away, this was my second guess.'

I ground my cigarette into Dad's ashtray, envisaging Naomi's face beneath the glowing tip. 'Perhaps the cliffs would've been a better choice, eh?'

She looked crestfallen. 'Please don't say that, Daisy. What Naomi and Patrick did back there was unforgivable, but it's so important after everything you've achieved that you don't let it get to you.'

'Easier said than done, though, isn't it? It's not as if I'm any closer to getting out of Bellfield. It's not like the thoughts have gone away or anything.'

'Of course they haven't. These things take time. But you must not forget the work you have done. Don't forget the days recently when these crazy thoughts have not gripped as hard. Maybe . . .' She paused. 'Naomi and Patrick have done you a favour.'

'A what?' I yelled, pushing to my feet. 'How do you work that out? Did you want them to find that bloody tape? Is that why you plugged me into it every day for the last month? To draw attention to me?'

'Of course not. Why would I do that? What I am trying

to say is that you have to take the positives out of situations and perhaps recognize that Naomi has helped you.'

'How?'

'Because she told me something about you that I did not know. I had no idea that you feel responsible for your mother's death as well as your dad's.'

I turned away from her, didn't want her to see that it was true. Scared this would be the final straw that pushed her away.

'Daisy, it is nothing for you to be ashamed of, whatever it is you're feeling. We will work at it and beat it the same way. With the same determination you are already showing.'

I thought about rolling another fag, but there wasn't a cigarette paper big enough to distract me from the enormity of what I was feeling. It had been with me so long, I couldn't fathom what I believed and what I didn't, where the truth ended and I began. Mum being dead was all I'd ever known and thanks to the hospital report it would always be linked with my birth. I mean, how do you explain that?

'Why does everything have to be so difficult?' I asked, rubbing the cut on my palm gingerly.

'Difficult how?'

'I don't know, just difficult. All the films I watched with Dad, any of them that were any good, they were all tense, they all had these plots where the characters had to get over things or work things out. And nearly always they did. By the time the two hours was up they'd found the answer, had the secret to life sorted and stored away in their head. Either that or they'd shot someone and felt better that way instead.'

Ade chuckled, her laugh warming the room.

'Hollywood has a lot to answer for.'

'It bloody does. It makes me wonder why I put myself through it. Why I constantly want to watch film after film.'

'Maybe you really believe that whatever answers you need are tucked away in a film somewhere. And maybe, Daisy, they are. Or maybe you already know the answers and you just need help to get them out of *here*.' She tapped the top of my head, before pulling me into her embrace. It was an action that revealed just how exhausted I really was.

'I don't enjoy feeling like this, you know.'

'I know. Nobody does.'

'There are times when I look at Naomi and Paddy and think they get off on it, feeling like they do.'

'I can guarantee you they don't.' She gripped me by the shoulders, breaking the embrace as she looked straight inside me. 'Everyone has their ways of coping. Those two smother theirs in aggression. It may be something you could learn a little from.' She grinned, enough for me to know that I should listen to her advice.

'Really?'

'The last thing I want is for you to copy anyone. Not me, not Paddy, Naomi or anyone. But ever since I met you, you have been apologizing. It would do you good for once to not say sorry. Just for once, maybe you could say, "You know, this isn't my fault."'

'But what if I don't believe it? What if things really are my fault? What if Mum dying really was down to me?'

I heard her groan, before she plodded over to the fire, tossing two large logs on to it.

'Prove it to me,' she said. 'You have as long as it takes for the fire to burn down to convince me. So go on and do your worst.'

She tossed these words at me as she flopped on to the sofa, leaving me exposed, despite the near darkness in the room.

'Well, go on, Daisy Houghton. I dare you.'

And so I began, waiting for the first apology to fall out of my mouth.

CHAPTER 43

The first charred log had fallen through the grate and I was no closer to explaining how I felt. I'd tiptoed around the truth, told her it was too difficult to explain, and so we'd sat quietly for half an hour, entranced by the flames. With every minute that passed I expected Ade to find another way of ordering my thoughts, but tonight there was nothing, just a soft humming from her lips.

The log slipping spurred me into life, though, reminding me that they were all that stood between me and the car journey back to my cell. If I was going to find some sense in what I was feeling, it had to be here and now, in a place that was familiar and comfortable.

'Do you know how long it took for you to be born?' I asked, not really knowing where I was going.

'You mean my mother's labour?'

I nodded.

'I'm not sure. I was sleeping at the time. I know it wasn't quick, as the nurse was late arriving.'

'Mum was in labour for almost seventy-two hours with me. It took so long the hospital sent her home three times before they finally gave her a bed.'

'That must have been frustrating for her.'

I pulled my legs into my chest, trying to push down a new wave of anxiety brewing there. 'That's just it. I don't know, do I? It's not as if I ever got a chance to speak to her about it. I grew up trying to beat stuff out of Dad.'

'He never wanted to talk about things?'

'It just wasn't his way, you know. I think he thought he was protecting me . . .'

'But you *wanted* to know, yes?'

'Of course I did. I wanted to know everything there was to know about her. Sometimes it was like he forgot that I never met her.'

'What did happen to her, Daisy? Because if you never met her, then I don't understand how you did this terrible thing?'

I breathed deeply, not knowing how to go on. How would she react: would she laugh at me or decide she'd had enough?

'You don't need to be scared of telling me, Daisy. Remember who you're speaking to, what I've done myself.'

I closed my eyes, took one last breath in and let the words come.

'The nurses weren't concerned when they sent mum home the first couple of times. Dad said it was normal for women having their first babies to have false alarms, but the final time he drove her there, he was convinced I was coming. They both were. The only person not convinced was me apparently.'

'I don't blame you. You were probably warm and well fed in there.'

My eyes never broke away from the fire as I went on. I didn't dare look at Ade.

'That was the problem, though. I didn't want to come out, but Mum's body needed me to be delivered. A few hours after they admitted her, she started getting really bad pains in her stomach.'

'You mean contractions?'

'No, she'd been having them for days. This was something different. Really sharp pains. Like someone was stabbing her.'

Ade stroked my hand as I spoke.

'How do you even know all this, Daisy? I thought your dad refused to talk about what went on.'

'I didn't hear most of this from him. He closed up whenever I asked him. But I found some papers a few months ago, a report from the hospital that he'd never thrown away. I was looking for something that filled in the gaps, you know? A photo, or a diary . . . anything really. But I hadn't expected something so official.'

'And you read it?' She sounded surprised.

'Of course I did. Wouldn't you? I'd spent years not knowing what had gone on. All I wanted to know was what had happened to my mum.'

'So what did this report say?'

'That the pains were down to me. That I'd started to show signs of distress as I moved lower, which pushed her blood pressure up. By the time my head started showing, she was in so much pain she was on the verge of passing out.'

'Daisy, what you are describing is what *happens* in labour. It must be a real shock to anyone's body to go through that.'

'She tried to hold it together, but the doctors said I was in such a terrible position that it was no wonder she was struggling. They tried to manipulate me into a better shape, but every time they did I resisted, until they had no option but to try and get me out as quickly as they could.'

'So were you born by Caesarean section?'

'No. At first they tried with suction, but when they did it was too much for her. One minute she was there and the next her heart couldn't cope.'

'She had a heart attack?'

I nodded. 'They worked on her at the same time as me, once they finally got me out. The cord was round my neck, but after warming me up I started crying. They shocked Mum time and time again. They massaged her heart and kissed her, but her body had given up. It just couldn't cope with what I'd put it through.'

Silence rolled around the room until a damp part of the log crackled, spitting a spark on to the rug. I crushed it with my trainer.

Ade didn't know what to say, so I filled the silence instead.

'Do you know what gets to me most, though? The thing that hurt most as I grew up? That I don't have a single picture of the two of us together. I've got nothing, *nothing*, that tells me how she felt about me. I mean, I know I love her despite never meeting her, but I don't have a clue how she felt carrying me. Was she excited, nervous, proud? I mean, I don't even know if I was an accident.'

'And would that make a difference?' Ade asked. 'Would you feel less guilty if you knew? If you had some evidence of how she felt?'

I shrugged. 'Dunno. Maybe. Maybe it wouldn't make any difference. I've had this in my head for so long that it's hard to make sense of any of it any more.'

Ade stood up and stretched her arms in front of her, cracking her knuckles as she threw a third log on to the fire.

'I thought I only got two logs' worth?'

'You did. But there's no way we're going home yet. Not when you've done so well already.'

She prodded the fire tentatively before sitting back on the sofa, the reflection of the flames glinting in her eyes.

It was easier to speak after that. I'd told her things I hadn't told anyone else and she was still there, listening. A bolt of lightning hadn't struck her after my words. Everything was as it was.

So I went on. Told her how Dad had compensated for his inability to talk by leaving kids' books in my room, stories about life without parents. It was the closest he could get to opening up about it.

'It sounds like he was doing his best. Other people wouldn't have made the efforts he made, even if they don't feel enough to you now.'

'I never blamed him for it. He was a brilliant dad, and it wasn't as if he didn't show me affection, cos he did. He just never got over losing her and I couldn't help but think that deep down he blamed me for her dying.'

'But why would he do that?'

'Didn't you listen to what I said? Her body couldn't cope with what I put her through. If I hadn't been so big, or in such an awkward position, then none of it would've happened. If it wasn't for me, he might not have smoked so much, or needed to hide inside endless films.'

'Daisy, you must distance yourself from this. Do you

really think you're at fault for being born? All this talk of your position and size, it wasn't your choice! But it was *their* choice to have you, and when you have children, then there is a health risk. What happened to your mum is tragic, a horrible accident, but to think it was your fault? No, Daisy, no. And you must say it to yourself time and time again, just as you did with the words on the cassette tape. Beat these thoughts down with logic. Think about them in other ways. Maybe Dad felt so sad because he felt responsible. Maybe he thought it was actually his fault.'

I shook off her suggestion dismissively, aggressively even.

'How could it possibly be his fault? That's ridiculous.'

She was on to me in a flash. 'Yes, it is ridiculous. It makes no sense at all. In fact, it makes as little sense as your ideas. He had as little to do with it as you did. Nothing at all!'

'But you didn't see him, Ade. You didn't have to sit and watch as he clammed up at the mention of her name. For the last few months it was like every time he looked at me, all he saw was Mum. And there was nothing I could do about it.'

'And you think that's why he crashed the car? Because he was so distracted by the way you looked?'

'No, of course it wasn't. He was in the car because of me. He was on the way to school.'

'What, to collect you? Were you ill or something?'

I pulled at my hair, not knowing how or if I could do this, whether I could complete the shame of telling her what I'd done with Hobson as well.

'Daisy? Don't feel agitated. All I want to do is understand. If there's something else, it's important you tell me.'

'What, so you can tell me it's not my fault again? You know, it's starting to feel a bit lame, all this. Some of what happened has to be down to me, doesn't it? I can't believe that all this has gone on and none of it is my fault!'

'Then you'll have to tell me, won't you? Because unless you do you'll never know, and instead you'll always be questioning it, letting it eat you away long after you leave Bellfield.'

'He was in the car because he found out about the self-harming. He saw the state of my arm and he lost the plot.'

'I thought you said he was on the way to school.'

'He was.'

'But that doesn't make sense. Why would he leave you when he'd discovered something so important?'

'Because he'd found out something else as well.'

'What?'

I said nothing. My mouth was suddenly as hot as the embers in the hearth.

'Whatever it is, you can say it. You know that.'

I had no idea where to start, but slowly it all came out. The problems with Donna in class. The way I pretended at parties and at school. She must have wondered where I was going until I got to Mr Hobson and how he'd been the only one I could trust, how he understood the way I felt. She didn't move as I told her about the walk along the path. In fact, it wasn't until I got to the kiss that she said anything at all.

'Daisy, you do understand the importance of what you're telling me, don't you?'

I bristled momentarily. 'Are you saying you don't believe me?'

'No, of course not. Why on earth would you lie about this? What I am saying is that this isn't something I can keep to myself.'

I grabbed at her hand, squeezing the life out of it as I told her she couldn't do that, that it wasn't his fault, that I'd liked him, invited him down the path, given him all the signs he needed.

She shook her head firmly. 'I don't believe that, Daisy, and even if there was an attraction between you, he should have known better. For him there is no excuse. He is your teacher and an adult. You knew it was wrong as soon as he kissed you. He should have known enough to not even find himself in that position.'

I argued with her, pacing around the room as the panic grew, but she was having none of it. She repeated back what she had heard, that his actions were typical of an adult trying to groom a teenager. That he probably didn't love films at all, that his mother was possibly even alive, that people like him looked for vulnerabilities and found ways to make you trust them before taking advantage.

I didn't want to hear any of it, but my confession had unearthed new steel in Ade that left her implacable. She stood in front of me, holding my shoulders firmly as I tried to walk.

'What you have told me has taken such courage, but unless we do something about it, then a lot of it will be in vain. Think about what he did, Daisy. Think about how he could be trying the same thing again, maybe with someone you know. You don't want that to happen, do you?'

I shook my head, limbs draining of energy.

'Then the bravest thing we can do is tell the police. They need to talk to this man and make sure that he can't move on and do the same again.'

A huge raking sob left my lips before I could stop it, a mixture of fear and relief.

'You must be so tired, my love. And you will be for a few days. But make no mistake, what you have just told me is incredible, and I promise that we will do everything we can to break all these thoughts down. They won't rule you for long. I won't let them.'

It didn't matter that the fire was dying now. There was enough warmth in her words and embrace to stop me shivering. She stood, holding me for long enough for my body to finally relax, and for my mind to wonder if this was how a mother's embrace really felt.

CHAPTER 44

I spent the next week feeling like I'd been turned inside out. Nothing made sense, every step I took was off balance, and for every minute I spent hiding in my room, I spent an hour in some office or other, whether it was at Bellfield or the police station.

Ade had been painfully true to her word, with the police arriving the morning after my admission, prepared but not fully ready to believe my story. For the first few hours they had me going over the full events time and again, the same questions, the same loaded comments, until I was convinced that they were trying to make me slip up. But as all I had to tell them was the truth, they seemed to leave a little disappointed.

It wasn't easy going over it all again. I was still feeling raw from the night before, so to own up to my own stupidity again so quickly felt like I was being rubbed with sandpaper. It didn't help that Ade was nowhere to be seen, leaving me with Bex, who'd explained that Ade had 'other things to attend to'.

What other stuff? She'd told me she was going to sort everything out, only to scarper the next day. Bex supported me, reining the police in when they pushed too hard, but I missed Ade and the fact that she believed me so implicitly. I couldn't help but wonder if Bex thought I'd played my part in what had gone on.

Once the initial interview was over, the police promised to pick up Hobson straight away, so I retreated to my room, forcing myself to plug back into the Walkman and my own words. I was desperate now, needed to be out of here so quickly that I'd do anything to speed the process along. And as Ade wasn't about to talk to, this was the only option I had.

The week crawled along in the same way. I was buffeted from meeting to meeting, seeing new officers, new psychologists. Even Evelyn pitched up, the first time I'd seen her since she deposited me at Bellfield. Not that she was hugely engaged, more disappointed that I was with Bex and not Eric. I swear her lipstick faded as she clocked us.

There were results from the endless meetings – important ones. The police picked up Hobson quickly and questioned him for hours. He'd been suspended from school and they were researching his family details, whether his mum was alive or dead.

I couldn't make up my mind what I wanted the answers to be. What was more difficult to accept? That he was a manipulator, or that I'd have to let go of my own feelings of guilt?

Bex was adamant, just as Ade had been, that it was all his fault, so I had to put my faith in them and wait it out.

I think this would've been bearable if the others at Bellfield hadn't worked out what was going on. Community meetings became torture, a daily opportunity for Naomi to dig away, telling whoever would listen that they had a right to know what was going on. At least in the meeting she did it in an articulate way; for the other twenty-three and a quarter hours she was in my face and behind my back. There were taunts and insinuations that I'd 'killed again', notes shoved under my door asking me where the bodies were buried. She was grinding me down to the point where I considered telling everyone what I'd done. Keeping it secret didn't seem so important any more.

Support came in an unlikely shape: the lumbering frame of Jimmy. He'd piped up for me in the community meeting that one time, but outside that session he'd been his normal distracted and elusive self. He was a proper Houdini who'd disappear for hours on end, which used to drive Eric to distraction, as he had to spend most of his shifts liaising with the police or combing the streets for him. I often thought Jimmy was playing him, because just as Eric was on the verge of panic Jimmy would materialize, phone clamped to his ear, eyes bulging with adrenalin or some other kind of high.

'Where have you been, Jim?' Eric would plead, but Jimmy's answer was always the same. 'Jammin' with mates. No biggie, just jammin'.'

I asked Eric one day if he thought it was true. Not that Jimmy had friends outside of Bellfield, but whether the whole music thing was in any way real.

'I used to worry about it when he first arrived, but not any more. Whether it's true or not doesn't matter for now. It's important to him and it gives him security. Once he knows he's safe here, he'll let us in.'

There were occasions when I wanted to push Jimmy on it myself, but that didn't seem fair. I did discover where he spent time during his disappearing acts, though: the laundry room in the basement. It was a grotty narrow space, even more non-descript than my room, the only decoration being half a dozen industrial washer/driers and a gallery of mould on the walls. Hardly the kind of place to linger, unless you were Jimmy.

I'd often find him there, backed up against the wall, eyes fixed as the clothes swirled round. It was like he was watching the telly. His eyes never left the screen, even when I was loading the machine next to his. He was so mesmerized that I found myself sliding down the wall next to him, focusing on the porthole as it tossed my clothes around, an untidy rainbow of socks and Dad's shirts. We sat there for a few minutes, until I found my breathing had slowed beyond its normal anxious patter. Was this what it offered him? A bit of peace? Each time I found him in there I sat next to him for a while, wondering if he knew I was even there.

It must have been on the fifth occasion that he finally spoke to me, when his machine reached the end of its cycle, breaking the spell.

'Sweet,' he whispered, stretching as I used to do when a film reached a satisfactory ending. 'Can't beat it, can you?'

I nodded, stretching my mouth into a confused smile.

'I'm not surprised you like it too. First time I saw you I knew we were alike, me and you.'

'That right?' I asked.

'Too right. You've got it, you see, just like I have.'

I had no idea what he was talking about. 'Got what?'

His arms blurred as he formed this dramatic X shape in front of him.

'The X-factor, mate, that something special. And that's the problem, you feel me? That's why the other two are gunning for you, just like they do me. Jealousy, mate, jealousy.'

He pushed himself to his feet in a long fluid movement, the veins in his arms pulsing with the effort.

'I've seen it before. Seen what they do to people like us. It's not pretty. Not pretty at all.' He fixed me with his eyes, until I swear he was looking inside my head, at all the anxieties rattling round inside. 'But don't you worry about it. The only thing you need to know is that I've got your back. Remember that and everything will be sweet.'

As the words ended so did his gaze, his attention flicking back to his phone, the screen blank as always. 'I've got to be somewhere. Take it easy. I'll catch you later.' And he strode towards the door, his fingers strumming an imaginary guitar at his side.

I didn't know what to think or do after that. Part of me wanted to laugh, while in some ridiculous way I felt reassured and protected. It felt good, whatever it was, so in celebration I slid to the floor and let the washer give me some therapy, Jimmy style.

CHAPTER 45

The news was greeted with a mixed response. Naomi looked pleased, so Patrick followed suit. Susie seemed close to tears as ever, while Jimmy took it as his cue to text furiously.

I was confused, so asked the obvious question.

'When you say *show*, what do you actually *mean*?' These were the first words I'd uttered in a community meeting since Naomi had exposed me and my heart skipped at the potential to be ridiculed again.

'It's exactly what I say. A show.' Bex grinned. 'A chance for each of you to share a talent or passion for something. It can be anything you like, as long as it is in no way harmful to anyone else in the group.' She fixed Naomi and Patrick for a second, making it clear she meant them.

'In six weeks it will be Christmas and, while I know that brings up insecurities for you all, it's important we try and celebrate. To acknowledge the strides you've made in the past year.' Bex paused, before adding with a grin, 'All carers will be sharing too, make no mistake.'

'And can we team up as well, do something together?' Naomi asked.

'All five of you? That would be great.'

Naomi sucked her teeth and looked disdainfully around the room. 'You're kidding. I was talking about me and Paddy.'

'Yep, that's fine, as long as you stay within the boundaries set.'

'So how long have we got to practise, then?'

'Three weeks. The stage will be set up for 7 December, so fix that date in your heads. No excuses. Everyone has to share something.'

You couldn't have written the script. It was almost malicious. 7 December: my birthday – the day I turned fifteen. Well, that ruled out my planned trip to the Bahamas straight away. Not that my birthday was ever a day to be celebrated, not with what it meant for Mum.

Dad had always tried to ignore the double meaning of the date, but every year, before we celebrated, he'd take some flowers to the tree he planted for her. I never objected to sharing his time. I didn't feel like I could, after my part in it.

But now, in the light of my new positive attitude, I forced good thoughts in, telling myself it would take my mind off the negatives. At least it would if I could work out what to share with the others.

I'd hardly say there was a buzz after the announcement. The staff thought it was hilarious, while Naomi and Patrick huddled up conspiratorially, glancing every now and then in my direction. Susie in particular was beside herself at the potential for further humiliation.

'What am I going to perform?' she wailed.

I shrugged. 'Can you dance or something?'

She pointed at her dumpy legs and frowned. 'Do I look like Darcey pissing Bussell to you?'

There was no answer to that, and I was pleased to catch sight of Ade, gifting me an opportunity to leave before I got sucked in further.

It was the first time I'd seen her in six days and I'd missed her enough to be irritated by her absence. I knew this was a job and that she had to take holidays, but her timing stunk. She knew it too, lacing her arm around me and giving me a squeeze.

'My friend,' she whispered. 'You must be angry with me, deserting you like I have.'

''S OK,' I lied.

'I don't believe you for a second. I owe you an apology and an explanation, one of which I can give you today. You'll have to wait for the other.'

She was talking in riddles again, which was my cue to spark up a rollie, as I knew it would hack her off.

'Do you want to walk today?'

'I've got class.'

'There are things we need to talk about. No one will mind. I've already told them we are going.'

I peered out of the window. It wasn't raining for once. The mist was hugging the grass instead, so I shrugged non-committally and went to grab my coat.

There was a spring to her step, another gear in her stride, and she was humming louder than normal. I hoped it was the things we had to discuss that were making her so happy.

'So how are you feeling after everything that's gone on?'

'Confused.' I wasn't going to lie to her. 'I've never been asked the same questions so many times.'

'These things are never easy. What that man did to you was so premeditated and manipulative that the police have to make everything clear for your sake. So he can't wriggle out of what he did.'

'Either that or they plain don't believe me.'

She shook her head adamantly. 'You see, there you go again, blaming yourself. Have you stopped to think that the police might just believe you?'

'Why should they? It's my word against his.'

'Not any more, it's not. Because of what you told them, they've made real strides towards prosecuting him.'

I slowed down, not sure if I was ready to hear what she had to say.

'The things he said about his mother . . . that she was dead? All lies.'

My head fizzed. I wanted to sit down but sucked on my fag instead, the nicotine adding to my head-rush.

'She is a sixty-seven-year-old woman living in Derby. She is ill, has been for a long time, but she is very much alive.'

Ridiculous as it seemed, part of me was disappointed. How could he have done that? To have dreamed up his story on the spot like that, all to kiss me? The rest of me just felt angry at him, and at myself for believing him. I mean, how could I have been so gullible?

I felt Ade grip me firmly by the shoulders.

'Hey! Stop that! I know what you're doing, reproaching yourself instead of him. Did you just hear what I said? Well, let me tell you again. Thomas Hobson is an abusive manipulator, and the news about his mother spurred the police on. They have been in touch with the other schools he's taught at. Other girls have come forward, with stories no different from yours. Like you, they blamed themselves, didn't realize they were being played in exactly the same way. They were too scared or too trusting to speak out.'

I listened to her intently, trying desperately to make her words sink in.

'What you admitted was brave. What you did helped these other girls, just as it helped you. This isn't the end of it. The police still have so much work to do, but you must believe what I say.' Her arms danced in front of her, mesmerizing me into listening. 'You must see this now. This is more power, more fuel for your mind. Look at the facts. Him kissing you was not your fault. It was *his actions* that made your father jump in the car that day, not yours. The guilt should always live with him, not with you.'

My head lurched back to the sight of Hobson by my hospital bed. His creased clothes and face, eyes that were felt-tip red. I hoped it was guilt that made him look that way, and that it would never leave him.

Ade let go of me, but held me with her eyes.

'This is a turning point, Daisy Houghton. You must use this information to prove that you are not the monster you claim to be. I have told you this before, on the night I met you. You are my lucky charm, don't forget that.'

After touching my cheeks lightly with her hands she marched on, not giving me a chance to ask what on earth she meant.

*

We power-walked around the headland that day, a weird sense of adrenalin and euphoria moving us along. We talked more about the police's discovery and what it meant, and how I should concentrate even harder on questioning the thoughts of guilt that came now, and batter them with logic, refusing them head space.

But for once we also talked of other things, things that didn't relate to the state of my head or the scabs on my arms. None of it was important, but that was the blissful part of it. It was throwaway stuff, banter, and for once I felt my age, like there was nothing sticking to me or weighing me down.

It must have been that feeling that led me to open my mouth.

'You know, I've been thinking –' which was a lie, as the impulse had only just grabbed me – 'that it might be the time for me to think again about Dad's ashes.'

'Mmmm?' mouthed Ade, although her body language suggested a greater, hidden excitement.

'I mean, I still don't want to have a load of people there. I'm not doing it for anyone else, but maybe we could do something round here, on the cliffs. Scatter his ashes or something?'

'I think that would be terrific.' She beamed, the corners of her mouth touching her ears. 'For your dad and for you.'

'How would it work, then?' I asked, a late moment of fear kicking in.

'What do you mean?'

'Well, what would I have to say? Who would I have to invite? Everyone back at Bellfield?'

'Daisy, don't let fear creep in. How you do this is entirely

277

up to you. It's your bravery making it happen in the first place. It can be just you, or everyone, or just me. No one will be offended. No one even has to know. You know, this is actually the perfect time for you to take more control and not let things happen *to* you. Make them happen *for* you instead.'

It was a rare time that one of her riddles made sense and I promised not to chew it over in my head. I'd do it when I was ready, when I was comfortable, and with the people who understood why I was doing it.

And if anyone didn't like it? Well, that was tough shit.

I'd make the choices. This was my goodbye. He was my dad, after all.

CHAPTER 46

Deciding to say goodbye to Dad seemed to anger someone, as it did nothing but rain for the next week and a half. And I'm not talking about squally showers or drizzle. I mean end of the earth, fire and brimstone, hammers falling from the sky. Stuff that none of us, mad as we apparently were, were prepared to set out in.

At first I took it as a blessing. I mean, I'm not religious or anything, but it gave me a bit more time to reflect on what I was doing and who I wanted there while I did it.

I was torn. Would it really do any harm to invite other people who knew Dad? Colleagues or school mates maybe, people I remember him drinking with as I grew up? Neighbours or kids I'd allowed myself to play with over the years? But none of them seemed right. That part of my life was so distant it felt like it didn't belong to me at all.

Which left me with everyone at Bellfield. But while I had no problem with the carers being there, it seemed like lunacy to invite any of the others, even Jimmy, whose concentration span extended only to the cycle of a washing machine. Somehow, I didn't think funerals were really his thing.

The rain gave me plenty of time to chew it over, too much

even. It affected the house as well, creating further divides within the group. Not only did it deepen Patrick and Naomi's hatred of the rest of us, but it also widened the distance between Susie, Jimmy and me.

They'd decided that we should pool together to do something for the show, and naturally Jimmy wanted this to be a song, a prospect that gave me the almighty fear.

I knew this show meant putting myself in the firing line, but somehow the thought of doing it on my own was more appealing. At least that way I could choose my own humiliation, rather than banging a tambourine as Jimmy wailed his way through some Beatles song or other. Quite what Susie planned to do was another matter, but I didn't fancy standing beside her as she did it.

I turned their offer down carefully, telling them I had plans of my own, and it was news that they met with a shrug before retreating to one of the classrooms, thankfully closing the door before picking up their instruments.

With the two pairs deep in rehearsals, immersed for hours on end, I was left to concentrate on myself, and doing what I needed to do to move forward and hopefully on from Bellfield.

The show was only a week away when the rain forced me into a corner. I'd listened to the Walkman so often that the tape was starting to wear out, my voice wobbling and distorting comically. Ade hugged me when I told her, praising my dedication, while ploughing even more time into my recovery. She took me to relaxation classes, acupuncture sessions, fed me little rewards for another week passing without cutting myself. I was starting to believe, starting to take pride that it had been twenty-three days since I'd let the fear take over me.

The last of my scabs had fallen away and although the skin was pink and sore to the touch, I wasn't repulsed at the sight of it. If anything the recovering skin spoke to me, told me how far I'd come.

The one person that managed to get inside my fledgling sense of calm was of course Naomi. It may have been paranoia, but every time I came back from somewhere with Ade, she'd be watching. Always from a distance, but that didn't dilute her sense of menace.

I knew what it was all about. She felt that I'd stolen Ade from her, and I worried that maybe I had. After all, she *was* there before me, with Ade as her key worker, and I couldn't help but remember her strop when I arrived and she discovered she had to share.

I was becoming paranoid about it, started cutting short conversations we were enjoying, almost prompting Ade to spend more time with Naomi.

I shouldn't have bothered. Naomi had pulled down the shutters as far as Ade was concerned. She refused to talk to her, did not show up for sessions, did everything she could to make it look as if she didn't give a shit. But I knew she did, as she singled me out more and more, telling me that Ade didn't care about me, that I was just a project, something to kill time before the next psycho arrived.

It got so bad, so relentless, that in the end I was desperate to get out of the house and away from her, and it was Dad who gave me the excuse to do it.

Ade was shocked when I told her I was ready, peering

out at the freezing fog before turning back to me with a look that said, 'Really? Today?'

I nodded quickly, giving myself no time to back down: Ade dashed for her coat, telling me to do the same.

We met at the gates, wrapped up like mummies, although Ade seemed to have found space for two scarves around her neck, which even to her must have been overkill. She gave me a squeeze as I arrived, before tapping her rucksack lightly. 'I have your dad in here,' she whispered, a surreal thought even by Bellfield's standards.

The pace along the coast road was slower than normal as the wind was blasting, testing our resolve. It blew the fog upon us and I felt its touch on my cheeks, its fingers cold and damp.

The anxiety started to prickle in my chest and instinctively I sparked up a cigarette. It was so cold that I couldn't tell when the fumes stopped and the clean air from my lungs began, but trying to work it out helped, diverting my mind from the fear.

I was two and a half fags in when the fog finally broke, a couple of hundred metres from a spot I'd come to love, where Ade and I had spoken on so many occasions. It was the one place where the rest of the headland disappeared, the one place on this bit of coast where you could see nothing ahead of you but sea. Even on the wilder days, there was a sense of calm here, and I had loved the thought that I could say *anything* while I was stood there, that there was no one to hear me but Ade.

'This is where we should do it,' I said, my voice emotion-less.

'Are you sure?'

'Completely. I reckon he would've liked it here. He could've smoked without anyone telling him to stop it.'

'Then it is perfect,' she said, and hauled the bag from her back, removing her gloves long enough to unzip it and retrieve a black metallic urn.

My stomach churned at the sight and suggestion that everything Dad was, not just his body, but his character, his achievements, everything, could fit inside such a small space. I had to fight the impulse to rip it from her hands and free him immediately, telling myself he had been there for months now . . . that another five minutes couldn't hurt him any more.

Hands shaking, I cradled the urn, surprised by how light it was. I felt uneasy, scared that I was going to mess it up, that I'd say the wrong thing or that the wind would blow him back into our faces.

'What do I do now?' I asked. 'I don't know what to do.'

'There's no right or wrong way. Just do whatever comes into your head.'

'Should I say something? You know, before I empty him out?' My pulse was quickening and I felt my edges begin to unravel, to crave my room and the cold metal of the nail scissors.

'Daisy, take a moment. Think about what you are doing here. Remind yourself of the bravery it is taking. Two months ago, two weeks ago even, you could not have done this, but now you can. Now you are here. Breathe deeply and think about what you want to say to him, about what you didn't get the chance to say before he died.'

'Should I say it out loud?'

'Out loud or in your head, neither is important as long as you believe what you are saying, that you are telling your truth.'

I pushed my hood down and pulled my gloves off with my teeth. The urn was so cold on my skin it burned. I twisted at the lid, feeling it give beneath my fingers, scared that the wind would whip Dad away before I was ready.

I was engulfed by things to say, a mad clutter of memories that I needed time to order. But it was time I didn't have, or want to have. I needed to do this before my nerve failed. Breathing deeply, I felt the wind gently rock me forward, making me confident I could push Dad slowly out to sea. My arm stretched out shakily in front of me and, as my hand rotated, his ashes slipped out, tumbling downwards until the wind took hold of them, embracing them gently, guiding them away from me.

A gasp escaped me as Dad's cloud surrendered to the fog and I mouthed goodbye three times, each word deepening the sense of what I'd lost.

I suppose I'd been grieving since the day of the crash, but this time it was different, now I knew he was gone without believing it was all my fault.

There was pain, and a weakening in every cell of my body, but still it felt good to let go, to let something of me join Dad in the wind.

It was part of me I didn't want to carry. It didn't belong to me any more.

CHAPTER 47

I peered above the duvet cautiously, expecting something hideous to welcome me to another birthday.

Sitting up slowly, I stretched the stiffness from my legs, trying to work out if I felt any different from how I had for the past year.

Nerves had been brewing for a few days, in part due to the prospect of facing a birthday alone and in part, ridiculously, because of the God-awful show that they'd hijacked us with. Three weeks had passed since they'd announced the plan, but it was mere hours since I'd finally settled on what I was going to share. I hoped the others wouldn't lynch me for it, because what I'd lined up was hardly sword-swallowing.

The pressure must have shown, as Ade had been around a lot in the run-up to the day, especially in the evenings, when she knew the fear tended to grip me the hardest.

'There will be times – anniversaries, significant dates in your life – that will threaten to overshadow your recovery,' she had said, 'even when you are well down the road. What is important is that you recognize it will only be a blip. If you keep questioning the dark thoughts they will pass, just as the date itself does.'

I took her at her word, challenging each thought, telling myself it was Hobson's fault Dad was in the car that day, not mine, and in the most part that settled me down. Since scattering the ashes, something had shifted in my head, moved me away from the guilt, squarely into the arms of grief itself. I wasn't blaming myself for him dying any more, I just missed him instead, and while this new pain was sharp, it rubbed upon me differently, making it easier to tell Ade what I really missed about him.

'He sounds like a special man, and he would not want you to be sad on your birthday. So we must do all we can to make sure this day equals any celebration you have ever had.'

It was a big statement, huge in fact, but the faith I had in her made me sit up and listen, wanting to believe that she could be right.

When I spotted a card pushed under my door, with her writing on it, everything in me lifted, hopeful of the promise being kept, but after ripping off the envelope and devouring her words, my resolve slipped:

Good morning, birthday girl. Happy 15th to you!
I wanted to be here to give you this in person, but I have an appointment that cannot be missed, loose ends that need to be tied up.

Enjoy a restful morning, Floss has promised to make you a breakfast banquet in my absence, and I should be back in plenty of time for the show.

Everything will become clear later . . .
Ade
X

I tossed the card to the floor, not quite believing what I'd read. What was it with her? What was this knack of disappearing when I needed her most?

On my birthday, when the police came to interview me, even when I first arrived she didn't show up. Did she have this in-built radar telling her to desert me when it actually mattered?

I fought hard to push the resentment down but couldn't. She'd spent weeks preparing me for an event she said would be hard, then buggered off on the day itself.

It didn't make sense and in my agitated state I didn't want to give it any more head-space, so instead I spent the morning growling at anyone who dared to even say hello, never mind wish me a happy birthday.

I skulked through breakfast, picking at the eggs that had been made for me, not bothering to clear away my mess afterwards. Instead I slouched in the dining room, rolling cigarette after cigarette, despite the carers telling me I wasn't to smoke in there. I was being a brat, doing a Naomi on them, but I couldn't help it, couldn't blow the fog away.

The buzz and excitement surrounding the show did little to help things either. Cliques were disappearing into rooms, costumes tucked under arms, smug smiles smeared on faces. Naomi was so full of herself she was in danger of overflowing. She danced around the dining room, circling me, pointing, mouthing the same word over and over again, 'You, you, you', her grin widening each time she sang. I had no idea what she was going on about, apart from knowing it was another of her threats. I hoped it was of the empty variety.

I started to fret about the paltry offering I had. Would anyone care what I was going to show them? Would it make sense, or change the way they looked at me? At the time it had seemed like a good idea, but as insecurity circled I wasn't so sure. All I knew was that I didn't want to sit around on the outside of everyone else's excitement.

The next few hours were tough. The toughest in weeks.

The fuse I'd lit downstairs was burning shorter. It felt like I had to go back to scratch and work out another idea, something more in keeping with what the others were doing. But everything seemed beyond me. I was no singer, could barely run never mind dance, and I certainly wasn't going to try and write a poem or anything. Can you imagine?

The fear was stinging, forcing me inside an endless cloud of tobacco, and by the end of the fourth cigarette I was doing all I could to keep myself away from the nail scissors. I paced the floor, speaking out loud, telling myself everything was fine, that it was only insecurity making me do this.

Rolling up my sleeve, I stared at my arm and its healing lines, reminding myself not to go back now. That tomorrow the fear would have subsided.

I wish I could tell you that I beat it on my own, that Ade's strategies were holding firm, gifting me a way out of the panic. But the honest answer is, I was losing, giving in to it. I'd pulled out the bottom drawer and ripped off the tape securing the scissors, my hand shaking as I tried to reason with myself.

But it was too late. The blade rested gently on my skin, the anticipation of calm overwhelming.

A knock at the door almost jolted me into piercing the skin. As the handle turned, I shoved the scissors under my pillow, desperately hoping I'd done it quickly enough.

'You all right?' asked Floss, eyebrows arched in concern.

'Kind of,' I gasped, relieved and guilty at the same time.

'You having an attack?'

I nodded. Didn't have the strength to lie.

'Have you hurt yourself?'

A shake this time.

'Want to give me what's under the pillow?'

'Do I have to?'

She smiled sadly. 'I'm not going to punish you, Daisy. We're all so proud of what you've achieved, so let's remove the temptation, shall we?'

My hand slid under the pillow and out again, palming the scissors to Floss.

'Well done,' she soothed. 'You strong enough for a quick walk?'

'Suppose.'

'Nice one. Bex wants five minutes with you. Ade too.'

I wanted to put a face on, be stroppy now Ade was back, but I couldn't. In fact, I couldn't think of anything I wanted more than her reassurance. So, puppy-like, I followed Floss out of my room and towards Bex's office.

They were laughing when I walked in. Didn't even bother to stop when they saw my grey, waxy face.

Floss gave them a heads up instead.

'Daisy's having a difficult day,' she said, 'but she's been fighting it. Winning too, eh?' She rubbed the small of my back encouragingly.

Ade circled the desk and embraced me. If she felt my arms stiffen at my sides, it didn't put her off.

'We've been expecting this, haven't we?' She sighed. 'And

I know I've let you down by not being here.'

I pursed my lips and gave her the tiniest shrug, as if it was news to me.

'There's a reason Ade hasn't been with you this morning,' Bex said, sitting on the edge of her desk. 'A good reason. Something that affects you, affects us all.'

I was in no mood for more Bellfield riddles and braced myself for another wave of therapeutic bullshit.

'You've impressed us lately,' she continued. 'It's hard to believe you're the same girl who joined us only a few months ago. And I know how much of that has been down to the work you've been doing with Ade and the trust you've built up between you. That's why we've called you up here first.'

I squirmed on the spot. Wherever this was heading, it had an ominous quality that I didn't like.

'Do you remember what I called you when you first arrived?' It was Ade speaking now, but I daren't take my eyes off Bex in case I missed something important from her. 'Daisy?'

My head jolted around to face her.

'The name I called you when I found you reacting to your medication. You remember?'

Of course I did. *Her lucky charm*. It was the one Ade riddle I'd never worked out.

'The day you arrived I received some news, good news that you brought with you. But I couldn't tell you what it was in case it all went wrong. Well, today they confirmed what I'd hoped. It really is good news.'

'Can someone please tell me what the bloody hell is going on?' I yelled, my voice cracking. 'It's like you talk a foreign language sometimes.'

My arsiness seemed to work as Ade reverted to the plain truth.

'I am pregnant, Daisy.' I saw immediately from her glassy eyes what this simple statement meant to her. 'We have been trying for years. My man and I have been prodded by practically every doctor in the north of England, but with no success. On the day you arrived they told me I had one more chance, using new drugs. I was elated when they told me, but I was scared. Petrified. But when you arrived, and I saw how distressed you were, I knew that in fact I was lucky. You have something very special about you, Daisy Houghton. Real strength. And I knew you were bringing some of it for me. And I was right, because today they have confirmed everything. I am finally having a baby.'

I shouldn't have hugged her so hard, but I couldn't help it. It was a mixture of the kindness in her words and the tears snaking down her cheek that made me do it. All the time she'd been going through this and I hadn't known. All the shit and doubt that I'd thrown her way and not once had she ever crumbled or told me to pull myself together. It was hard to believe anyone had that strength. So I told her exactly that, which drew a laugh that rumbled up from her belly.

'We are both strong,' she said, breathing deeply, 'and that is why you will not miss me when I'm gone.'

My arms froze, still wrapped around her. What did she mean? I pressed my tummy against hers, trying to gauge the size of her bump. I was no expert, but it wasn't like it was imminent or anything.

'Gone?' I asked, trying to keep my voice steady. 'You're not going anywhere yet, are you?'

Our embrace slipped, broken by Bex.

'I'm afraid we have to put Ade's health at the front of this now. We can't have her at unnecessary risk.'

I was gobsmacked. 'You think I'd hurt her?'

'No, no, no,' Ade insisted. 'Of course not. But you have seen this place. You have seen the passion that runs through it. Things flare up quickly, without warning. It's not a place I can afford to be.'

'It's not a place you want her to be either, is it, Daisy?' Bex again.

Of course I didn't, and I felt guilty for even thinking of myself before her. But I couldn't help it. The other staff were OK, but they didn't get me, not like she did. She'd been a cutter, been where I was now. If she wasn't there guiding me along, I'd fall off again. I mean, I nearly had an hour ago, and I'd had no idea this was going on.

'I know what you are thinking,' Ade whispered, 'but you will not break down again, not after what you have achieved. The things you have learned, your strategies, they need applying whether I am here or not. They are your weapons and with them intact there is little that can touch you.'

I straightened my back, my chin lifting defiantly, trying to show that I agreed, although everything inside me was crumbling.

What was I going to do? How the hell was I going to get out now?

'You are in touching distance of a foster placement, Daisy. You were only ever here to gain understanding of what was going on. And now you have that . . . well, I have already been making a case to your social worker.' She paused a second, long enough for me to catch a whiff of unease. 'And she has listened to our thoughts.'

I knew what that meant. That bitch Evelyn didn't believe any of it. She'd always thought I was mental and while I was here I probably kept her paperwork levels down. Anger bubbled, splitting my thoughts, leaving me incapable of saying anything. All I could do was squeeze Ade's hand in support and try not to collapse in front of them.

'We haven't told any of the other residents yet,' said Bex. 'We wanted to let you know first. It's important you keep it to yourself, at least until tonight. Apart from Naomi, we'll tell everyone at the end of the show.'

I cringed, not liking the idea of being in on a secret. Naomi's threats after the last time still echoed, but on the other hand she hadn't spoken to me properly in weeks. I couldn't see that changing before they told her.

'No worries,' I lied. 'I'll even look surprised when you tell everyone if you like.'

Bex seemed chuffed, relieved. 'We knew you'd understand, Daisy. And we are all here for you. We'll have you in a foster placement as soon as we possibly can.'

'I know you will,' I grimaced through a tight jaw. 'Not long now, eh?'

I reinforced the words with a glance at each of them, seeing the pride on their faces.

But Ade? There was no pride. She was elated by her news, but she wasn't buying any of my lies, and as I slumped out of the room I could feel her eyes burning into my back.

CHAPTER 48

The classroom was transformed. Desks had been removed and the tatty painted walls lined with flowing drapes, while a stage stood proudly, taking over half the space.

It was eye-rubbing stuff, like stepping on to a film set, and I watched the same sense of wonder creep over the faces of the others as they made their way in. Even Naomi, stony-faced as she normally was, couldn't help but wander around, taking in what the staff had done.

I paid special attention to her, to see if she was distressed by Ade's news. They'd worked together ever since she'd arrived and, although their relationship was strained, I couldn't believe it wouldn't affect her.

After a couple of minutes in her presence, though, it appeared I was wrong. There was no anger on her face, no evidence of tears, or even signs of agitation from a slanging match. She looked excited. Playful even.

She and Paddy were dressed identically in black suits, white shirts and black ties. Neither suit fitted well: hers was turned over endlessly at the cuffs, while Paddy's buttons strained to keep his belly in check. They didn't care. In fact, they carried the look with a swagger, an arrogance, like they knew they had something special lined up.

There were broad grins everywhere I looked. All the staff, Eric included, were tarted up like some girl band. Even Jimmy and Susie were dressed similarly, in jeans and matching shirts.

Breathing deeply, I forced any nerves away. I'd spent the rest of the afternoon fretting and pacing, and was so sick of the ball of anxiety in my gut that I just wanted it over now, so I could pull the duvet over my head and wake up on a day that wasn't loaded with meaning.

Climbing on to the stage, Bex called everyone to order and I plonked myself next to Jimmy, as far away from the other duo as possible. He was showing no sign of nerves, casually spinning his mobile phone in his hand like it was a microphone. Susie looked on adoringly. It would've been sweet if it wasn't so comical.

'Right, then,' Bex boomed, like she was manning the waltzers on the seafront. 'Look at you lot, you're amazing! And look at the room as well. Have you ever seen such a transformation? Let's have a massive cheer for Floss and Eric, who've spent all day putting this together.'

Everyone whooped as they bowed theatrically, Eric looking ridiculous in a long black wig, bra and hot pants. Quite what our social workers would've made of it I didn't like to think.

'It seems perfect to be having this event tonight. To bring us together in a way other than the community meeting. The fact you've all embraced the idea of sharing shows me how much work you've put in this year. Whether you're any good at singing or dancing – and believe me, the staff definitely aren't – isn't important. What matters is offering a glimpse of yourselves, so you can see just how much you are worth and how much you have to give.'

Naomi and Paddy sniggered, pushing their fingers down their throats.

'Yes, thank you, you two. You've done more rehearsing than anyone else, so don't try and tell me you haven't enjoyed yourselves.'

Naomi flashed Bex a 'whatever' sign and told her to get on with it. And thankfully she did, announcing with great glee and excitement that the first act on stage was the Pussycat Dolls.

With that the lights went out, sending a small buzz round the room. There was a lot of shuffling and banging, until a voice whispered 'Ready' and the lights flashed on again, accompanied by deafening music.

And there they were, held motionless in the most ridiculous poses. Bex, Eric, Floss, Maya and Ade, all of them pimped to the max. A terrible collage of PVC, fishnets and lip gloss. It was the most horrific sight imaginable, but as the next five minutes passed, the funniest as well.

It didn't matter that there weren't many of us in that room, the noise we were making could've come from a packed stadium. They were raising the roof and we loved it. All right, none of it was on time or even vaguely impressive, but it was hilarious, like the best pantomime we'd ever seen. I'd certainly never seen Ade do anything like it, and as she strutted across the stage, I forgot completely she was pregnant, or about the awful hole she would leave behind.

The end of the song came too soon for us, but not quickly enough for the 'Dolls', who were on the verge of collapse. It looked to me like our applause and cheers were the only thing keeping them vertical, and they were speedy to refuse an encore, with Bex calling for Patrick and Naomi to take their place.

The pair of them couldn't have bounded up there any quicker, diving to retrieve a hat each from the back of the stage. Striding to the centre, they stood back to back, arms folded, chests puffed out. This sight alone earned whoops from the crowd, so when a song from *The Blues Brothers* cut through the silence, the atmosphere was ratcheted up even further.

It was gobsmacking just how slick the whole dance was. Not that Paddy was a mover or anything, he was far too clumsy for that, but he held the space with enough finger-clicking and menace to allow Naomi to work her tricks around him. The last few months had proved to me how good an actress she was, but here she was in Oscar-winning territory. She dived around the stage like a gymnast, spinning her hat in her hand as she mimed into the microphone. Everyone knew the song and so once the chorus kicked in it turned into a giant karaoke, all the carers punching the air as they sang, 'I need you, you, you.'

Naomi pointed back at them in turn, but not aggressively. There was something different about her, she looked without any ulterior motive, like she was truly enjoying herself for once.

She turned and cartwheeled, kicked and punched until the music finally gave way to applause that even I couldn't ignore. They stood there, wheezing, a look of wonder on their faces as they soaked up the roars. Bex leapt on to the stage, embracing them both, telling them to bow again and again. They didn't need encouragement. In fact, they probably would've still been there if Jimmy and Susie hadn't been up to replace them.

It was funny how the atmosphere changed once they settled in front of us. Jimmy stood bolt upright, still fiddling with his phone as a mike stand was placed in front of him, while Susie sat further back, eyeing a tambourine like it was a bomb rather than an instrument. I saw Eric at the side of the stage, an acoustic guitar strapped to his front, and he clung to it grimly, his earlier euphoria lost.

Everyone was thinking the same thing. Was he going to do it? Was Jimmy actually going to sing?

I felt the scars on my arm prickle, my mouth forming the words to tell him not to do it. But to my left was Naomi, whose sneer was begging him to open his mouth and humiliate himself.

The only person who didn't look edgy was Jimmy himself. He flicked at a few keys on his phone before sliding it into his back jeans pocket.

'This is a song,' he shouted into the mike, a screech of reverb chasing his words round the room.

This drew a laugh from the Blues Brothers, who mocked him, crowing, 'Not the way you'll sing it, it won't be!'

But Jimmy either didn't hear or didn't care. He just went on.

'It's not a new song or nothing. It's not one I've sung

for a long time either, for obvious reasons. But it's mine and this seems like a good time, so anyway . . .' And with that he motioned to Eric, who started to pick at his guitar strings.

I watched Jimmy close his eyes and suck in the biggest breath I'd ever seen. I practically felt the air around me rush in his direction and I tensed, scared of what he was opening himself up to.

But I needn't have worried, for as soon as the words left his lips, we were held by them:

And should you look tonight . . .
And see what I have seen . . .
This perfect light
This perfect light . . .

And so I stand alone
Imagine that it's you
In the moon tonight,
It's you in the moon tonight . . .

His eyes were closed as he sang, but that wasn't out of fear. From his stillness it was clear he believed in what he was doing.

And his voice?

Well, it was Jimmy's voice, except mellower somehow. It wobbled at the end of the lines in a tuneful way, and I took such delight in seeing Naomi's jaw drop as she realized she'd been trumped. Jimmy could sing. He really could. OK, it wasn't polished or anything, but there was such honesty in his words that we let him pull us along:

And how I want to be held . . .
But I bathe in the moon tonight
The only moon
I bathe in the only moon . . .

Jimmy's foot began to tap as Eric's guitar picked up, doubling its tempo, driving the tune on. Susie threatened to ruin it all with some God-awful tambourine bashing, but thankfully grew tired when Jimmy started to sing again, his voice rising and falling:

But it's not enough to think that it will just happen
It's got to come from the moon and from me and from you
Look to the stars and follow their pattern
And make your way in the hazy blue
The moon sees us both and it makes me remember
The nights when we stood and were hidden from view
But now I can only stand here and keep looking
It's got to come from the moon
And from me . . .
And from you . . .

The guitar stopped dead, before the slower tempo fed back in and Jimmy took one last breath:

And just keep looking . . .
Just keep looking . . .
Look to the moon
Look to me
And look to you . . .

The last pluck of the guitar gave way as Jimmy's voice did and there was a moment's stunned pause before the avalanche started. A noise that eclipsed anything that had gone before, even without Naomi joining in. She turned to Paddy, mouthing something to him. I didn't need to be a lip-reader to know what it was. She didn't believe he'd written it, in fact she probably thought he was miming, but to me it didn't matter if they were someone else's words. It was extraordinary, from start to finish, the most unexpected thing I'd heard since I'd arrived. And that was saying something.

We clapped for so long that our hands hurt. There were tears from Bex, who bounded up to embrace Jimmy. He stood there as motionless as before, eyes finally open. He soaked up every last drop. In fact, it wasn't until the room was silent that he looked awkward and his hand reached for his pocket, retrieving his phone before pointing at it, speaking once more into the microphone.

'Sorry, I really need to take this, yeah?'

And with a leap from the stage, he bounded out of the room, shouting into his broken phone.

It was the perfect moment to end his performance, something that drew laughter as well as tears. Bex was finding it hard to know which to let out first.

After a short pause to collect herself, she turned to us again and brought me straight back down to earth with a splatter as loud as Jimmy's applause.

It was my turn, but how was I going to follow that?

CHAPTER 49

My fingers shook as I tried to slide the DVD into the player. I blew on my knuckles, hoping it would steady them, which drew a snort of derision from certain members of the audience.

After Jimmy's song there was a huge swell of expectation in the room and my chest hammered at the knowledge I was about to slow things right down.

Trying to rationalize it, I knew I had two options: go ahead with my plan and humiliate myself, or leg it and face the same result. The second option was tempting, but somehow I found the balance to stay put. If I was going to get by without Ade, then I had to start fronting things out.

The DVD player whirred into life and the TV followed with the first press on the remote control. I stood chewing my lip as the copyright screen took an age to complete, ignoring Naomi's exaggerated yawns.

Eventually the menu screen appeared and I selected the right chapter before turning to face everyone, immediately wishing they would dim the lights as they had before, so I could talk to a load of silhouettes.

'Er, dancing has never really been my thing. Singing neither. This is the thing I love –' I motioned to the screen behind me

– 'not so much telly, but films. My dad was a movie nut, so for as long as I can remember I have been too. I've spent more time watching them than anything else, so today I wanted to show you the best scene from my favourite film.'

There was a titter from the floor in front of me. 'You're kidding me, aren't you?'

It was Naomi, of course.

'Er, can you keep your opinions to yourself?' hushed Bex, tapping her on the shoulder.

'Well, it's hardly impressive, is it? Me and Paddy spent hours getting our stuff together and you're going to let her get away with pressing a button on a remote control?'

'This is about sharing something. No one said it had to be a performance.'

Naomi turned her snarl back towards me. 'Come on, then, get on with it. I'm dying for a fag.'

I swallowed the urge to tell her where to go, thinking carefully about what to say.

'There's loads of films I could say are my favourite, but *The Shawshank Redemption* is the one I watch if I need cheering up or am feeling ill. It's not a comedy or anything. It's about a guy who's sent to prison for allegedly killing his wife –'

'No wonder she likes it . . .' The temptation was too much for Naomi.

'Once more and I'll ask you to leave,' shushed Bex.

'We know he didn't do it, but he can't prove it, and so he spends years, decades in Shawshank, where the guards all take advantage of him, making him do their tax returns and fiddling the prison books. All the way through it looks like he's going to die in there, until . . . well, until this bit . . . I'll shut up now and let it speak for itself.'

I hit the play button, turning the volume button up as high as it would go, feeling the goosebumps on my arms as the familiar scene started to unfold.

One of the carers flicked the lights off and that was it, I was transported. I could've been anywhere and as long as the film was playing I didn't care what the others thought about it.

The first thing they saw was the prison governor finding the hole in our hero's cell wall, then stirring music as he realizes that the prisoner he needed locked up more than any other has escaped.

It was like watching it for the first time again and I felt my whole body tense as the hero pulled his way through the sewage pipe. By the time he splashed from the human waste into the river outside the prison, tears were gathering in the corners of my eyes, and as he stood in the pouring rain, arms outstretched in joy as the camera spun above his head, I was completely in its grip, forgetting to turn it off as the scene ended.

The lights burned my eyes as I was thrust back into the spotlight and I tried to brush the tears away casually without anyone noticing. I'd had no clue, when I came up with the idea, that this scene would affect me again. After all, it was like the twentieth time I'd seen it.

It was too late to worry about it now. There were a dozen pairs of eyes all focusing on me, all of them asking the same question.

'OK. Now what?'

I swallowed hard, any thoughts I'd prepared sailing clean out of the room. I had to say whatever came into my head and I had to say it before the knives flew from the front row.

'I d-didn't pick this film because it's set in a prison,' I stuttered, 'and any similarities between the reprobates in it and the ones here are purely coincidental.'

There was a polite laugh from a couple of the staff and another 'humph' from the Blues Brothers.

'This has been my favourite for a few years now, long before all the stuff with my dad happened, and to be honest I haven't watched it since he died. In fact I haven't watched any films since then.'

The realization shocked me. Had it been that long?

'I suppose I felt like I haven't deserved to watch anything. Why should I surround myself with something I love when I felt so responsible for all the bad stuff going on?'

Ade was watching me, wondering if all her hard work was unravelling in front of the whole community.

'I guess what I'm trying to say is that I can identify with the guy in the film, even if I'm not really like him. This isn't prison, even if it's felt like one from time to time. And I'm not a prisoner either. At least not any more. For way too long I've felt like a bad person and I know some of you reckon I am as well. But that's not who I am.

'And the reason I love this film and this scene so much . . . ? It's because I'm waiting for my moment like his. Did you see what it meant to him, the smile on his face? All that stuff in the prison, the years of torturing himself? In that moment, it doesn't matter any more. It's all in the past. And I can't wait to feel like that. I'm waiting for that moment where all the guilt and all the bad stuff I think about myself washes away.'

I paused briefly, to see if anyone was with me, and they were certainly listening.

'I didn't think I'd ever have that moment. But now? I'm looking forward to it, because I know it's coming. I just hope it's soon.'

I didn't know what to say after that. There was nothing left in my head, so I crouched down, ejected the DVD, turned off the TV and walked, head up, back to my seat, listening to the applause and ignoring the jeers. It was over and I didn't have to fear it any more.

CHAPTER 50

It wasn't the rapturous reception the others had got, but there were enough nods and smiles from the staff for me to know that I hadn't come off as badly as I'd feared. All I had to do now was keep my head down, sit through Ade's announcement and scoot off to bed. Tomorrow couldn't be as eventful as today.

We watched as Ade clambered on to the stage and I could see the tension in her face. I had no idea how she was going to break the news. I just hoped they'd done as they said and told Naomi.

'You certainly know how to put on a show,' she said, beaming. 'I don't think I have ever been so moved, entertained and tickled in such a short space of time.'

She took a deep breath, and I held mine in anticipation.

'Today, though, is a special day for other reasons . . . not just because of what we have seen tonight. I actually have two more things that I need to tell you about. Both are good news, and the first is to do with our friend Daisy, who is fifteen today.'

There were polite whoops as the focus turned to me, and if I'd had the time I would've slid down my chair to hide.

'As you know, Daisy has had some issues to work through since she arrived, some of them to do with the death of her father, but some that are older than that.'

I saw Paddy roll his eyes at Naomi, whose jaw was stiff and tense.

'What you might not know is that Daisy wasn't lucky enough to ever meet her mum, and that has been difficult for her to accept. As much as I'd love to be able to remedy this, I can't. But I did make Daisy a promise a few weeks ago and I hope that this birthday present will in some ways help me keep that promise.'

From behind her back she pulled out a CD and, after waving it in the air, she asked Eric to do the honours, which he duly did, sliding it into the DVD player.

'Now, this may not make much sense to you, but it's important that we all support Daisy. She has made incredible progress, despite tensions between some of you, and that's why I want you all to see this. I hope this may make up for me letting you down earlier, Daisy. Happy birthday, lucky charm.'

The lights disappeared and all eyes were sucked back to the TV.

At first there was little to see. The picture was scrambled, a snowstorm invading both the top and the bottom of the screen, but slowly it started to settle and instead of the snow there was now a beach. The picture quality wasn't great, it was overexposed like an old Polaroid, with the camera pointed out to sea, a woman's back the only thing blocking the waves as they rolled in.

'For God's sake,' moaned Naomi. 'Is this *You've Been*

Framed or something? Can we cut to the funny bit where she falls over?'

It was like whoever was holding the camera heard her, as they started to walk towards the woman, and as he called her name, everything fell into place.

'Lydia!' the voice called. 'Lydia! Lyds!'

It was Dad's voice, the familiarity of it shocking me upright in my seat. Not just that, though, the name he was calling was Mum's, which meant . . .

I stopped the thought in my head, terrified of disappointment, but the camera rolled on and finally the woman turned to face him.

There was no disappointment, just shock, as for the first time I was confronted by the sight of my mum in something other than a photograph.

As a gift that would've been enough to satisfy me, but as I tore my gaze away from her face I saw the shape of her body, and the swollen bump where her stomach should've been.

It had to be me in there, but I didn't understand.

Where had Ade found it?

My pulse quickened in excitement and I lifted myself off my chair, gripping the front of the stage hard.

'I was beginning to think you'd fallen asleep?' I heard Dad say to her.

'What, standing up?' She laughed.

'Well, you have been knackered lately.'

'No wonder, what with this one booting me every five minutes!'

'Is she kicking now?'

I watched Mum's face soften and nod.

'And how does it feel?'

Dad zoomed in as her hands slid down and held her tummy.

'How do you think it feels?' She laughed, before speaking a line I never thought I'd hear. 'It's my daughter belting the crap out of me. It feels amazing.'

It didn't matter that the screen went fuzzy again. It didn't matter that the snowstorm took over and the lights went back on. All that mattered was that line, looping endlessly in my head. I could think of nothing else. No one would ever be able to take it away, even if the disc never worked again. I fell back into the chair, my eyes leaking everywhere, but I didn't care who saw. I wasn't going to let anything spoil the moment.

Ade walked back to the centre of the stage, her eyes misting too.

'Happy birthday, Daisy,' she said. 'Do you like your present?'

I stuck my thumbs up.

'Well, you should thank your dad, not me. He hoarded a whole load of old tapes. The hardest bit was finding a video player. As soon as I found that I just had to sit and watch until your mum showed up. I guessed she would in the end.'

This brought a ripple of applause from Bex and the other carers, and edged Naomi ever closer to the end of her leash.

'Have we finished now? Or do we have to flick through their holiday snaps as well?'

She ignored the stern looks of the staff and pushed herself to her feet.

'Seriously,' she moaned. 'From the way you lot go on about her you'd think she was the only person living here. So if we're done I'm going to go and have a smoke. I reckon me and Paddy deserve it after what we laid on.'

She made for the door, only for Ade's voice to pull her grudgingly back.

'Naomi. Patrick. Please. Sit down for one minute. There's something else I need to tell everyone. Something important.'

Naomi growled, every muscle in her body tensing as she threw herself back into her seat. 'Make it quick, will you?'

Confusion buzzed through me. I studied Naomi, to see if she was acting dumb like I was. She had to know, didn't she? I mean, why on earth wouldn't they tell her like they told me? Ade was her key worker too.

'I have one more piece of news that is important. You see, today is going to be my last day on shift here. For a while at least. I discovered today that I am having a baby. So until it has arrived, I have to step away. I know it will be a bit of a shock to some of you, but I hope that you can all be pleased for me as well.'

I sat with my head down, my nerve not strong enough to look up and feign ignorance. But when I did, I found Naomi's boring a hole in me and I knew my fears were true.

She didn't know. The pain was all over her face and she stared at me without blinking.

'You knew,' she mouthed to me. 'You knew. Didn't you?'

I should've acted more. Or better. Or both. I tried, but failed, as she wasn't buying into whatever look I managed to give her.

'Bitch,' she mouthed again, before shouting it, loudly, startling everyone. 'BITCH!'

I wasn't sure if it was aimed at Ade or me. Probably both, not that it mattered. With a screech, her chair flew backwards and I braced myself, expecting her to throw herself in my direction, but she didn't. Instead she sprinted for the door, her hat flying off in the process. With a final flourish, the door slammed shut behind her, the echo tearing its way around the room, causing the drapes to flutter like kites.

There was silence around the room for a heartbeat or two, until Susie broke it. Climbing to her feet, she clambered on to the stage and hugged Ade a little too tightly.

'Congratulations,' she said, beaming. 'We aren't half going to miss you.'

Everyone else took that as their cue, whether it was news to them or not, and I stood in line, waiting to tell her again just how pleased I was.

Typically, though, Ade deflected any talk of herself away and focused instead on me.

'You should be so proud of yourself. To tell everyone what you did, today of all days . . . Incredible, Daisy Houghton. Incredible.'

'But what about Naomi?' I whispered in her ear. 'I thought you said you were going to tell her too.'

'And we tried. Several times. She wouldn't come to Bex's office or the staff room. She even locked herself in her room. In the end we had no choice but to tell her tonight with everyone else.'

'She looked gutted. What do you think she'll do?'

Ade shrugged, upset herself that Naomi had reacted as

she had. 'She'll do what she always does. She'll shout, and break a few things, but she'll calm down finally. I'll go look for her. It's not like I can leave until we've smoothed things out, is it?'

'Suppose not. You want me to help?'

'You know what I want you to do? I want you to take this DVD to your bedroom, put it into the player and look at it again. I spent hours looking through your dad's tapes. Pretty much every night for the last couple of weeks. But I'll tell you what. Seeing your face as you watched it? It was worth every single second.' She looked at me, head cocked on one side. 'Do you think it'll make a difference, like you hoped it might?'

'It already has,' I said, grinning. 'It's the best present I could've asked for. Thank you.'

'You are welcome,' she said. 'Now go and watch it again.'

I didn't need telling twice, so I hugged her, making her promise to say goodnight before she left.

It had been a long day, and a knackering one at that, but for once I didn't notice the stairs up to the girls' landing. I practically floated up them, knowing that my mum would be waiting at the end of the corridor.

CHAPTER 51

The power of the footage didn't dwindle on second viewing, or the third or fourth.

I watched it greedily, barely blinking, looking for signs that Ade had fooled me with an elaborate hoax.

But however I tested it, it made no difference. That was my mum stroking me, telling me I was amazing, and nobody was going to dilute the joy that brought with it.

I was so pumped up I'd forgotten all about the tantrum that followed Ade's bombshell. In fact, I don't think I'd have given it a second thought had a fist not hammered on my door, shaking the walls like a flimsy film set.

With my head full of Mum, I didn't think about who might be there and flung the door open . . . to find Naomi.

She filled the doorway and in a couple of strides forced me backwards until I tripped on to my bed. Before I knew it, there was a hand around my throat, the other pinning me to the mattress.

'I warned you, didn't I, bitch?' she spat. 'The last time you kept secrets from me I warned you.'

'I don't know what you're on about,' I said, grimacing as I tried to lever some space.

'Don't give me that. The news about Ade leaving, you knew, didn't you?'

I couldn't say a word as her grip was cutting off the air to my lungs.

'What is it with you?' she screamed. 'I thought you might be different from the others, but you're not. Whenever I have something special going on there's always someone who has to ruin it. Someone who hoovers all the good stuff up. It happened with Mum so many times, but not now. I'm not going to let it.'

She was sweating, spit spraying from her lips as she tightened her fingers around my neck.

'They tried to tell you,' I gasped. 'But they said you wouldn't listen.'

'Well, they should've tried harder,' she yelled, and for the first time I saw weakness in her as tears mixed with perspiration. 'Would it have been so hard for them to try again? Am I not even worth that?'

'Course you are.'

I would've said anything to get her off me and she knew it.

'Listen, I haven't finished with you. You may think you're on the way out of here now, but let me tell you something. I've seen them promise the same thing to a load of kids, and never, not once, have I seen it come to anything. No one wants kids like us – why would they? So you can sit tight and think about how difficult I'm going to make life for you. Because I will bide my time and pick you off when I want to. I've bigger things to look after tonight.'

She forced my neck into the bed before backing away to

the door. The air gushed into my chest, but I was unable to stand as my head was spinning with the shock.

I knew instantly what that last threat meant. She wanted to square things off with Ade and I knew I couldn't let that happen, not with her being pregnant.

Steadying myself against the headboard, I pushed myself upright, eyes falling on the window. It was a hideous night, the wind gusting against the house, daring anyone to step outside.

I was about to head to the door when I spotted a figure walking on to the path. Despite the hood pulled over her head, I knew it was Ade. She turned in a tight circle, looking for someone I guessed was Naomi.

I rattled the window, trying to open it and warn her, but it wouldn't give. So I hammered instead, bending the plastic further than I thought was possible, but the wind just carried my warning away.

I pulled on my trainers and jacket, turning to the window one last time to see Ade move through the gate and on to the coast road. I breathed a sigh of relief, knowing where she was heading. Maybe she and Naomi had walked the cliffs as well. Maybe there was a spot where she thought Naomi might be. As long as I could get out there quickly, I knew everything would be all right.

But it wasn't. For as Ade disappeared from view I heard a door slam and saw two more figures hit the path, hunching together to light cigarettes. Naomi and Paddy.

At first I thought it was a coincidence, that they were outside to let off steam, so I watched, waiting for them to finish up and step back through the door. But as they stubbed out their smokes they didn't turn back. Instead they pulled up their hoods and followed Ade's steps, turning left at the gate too.

I swore, realizing that any coincidence ended there. They knew where she was heading, and my mind reeled at the thought of what they might do once they caught up with her.

Without a second thought I stumbled from my room, leaping down the stairs . . . anything to get me outside quicker.

As my hand fell on to the front door handle there was a shout behind me.

'Daisy!'

It was Bex.

'Where you headed?'

'For a smoke.'

'Do you really need one? It's hammering down out there.'

'Depends if you want me to get lairy or not.' I wanted to fob her off as quickly as possible.

'OK, but be quick, you hear?'

I pulled on the handle, but her voice came again.

'You haven't seen Naomi, have you?'

'No. Why?'

'Ade was looking for her. If you see her, can you let her know?'

I nodded fearfully, hoping this conversation wouldn't stop me finding Ade before Naomi did. The alternative didn't bear thinking about.

By the time the sea rolled into view I was soaked, my jeans clinging to my legs, slowing me to a waddle.

I thought about my conversation with Bex and wondered why I didn't come clean about Naomi. Was it paranoia that stopped me? Maybe it *was* just coincidence that Naomi had followed Ade. It was possible, but unlikely, and now with no signal on my phone there was nothing I could do to put things straight. I just needed to find Ade and quickly.

The rain was bouncing now, ricocheting off the tarmac like bullets. It was so heavy that I had to squint to make sense of where I was.

Fortunately, the route had become familiar and I felt my way instinctively, disappointed when, at every landmark, there was no sign of Ade. She was obviously determined to find Naomi, which meant I had no option but to follow.

Ten minutes on and I reached the coastline, turning instinctively to the path that ran along the cliff. Head down, shielded from the rain, I wasn't aware of what was in front of me, so when I came up against something in my way I presumed I had taken a wrong turn.

Except I hadn't. The thing blocking my path wasn't a wall or a fence, but a person. A person I didn't want to see. Patrick.

'Whoa, whoa, whoa,' he said, trying to smile. 'Where are you off to?'

I peered around his bulk to see what he was hiding, but there was only more rain.

'Nowhere,' I lied, hoping he'd believe me. 'Trying to blow off some steam after Ade's news. You?'

My question stumped him and he shifted from foot to foot, bumbling something about being upset himself. I stared at him, trying to guilt him into telling the truth.

There was no chance. Instead he stood still, every inch of him blocking me.

'Right,' I murmured, a hint of desperation creeping in, 'I'll catch you later.' I tried to scoot around him unsuccessfully, his chest bumping up against mine.

'You don't want to go down there,' he gabbled.

'Why not?'

'Just been down meself and turned back. The wind's whipping up something savage. Girl as light as you? It'll have you over the edge.'

I smiled thinly. 'I'm sure I'll be all right. I had a big tea,' and tried again to sidestep him.

This time an arm stopped me, threatening to remove my head from my shoulders.

'Did you not hear what I said? You don't want to be down there right now.'

I squared up to him, a horrible mismatch.

'I appreciate your worry, Paddy, I really do. But it's a bit late for the big brother act, isn't it? Let me past, will you?'

It was a mistake to try and wrong-foot him, an even bigger one to try and push him in the process, as all he did was step forward and wrap his arms around me, lifting and crushing in a single movement.

'You never listen, do you, you silly cow,' he moaned. 'Well, this time you're going to have to. I know why you want to be down there, but you're going to have to wait. Naomi and Ade need to talk. There's stuff to be said, so you can stay here until they're done, got it?'

His arms tightened around my chest as he walked me

backwards. His face was in mine, his breath rank, a mixture of cheap booze and cigarette smoke.

I peered over his shoulder but there was nothing to see, and no way out of his grip. I struggled, looking for somewhere to bite him, but every inch seemed to be covered in waterproof coat.

He marched me away from the coast, leaving me out of ideas, but then something weird happened. The ground seemed to twist on its axis, like some kind of tremor had hit, and before I knew it, both Paddy and me were lying on our sides. The only difference between us was that my eyes were open, while his were firmly shut.

A shadow loomed above and I raised my hands instinctively, fearful of the new danger. Two long arms reached down: bare arms without any sleeves or jacket covering them.

The massive hands held me firmly, setting me back on my feet, and fearfully I peered beyond the arms to their features, coming into focus.

I half screamed in fear and delight as Jimmy's face pressed up against mine.

'Daisy? You all right?'

I nodded, scraping my hair back. 'Where the hell did you come from?'

'I saw you all heading out the gates and didn't like the look of it. Thought you might need the help.'

I threw myself around him, squeezing hard, as I looked down on Paddy.

'Is he going to be all right?'

'Oh aye. I only gave him a tickle.' He grinned. 'But I don't think he'll be too chuffed when he wakes up.'

'I need to find Ade,' I shouted against the rain. 'Have you seen her?'

He shook his head. 'I followed you out the gates. Guess she must be further along the path.'

'Can you keep an eye on Paddy –' I gestured – 'in case he wakes up? I don't want him chasing me.'

'No worries. Just be careful of Naomi, will you? She's off her head, that one.'

I nodded before stumbling onwards, remembering that the others had said exactly the same about him.

The wind was raging now, throwing the storm on top of me. It was so disorientating, I kept as much distance from edge of the cliff as possible. The rain played tricks, shapes rearing out of the darkness, but each time I thought I'd found them it was just a rock or a tree stump. It took a good five minutes of further stumbling until I finally saw something that set my heart pounding. Two shapes, but this time they were moving too much to be branches.

One of them was pacing forward, forcing the other back. Was Naomi going for Ade? All I could think about was the baby.

Naomi wouldn't hurt her, would she? I knew she was pissed off, but surely she wouldn't . . .

It wasn't easy sprinting into the wind, especially with the track boggy underfoot, but I had to try, and within a minute I'd closed the gap to about forty metres.

At this point I slowed, shuffling into a line of trees on the edge of the path. I picked my way around the roots, not daring to take my eyes away from the situation ahead.

The figures were clearer now and I could see that one of

them had something in her hand. I strained into the darkness, hoping it wasn't what I thought it was.

A knife.

There was no mistaking it, despite the darkness, and I knew it had to be in Naomi's hand. But the weird thing was, she wasn't pointing it at Ade. Instead the blade pointed back towards herself, towards one of her own arms.

I stumbled on, maintaining cover, straining to hear their conversation. Fortunately, the wind carried their words towards me.

'Is this what I have to do to get your attention?' Naomi screamed, sliding the blade closer to her wrist. 'Cos I'll do it if I have to.'

Ade looked horrified, hands raised in submission as she fairy-stepped forward.

'Of course it's not. Just give me the knife so we can put things straight.'

'I've wanted to talk to you for months, but you haven't had the time for me. Not since that cow arrived. I mean, what's so friggin' special about her anyway? She's a cutter, so what? So am I? What did I do wrong?'

'You haven't done anything wrong. I care for Daisy like I care for you. If you were feeling left out you should have told me, or Bex, or anyone. No one wanted this!'

'Yes, you did. You've wanted rid of me for ages, same as Mum did. Daisy arriving just gave you the excuse to push me.'

'That's not true!' Ade shouted. I'd never heard her voice as desperate as this. 'We'd do anything to make you happy, to help you take steps forward.'

'Then prove it,' Naomi cried through huge racking sobs. 'What do you want me to do?'

'Keep working with me. Daisy doesn't need you any more. They'll ship her on any day, but I still need you. See me once a week or something. I'll do the stuff you've done with her, I'll do whatever you say.'

It would have been simpler for Ade to agree with her. To say whatever she had to say to get the knife out of Naomi's hand and the pair of them off the cliff.

But that wasn't Ade's way. Instead she shook her head and told her that she couldn't do it.

'Why not?' Naomi screamed, on the verge of a tantrum. 'Why not me? Why choose her?'

'I haven't chosen anyone.' Ade's voice was calm again.

'Liar!'

'It's the truth.'

'You're a friggin' liar!' Naomi roared, taking a step forward.

And with that step everything changed, because the knife was no longer facing towards herself. Now it was pointing straight at Ade, at her belly.

They paced towards the cliff edge, like some kind of sick dance, Naomi leading with every step. Maybe the rain was blinding her, maybe she didn't realize how close they were to the edge, but Ade knew, as she tried to spin away and bring them back from the sea. Fear seemed to cover her entire body, her legs buckling, reducing her to all fours before she could regain her balance.

'Tell me the truth,' Naomi roared. 'Tell me why you chose her instead of me.'

'I can't.'

'Tell me!'

'There's nothing to tell.'

'You're just like the others. Like all the others before you.' The devil was in her now, possessing her every expression, every word. 'In fact, you're worse, because they never promised me nothing. But you? You told me everything was going to be all right. You promised.'

'Naomi, you are scaring me now. Whatever I have done to let you down I am sorry, but there are people you can talk to, people other than me who will understand.'

Her response cut through the wind and was so emphatic that I knew I had to do something.

'NO!' she bellowed. 'NO MORE PEOPLE. I can't do this any more. In fact, I should've done *this* a long time ago. Maybe then people would have taken me seriously.'

We moved in tandem. Me powering forward as Naomi's arm arced upwards. Me diving forward as her elbow whipped straight.

I saw Ade flinch, her feet perilously close to the edge.

I don't think she saw me, though, until it was too late, until my body passed between hers and Naomi's.

Naomi saw me, but only once the blade had sunk its teeth in. I saw her eyes widen, her mouth open and her hand release the knife, leaving it to dangle from my arm.

It didn't hurt as it entered. Instead I smiled, relief flooding in as the blood flooded out. I'd never moved so fast, or imagined that I could actually get there in time, but I'd done it, I'd done it, I'd done it.

It didn't matter that my balance left me, or that the

ground was wet through my clothes. Instead I saw the camera spin above me, swirling among the rain, giving me the moment I'd talked about earlier in the evening.

It was odd, seeing myself in my own movie, but it felt good too, like I'd done the right thing, and I smiled as Ade propped my head in her hands.

The smile didn't leave my face. Even when the shadows swept in, taking the rain – and everything else – away.

CHAPTER 52

My eyes opened to strip lighting, nausea and a strong sense of déjà vu.

There was only one place that smelt as unhealthy as this and it was hospital – not a place I remembered with any kind of warmth.

Without looking I knew the layout of the room: the iron bed, cheap wooden dresser to its left, semi-comfortable PVC armchair to its right.

My stomach lurched as I remembered Hobson sitting there during my last stay and as the fug cleared from my head I became aware of a presence again, could hear gentle snoring rolling off the walls.

I dared myself to see who was there, only for a lightning bolt of pain to stop me, causing my stomach to flip.

The pain was white hot, screaming from the very top of my left arm, just before the shoulder joint. Gingerly, I lifted the gown to find a swathe of padding, its centre point dyed a ruddy red. I peeled away the tape that held it down, ignoring the nagging of my skin, and surveyed the damage.

It was a cut all right, not the long shallow ones I'd inflicted on myself but a short, ragged gouge, as if the knife had gritted its teeth to bury its way in. The knives in the kitchen at Bellfield always were on the blunt side.

The other difference was that I didn't feel ashamed of this scar. There was a story behind this one with a bit more dignity. Maybe in time it would be one to show off instead of hide away. Well, maybe.

Any further inspection was cut short by a stirring beside me, a hand resting gently on my arm.

'Well, well. You are finally awake, Daisy Houghton.'

The warmth of the palm was enough to tell me it was Ade and I forced my upper body to turn forty-five degrees, swallowing the bile that rose in my throat.

Was she OK? Had I done enough? What about the baby, how would I know?

My eyes sped to her belly and the other hand resting gently upon it. Her body shook with a low chuckle that set me at ease immediately.

'It's OK,' Ade sang. 'Naomi didn't quite reach her target. Something else got in the way.'

My head fell back on to the pillow as the room tilted slightly. I felt a tear of relief as well as pain roll off my cheek, only to be caught by Ade. Her fingers soothed my face as she wriggled closer.

'I was right all along, wasn't I?' she asked. 'My lucky, lucky charm.'

I said nothing, just closed my eyes and let myself fall back into a dreamless state.

The doziness lingered for a while, though not as long as the nausea, which threatened each time I dared to change position. The other constant in the room was Ade, who seemed to be in the same place each time I woke. The only thing changing were the clothes she wore.

'Maybe I should try and stay awake for more than ten minutes,' I suggested.

'Or maybe you should listen to your body until it's ready. I don't have anything in my diary now for, ooh, six months. Until then, I'm welded to this chair. In fact, they might have to cut me out of it to deliver this baby.'

Laughing wasn't a good idea. It stretched the stitches, but the giggle felt good all the same and I made a mental note to try it again soon. It had been too long.

I knew as well that there were other things to ask about. What had happened to Naomi? Had Jimmy managed to keep a lid on Patrick when he'd woken up? But whenever Ade saw these questions forming in my mouth, she told me not to rush. So I listened, swallowing down each thought that came, even the biggest of them all: 'What happens to me now?'

But the questions didn't go away, no matter how I tried to dismiss them. Would I return to Bellfield? What did that mean for Naomi? They wouldn't put us under the same roof again, would they? If not, then it had to mean a foster family, but was I normal enough to fit in? Would anyone dare take a chance on me?

These questions dogged my waking moments, to such an extent that I almost hugged Evelyn when she finally made an appearance.

'Well, you have been in the wars, haven't you?' she tutted, shuffling the papers that fell out of my now full file.

Attempting a smile at Ade, she perched on the edge of the bed and paused to find the right words.

'It's been so pleasing . . . surprising, to hear of your progress from Adebayo here.'

I searched her face for sincerity as the words trickled out.

'In fact, everyone at Bellfield has vouched for the resilience you've shown in the last six months. They feel very strongly that the community doesn't offer you the kind of care you need now. That you'd be better off – with support, I might add – in a more traditional family set-up.'

I looked at her blankly. Her riddles were as bad as Ade's.

'With a foster family, Daisy,' she said, pronouncing each word emphatically in case the doctors had given me a lobotomy. 'I have to say that I would rather undergo a period of evaluation before making such a leap, but in light of the shenanigans this week, it wouldn't be appropriate for you to head back to Bellfield.'

My head whirred.

'You mean because Naomi's still there?'

Why on earth would they do that after what she did? I didn't like to think about how she'd target the others, Jimmy in particular.

'You mustn't worry about Naomi, or anyone else, Daisy,' interrupted Ade. 'This is not about them, it is about you.'

'But you have to look after Jimmy,' I gabbled. 'He followed me after I saw Naomi and Paddy. He laid Paddy out, gave me the chance to . . .'

Ade's hands pointed up in submission. 'We know what Jimmy did, he told us. Several times. I've never seen him so proud in his life.'

'So you have to keep her away from him. Paddy too!'

'Relax. Jimmy is fine. In fact, he's enjoying the attention now that Naomi and Patrick have moved on.'

I heaved a sigh of relief and sagged against the pillows.

'Moved on? Bex hasn't kept them together, has she?'

'It does not matter where. All you need know is that we've found somewhere that will help them with their issues, somewhere where they will receive more time and attention. And no, they won't be in the same place.'

'I'm surprised you're even concerned about Naomi after what she tried to do,' added Evelyn, scrawling illegibly on a pad. 'What you need to focus on is being healthy.'

'So where does Daisy stand?' Ade asked. 'Have there been any developments?'

'As a matter of fact there have,' Evelyn replied, and with a flourish she produced a second file.

'As I say, we haven't had a lot of time to put a placement together, and this couple, while incredibly keen to have you . . .' She paused, as if searching for the right words.

'What?' I asked. 'Are they Satanists or something? Because, to be honest, it doesn't matter to me.' I just didn't want to go back, not if Ade wasn't going to be there.

'Well, it matters to us. The last thing you need is unnecessary upheaval. We want this to be a long-term move for you, Daisy.'

The gravity of that statement floored me. She was talking about a new family – people who would replace Dad – and I still didn't know if I was ready for that.

'And they know about me, do they? They've read my file? Know about the cutting and everything?'

'Of course. They know everything we know about you, and despite their lack of experience of young people with your kind of needs we think you will really get on with them.'

I noticed a crease on Ade's forehead and for a second dreamed of her volunteering to take me in herself.

'But Daisy wouldn't be their first foster child, would she?' she asked.

Evelyn flicked through the file, tapping a section of interest.

'No, no. They have fostered before. A boy. A bit younger than Daisy, but not without his own challenges by the looks of things.'

I didn't like the shake of the head that accompanied those words, but before I could question her, Ade jumped in.

'But you have met them?'

'I have.'

'And you think Daisy will like them.'

'I'm sure she will. In fact, you won't have long to wait to find out. I've arranged for them to come and meet you both this afternoon.'

My scars prickled with fear. Ade's hand fell on to mine and squeezed gently. This was all moving so quickly, I just hoped I could keep up.

CHAPTER 53

It had never occurred to me that there was someone in the world who smiled more than Ade, but I was wrong.

Jan Scott's grin was wide and enthusiastic, though it wavered at the edges occasionally. It didn't have the confidence or reassurance of Ade's. She plastered it on to her face as soon as she saw me, but I'd seen the look that preceded it: a nervous frown, hands shaking slightly as they fidgeted with her handbag.

To be fair, she banished the long face as soon as our eyes met and for the next fifteen minutes she talked non-stop about absolutely nothing. It wasn't even small talk, it was just noise. She was sounding me out, testing me, working up enough bravery to touch my hand occasionally, to see if I would bite her if she did.

I didn't dislike her. It didn't look as if she was hiding an evil streak. She was just trying too hard, like she had to make up for something she'd already done. I had no bloody idea what that was.

The husband, Grant, was a different story. He smiled and waved when introduced, but was happier to sit in the background and let Jan go into overdrive. Maybe he didn't like the look of me, or perhaps he was just cautious. Either way he didn't get in my space like she did. Instead he hovered by the window, offering the odd nugget of conversation or chewing at the skin on the side of his thumb. He was friendly, but there was something he wasn't comfortable with. I caught him rubbing at a series of scars that pocked his right cheek, like they were suddenly throbbing.

'We haven't had time to decorate a room for you, I'm afraid,' Jan said in a rush. 'Perhaps it's something we could do together, once you're in and you've scoped out the space.'

I smiled politely. What did you say to that?

'As long as there's room for a lot of movies, I'm sure the room will be great,' offered Ade.

What followed was a long meandering conversation about the films they loved, although it was clear they never went to the cinema. Instead she talked about videos they'd seen and looked blank when I mentioned Blu-rays.

'Is that an underwater film?' she asked, and didn't look cross when I giggled. In fact, it was the first time I'd seen a true smile appear. It suited her too: stopped her looking so completely terrified.

They stayed for an hour or so, long enough for Jan to get every bit of information out of me that she could: what I ate and didn't eat, my favourite colours, my star sign. She peppered me with so many questions that Grant eventually told her to ease off. 'Let the girl have some secrets,' he quipped, daring a wink in my direction. At which point I decided he was all right too.

It became clear that there was a lot to do and not a lot of time to do it in.

My shoulder was healing well. The gash was clean and, apart from some muscular damage, Naomi's knife had avoided anything important. The doctors were making noises about the bed being needed and didn't seem too concerned about where I ended up next. That wasn't their problem.

It was agreed that I would be ferried by Ade to the Scotts' the day after tomorrow, news that was greeted with a new level of frenzied clucking from Jan. As they scurried out of the door I heard there were beds to turn down and shelves to put up. No wonder Grant looked exhausted, though to his credit he didn't take it out on me, offering a smile and a thumbs up after Jan planted a wet kiss on my cheek.

'It'll be fine,' he said, 'once you get used to living with the whirlwind here.'

And out they blew, a gust spiralling in their wake.

'Well, they were nice, weren't they?' said Ade, as flustered as me.

'Among other things,' I replied, nodding, 'including bonkers.' I paused and took a long swig of water. 'I reckon I'll be happy there. I should fit right in.'

I giggled again, we both did. And again it felt good.

My room at Bellfield was restored to a cell. Apart from a few Blu-Tack stains, there was no evidence anyone had been here at all. It was as hideous and cold as the day I moved in.

It hadn't taken long to pack. I never had gone shopping, so after sorting my underwear, jeans and a handful of Dad's shirts, I was done. I folded the shirts carefully, laying them flat in the case and choosing a fresh one to wear. I wasn't ready to give them up, not yet.

Speed-packing seemed the right thing to do. I knew in my head that Naomi and Patrick were miles away, but every creak or bang from outside seemed to threaten their return and, as the anxiety spread through my chest, I felt the scars on my arm ache, reminding me they hadn't faded yet.

As usual, Ade was bang on the money, reading my every thought.

'Don't be surprised if the next few weeks are tricky. New surroundings, new school, new friends, all these things may cause you some anxiety. What doesn't change, though, is your way of dealing with things. Keep the logic going. Bat away those silly thoughts with evidence of what you've done, how far you've travelled.'

'I'll try. It just seems so tiring, the prospect of it all. Maybe it'll be easier if I keep a low profile, don't make friends too quickly. I mean, it didn't do me any favours here, did it?'

'Well, no, but again, don't be blaming yourself for that. You did what you had to do to survive those first few weeks. It's only what anyone would have done.'

'Suppose so.'

'People will surprise you, Daisy. It may not feel like it now, but you must believe me. It's no good hiding yourself away, ignoring the potential to make new friends. You have so much to offer.'

'But how will I know who to trust?'

She blew hard, a raspberry bubbling from her lips. 'You'll just know. Someone will come along and they'll . . . I don't know, get you. They'll understand what you're about and you'll want to tell them too. You won't be able to stop yourself. That's how you'll know it's right.'

'But if I tell them about what's gone on then they'll just run a mile.'

She swiped her hand at me in jest. 'There you go again! Where's the evidence that will happen? Did I sprint off when I found out about your mum or dad? Did Jimmy? Or Susie?'

I shook my head. She had me again.

'You have to stop apologizing so readily for the bad luck you've had. Every time you feel the urge to say sorry, I want you to stop and work out if it's really necessary. Because I'll bet you, nine times out of ten, you're not to blame.'

'I'll try.'

I meant it too. It would just take some practice, not to mention a lot of lip-biting.

'Do you have everything packed?'

I nodded.

'Want me to give you a few minutes alone to say goodbye to your room?'

I fixed her with a stare.

'You are kidding me? I've already wiped this box from my memory. I'll miss you, and some of the others of course, but I'm looking forward to windows I can actually smash if I want to!'

She giggled and I stored up the sound, wondering when I would hear it again.

A small crowd had gathered in the hallway. They applauded us both as we walked down the stairs and I framed the moment, another scene to remember in my ridiculous movie of a year.

It was odd looking at the group without seeing Naomi

and Patrick at its centre, agitating everyone around them, but it felt great to be able to walk around without expecting a slap to greet me.

As much as I wanted to leave, it was hard to say goodbye. I couldn't imagine how many kids the staff had packed off over the years, but the emotion on Floss's and Maya's faces was real. No actresses were that good.

It was Jimmy who really shocked me, not that that should have been a surprise. His long arms snaked around me, threatening to reach around my shoulders a second time.

'Don't be a stranger, yeah?' he said, and grinned.

'I'll give you my number if you want. You can send me a text, let me know how the gigs are going.'

'Can't see that happening. This phone's been on the blink for a while now. Must be the SIM card or something.'

'Or the lack of a battery?' I chanced.

He looked at the back of his phone and gave a sheepish grin.

'Could have something to do with it, I suppose. But keep that under your hat, eh?'

He offered me a scrap of paper and I scribbled my number on it. I had no idea if he'd ever use it, but it would be entertaining if he did.

Goodbyes over, there was an awkward moment as we worked out how to leave, but fortunately it was broken by a rap on the front door.

Susie broke ranks first, dashing towards it with a shout of, 'SHE'S HERE!'

'New resident, Daisy,' Bex said, smiling. 'I'd better get

there before Susie smothers her. Wouldn't look good to kill her on her first day, eh?'

She squeezed my hand before walking away and eventually the other staff and even Jimmy did the same.

'You ready, then?' asked Ade. 'We can leave through the school block, avoid the crowd.'

'Sounds good to me.'

I gasped as I felt the weight of my box of DVDs. But I didn't turn back as we moved through the labyrinth of corridors. There wasn't a great deal to say goodbye to, or remember fondly, but as we approached the last door an ear-splitting scream echoed through the hall, followed by a crash and a flurry of voices.

Ade opened the door and a shaft of cold light shot in. I walked into it without hesitation. Whatever was going on back there had nothing to do with me. This time, I *knew*, it wasn't my fault.

ACKNOWLEDGEMENTS

I couldn't have written this story without the support of a lot of people, such as Haydn (trailers), Jason (website), the two Matts (Williams and Hutchinson), Madeleine Buston, plus colleagues at work, in particular Rob Cox, whose feedback was spot-on and only occasionally sketchy. It would be remiss of me also to not mention the drivers of the X68 bus too, who steered me home safely while writing.

I'm also very grateful to the booksellers and librarians who have supported me over the past year, especially the Booksellers Crow, John Newman, Jo De Guia, David, Dave, Tamara and George. Much love as well to Carol Webb at Forest Hill School, who has the finest library in old London town. Her students are rather spectacular too.

Cheers also to folk who've endlessly boosted my confidence. In particular, Jenny the Wondrous Reader, the Cherub Represents group, cousin Andrew, Zammo, Marcus and Bek, who always goes above and beyond the call of duty. I'm also very grateful to Stephanie Purcell and Alejandro Reyes for their help and expertise, not to mention Latino spirit.

Thanks also go to the good people of Puffin, especially to Tania, Emma, Adele, Katy, Sarah, Samantha, Jennie, Brigid and to Shannon Park, who is as brilliant as she is persuasive – thank you, my friend.

The song that Jimmy sings is called 'The Moon' and was written nearly twenty years ago by my friends Will and Waggy. Thanks so much for letting me use it, chaps. I never get tired of hearing it – it's an absolute cracker.

It's a funny thing, this writing lark. I started on one thing, only to find myself somewhere completely different, somewhere I didn't think I'd ever go. As a result I must thank the people who, twelve years ago, wrote, called or drove down the A63 to sit, play pool and kick my arse into action. Without you, I wouldn't have written about Daisy, or Billy for that matter. I owe you one.

Finally, thanks to my friends in the Palace and beyond. You know who you are.

And finally-finally, to Laura, Albie, Elsie and Little Stan, who make my world turn and my head spin.

Crystal Palace, June 2011

GET INSIDE YOUR FAVOURITE BOOK

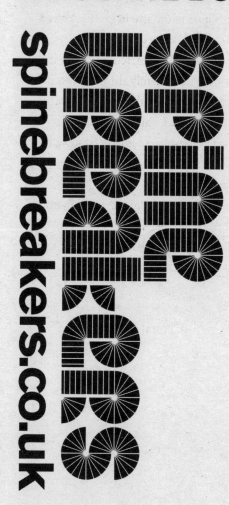

spinebreakers.co.uk

spinebreaker (n)

story-surfer, word-lover, day-dreamer,
reader/ writer/ artist/ thinker

SIX SPINE-TINGLING BOOKS

as chosen by the Spinebreakers crew

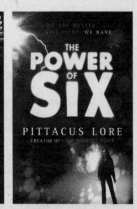

The list continues at www.spinebreakers.co.uk

DO YOU WANT TO JOIN US?

If you are a story-surfer, word-lover,
day-dreamer, reader/writer/artist/thinker
. . . BECOME one of us.

spinebreakers.co.uk

GET INSIDE YOUR FAVOURITE BOOK

He just wanted a decent book to read ...

Not too much to ask, is it? It was in 1935 when Allen Lane, Managing Director of Bodley Head Publishers, stood on a platform at Exeter railway station looking for something good to read on his journey back to London. His choice was limited to popular magazines and poor-quality paperbacks – the same choice faced every day by the vast majority of readers, few of whom could afford hardbacks. Lane's disappointment and subsequent anger at the range of books generally available led him to found a company – and change the world.

'We believed in the existence in this country of a vast reading public for intelligent books at a low price, and staked everything on it'
Sir Allen Lane, 1902–1970, founder of Penguin Books

The quality paperback had arrived – and not just in bookshops. Lane was adamant that his Penguins should appear in chain stores and tobacconists, and should cost no more than a packet of cigarettes.

Reading habits (and cigarette prices) have changed since 1935, but Penguin still believes in publishing the best books for everybody to enjoy. We still believe that good design costs no more than bad design, and we still believe that quality books published passionately and responsibly make the world a better place.

So wherever you see the little bird – whether it's on a piece of prize-winning literary fiction or a celebrity autobiography, political tour de force or historical masterpiece, a serial-killer thriller, reference book, world classic or a piece of pure escapism – you can bet that it represents the very best that the genre has to offer.

Whatever you like to read – trust Penguin.

read more
www.penguin.co.uk